# WAY
# OUT
# WEST

WAY OUT WEST
First published in 2024 by
New Island Books
Glenshesk House
10 Richview Office Park
Clonskeagh
Dublin D14 V8C4
Republic of Ireland
www.newisland.ie

Print ISBN: 978-1-84840-909-5
eBook ISBN: 978-1-84840-911-8

British Library Cataloguing in Publication Data. A CIP catalogue record for this book is available from the British Library.

Set in 11.5 on 16pt Adobe Caslon Pro
Typeset by JVR Creative India
Edited by Neil Burkey, neilburkey.com
Proofread by Michelle Griffin
Cover design by Fiachra McCarthy, fiachramccarthy.com
Cover image: *Gray and Gold* (detail), 1942. John Rogers Cox. Courtesy of The Cleveland Museum of Art.
Printed by FINIDR, Czech Republic, finidr.com

New Island received financial assistance from The Arts Council (An Chomhairle Ealaíon), Dublin, Ireland.

New Island Books is a member of Publishing Ireland.

10 9 8 7 6 5 4 3 2 1

# WAY
# OUT
# WEST

## ANTHONY GLAVIN

NEW ISLAND

# Also by Anthony Glavin

### NOVELS
*Nighthawk Alley* (1997)
*Colours Other than Blue* (2016)


### SHORT STORIES
*One for Sorrow and Other Stories* (1980)
*The Draughtsman and the Unicorn* (1999)


### POETRY
*The Wrong Side of the Alps* (1989)


### AS EDITOR
*The Best of Benedict Kiely: A Selection of Stories* (2019)

*For Brother Mike*
*(1941–2014)*

**I**

# 1

A storyline is seldom the shortest distance between two points – say Ireland and America. And fact is that Fintan first headed east across the Irish Sea – to London – not west across the North Atlantic. Yet picture this for openers: a little village on the southwest Donegal coast, cottages scattered across a long glen that sweeps back up from the sea. Blue skies that soar over brown hills whenever the grey rain relents. The same hills green with bracken in spring and flecked with purple in the summer, the blooming heather like specks in a swathe of Donegal tweed.

Picture too a three-room whitewashed cottage on the north side of the Glen, with blue trim and a small byre, a turf shed and a small loom-shed. A cottage still thatched in 1955, when Fintan was born, but it was re-roofed shortly after with grey fibreglass sheets by his father, Packy. In early memories the new roof crackled as it expanded in the morning sun, and nettles stung his hands as he foraged beneath the fuchsia hedge for eggs from a hen that refused to lay in the byre. Also, the pungent scent of sheep dip, and the milk his mother, Mary, left out to sour for bread-making. Her hand, gentle on his brow when he fell ill with scarlet fever. Or the sound of Texarkana singing 'The Streets of

Laredo' by the open fire in Molly's pub, the first time Mary sent him, at age seven, to fetch his father home.

Imagine Texarkana so – a tall man crowned with a shock of white hair who had peddled his wares around Texas for fifteen years before coming back to Glenbay to swap lies about America with a fellow villager, Dakota, who himself had returned from an even longer stay across the Big Pond and put a second storey on his house. 'They're wild for the second storey in America,' Dakota had informed his sister Nora, before ordering the best of Bangor slates for their new roof. Be that as it might, the Vaseline (as Nora was known behind her back) refused to mount the stairs in the fifteen-odd years she would live with a second storey over her head. At that point over ninety, Dakota only left the house for Sunday Mass, where Fintan might see him lurching suddenly sideways, like an outsized crab, as he returned from the Communion rail.

'Why the Vaseline?' Fintan had asked at home, only to be told by his father not to be so nosy. 'Why Texarkana?' he later chanced, after the ex-pedlar had died, guessing it was more the kind of thing you might inquire. 'It's a place he lived in America,' his mother answered, Packy being little given to speech at home, and even less so to Fintan or his younger brother, Frankie. Nor had Packy much notion of Texarkana or Dakota – the localities that is – having never ventured any farther west than where their parish met the Atlantic, nor farther east than Donegal Town. 'A great place, that,' he sourly observed of a postcard of Paris Mary had once shown the boys. 'You'd hate to live there. See nothing but spires in the morning.'

Imagine this then – a village that included amongst its returned émigrés not only Texarkana and Dakota, but Montana and James the Yankee, although James had passed away a few years before Fintan was born. But Montana, rigged out in a three-quarters ranch coat, string tie and Stetson, still walked down most days to Molly's for a few bottles of stout. 'Montana's rich,' Packy often remarked, believing that anybody who had been in America must have come back with plenty of cash. 'Rich my ass!' snorted Mary's brother, Uncle Condy, when Fintan, aged thirteen, quoted his father. Not 'arse' but 'ass' – yet another echo of America, where Condy Cunnea and his father Cornelius, Fintan's grandfather, had themselves both worked.

Certainly Condy lived like he had little money, a tattered woollen gansey hanging off him like a torn swathe of blanket. His cottage over the hill in Pier, Fintan's mother's home place, was rough and ready too: a blackened tin on the range that did for boiling an egg, the plastic basin of rainwater outside the door to rinse his boots, and more often than not a cock atop the dung heap beside the tiny byre that was home to a lone cow. That said, Condy had invested in an electric fence around the meadow beyond the byre to keep the cow in line, a single wire powered by an old car battery. Plus Condy had a car, an old black, humpbacked Morris Minor. Further evidence, Fintan reckoned, of the decade his uncle had spent across the water.

Like her father and older brother, Fintan's mother had also ventured out to America, having left Pier at eighteen to work as a nanny to the two daughters of a young Irish-American doctor and his wife in Chicago, where she stayed for five years before returning to Glenbay to look after her dying mother. Three years later she married Packy Doherty, a taciturn man nearly fifteen years her elder, a weaver who fished salmon in spring and kept sheep year-round.

It was Mary so who told her sons of a world beyond the parish of Glenbay. Showed them the postcards of Paris she'd found in a trader's stall at the Carrig sheep fair, or photographs of the Black babies in *The Messenger* from Mass with its bright red cover. Mary too who described the snow that froze into dirty lumps along the Chicago streets, or the wind off Lake Michigan like a knife blade on your nose and ears. Though truth be told she spoke little of herself in America: at most a few words about her charges, 'Two wee girls who'd be young women now,' and their father, the doctor, 'a perfect gentleman'. But Mary had also witnessed another way with children within that household, and so in small ways was markedly attentive to her own – cuddling her two sons when they were little, gifting them a watercolour box one Christmas, encouraging them to draw on old sheets of wrapping paper, or reading the odd passage aloud to them from whatever book she took up in the evening.

Fintan in turn occasionally questioned her about America, if his father was out. She laughed when he asked had she ever seen a cowboy, and merely shook her head whenever he asked why she hadn't stayed on over beyond. Yet one afternoon, when Packy was mucking out the byre, she took down a little black-and-white photograph from a tea caddy atop the dresser to show to Fintan. A photograph of a striking young woman in a long-sleeved blouse and high-waisted skirt, her long dark hair tidied into a loose knot at the crown of her head. Fintan looked quickly up at his mother beside the dresser, then back to the photo, where she stood, nay posed, by a flower bed beneath the railed veranda of a massive wooden house, all clapboards and big windows. Of course Fintan didn't know to call it a veranda yet, nor the clapboards clapboards, not until he hired on, some fifteen years later, to cover the weather-beaten boards on a succession of Missouri houses with wood-grained plastic siding, on behalf of an outfit called Vinyl Is Final that made sure to have moved on to another state by the time it took, generally a year or two, for the cheap-grade plastic to begin to crack and peel.

Fintan had never seen his mother in a costume like that, never seen her in anything fancier than the best dress she kept for Sunday Mass, while alternating the several dresses she kept for everyday use, unlike Packy, who might don the same muddied trousers and jacket for days on end. 'Was that the gentleman doctor's house?' Fintan asked, ignoring his brother's outstretched hand as he handed back the photograph.

'A summer house they had on Lake Michigan,' Mary said, taking care to show Frankie the photo before replacing it in the tea caddy. 'Homes,' she said, 'Huron, Ontario, Michigan, Erie and Superior,' she recited, offering a geography lesson that would stand Fintan in the years to come. And then – as if whatever had prompted her to take out the photograph held sway – she turned and whistled a three-note call. 'A whip-poor-will,' she told her sons, 'which sang me to sleep each night beside that lake.' And that night in the lower bedroom Fintan tried to picture the interior of the huge

7

wooden house, puzzling why anyone needed a second home – 'a summer house' – that was four times the size of their Donegal cottage.

But mostly it was America itself he conjured, fashioning six-guns from bits of timber with his best mate Rory O'Gara, making granite-faced Craig Beefan, behind his cottage, into a landscape of mesas and buttes, imagining the gorse-lined stream that divided the north side from the village proper to be an arroyo choked with sagebrush. Indeed he was abetted in such by Father Boyle, the parish priest, who preferred to hear confession in the parochial house kitchen, where he could take snuff and watch telly. 'Bless me, Father, for I have sinned,' Fintan would begin, sitting on a bench beside the priest, who kept one eye on the small black-and-white telly in the corner, the first in Glenbay, and tuned, it seemed, to a perpetual Western, so that hoofbeats and gunfire often punctuated the litany of Fintan's sins, such as they were, as the elderly priest struggled to both grant absolution and stay ahead of the posse.

One summer night Mary took Fintan, aged nine, to the Spink, a large green corrugated-iron shed below the chapel, which, together with Molly's pub and Barney's shop-cum-petrol-pump, made up most of the village's main street. At the back inside the Spink, Andy the Post stood behind a 16-mm projector that soon began to noisily spool out, over the heads of a benched audience, *The Return of Frank James*, onto a pull-down screen on the far wall.

Dakota had died earlier that summer, but Fintan would hear a few years later from Uncle Condy how the old man had walked one night out of the Spink halfway through

*San Francisco* with Clark Gable and Jeanette MacDonald. Dakota had said nothing in Molly's afterwards, but he told Condy several weeks later how he had been in San Francisco, barely twenty years old, in 1906. 'He was in the toilet of a pub when the first tremor struck,' Condy told Fintan, 'jamming the door. But then a second tremor freed it up and he got out.' His uncle also recounted what else Dakota had described: fires burning everywhere, dead bodies buried in the debris. And live bodies, trapped waist-high in rubble behind walls of flame, beyond the reach of rescuers, pleading for their lives, until the army simply shot them dead. 'Out of mercy,' Condy explained to his wide-eyed nephew.

*The Return of Frank James* had impressed itself on Fintan, who woke later that night – loud voices and chairs scraping the kitchen flags – after Packy and Montana landed back from Molly's, along with a naggin of whiskey bought with the latter's Yankee dollars. 'Is Daddy after robbing a bank?' Fintan tearfully asked Mary when she came into him. 'Hush,' she replied, 'don't wake Frankie' – the same Frankie capable of sleeping through a hurricane.

According to Condy, Dakota had confessed to Father Boyle upon his return from America, saying, 'Bless me Father, for I have sinned – all sins, bar murder!' And how, a few years later, at a funeral Mass when mourners still gave a name and townland along with their offering at the table inside the chapel door, your man had hollered out – 'My name is Freddy McIntyre from South Dakota, the Land of God!' – loud enough to raise the chapel roof. But Fintan had never told Condy in turn how another of his fellow returned Yanks, Texarkana, had swivelled round one morning at the boreen below the chapel to show him and Rory his thing, like a mouldy yellow carrot, hanging from his open flies.

\*

That autumn after his first Western, Mary found him several books at the same Carrig sheep-fair stall where she'd seen the Parisian postcards, encouraging him throughout that winter to read at night same as she did, while Packy talked to Jack Gara, their nearest neighbour, who called in most evenings. Fintan's favourites were a dog-eared anthology of adventure stories, set everywhere from the Alps to Africa, along with a hardback of Greek myths, which also had bits of Homer's *Iliad* and *Odyssey*. 'Go out and get turf, you,' Packy, who read nothing but the weekly *Democrat*, might mutter when he saw Fintan with a book, even if the kitchen creel were in no ways low. But Packy would often go out then – to the loom house or the byre – leaving Fintan to read on while Frankie pushed a little red-metal double-decker bus around the kitchen flags in front of the range.

There were, of course, other chores. Climbing the hill behind the cottage after the sheep, or helping his father with the turf in the bog high up on the north side once April arrived. The worst of the bog were the midges, which flew into eyes, ears and nose on close, warm days. The best of it was the descent home, sitting atop the trailer of turf, which crested and plunged like a wave-tossed boat behind Rory's father Connie's grey Ferguson tractor, prompting Packy to intone 'Hateful old hill' as he clung to the trailer-side.

Gathering the sheep would have been easier, had his father been any ways handy with a dog. But each successive canine he got was ever more useless per Packy, who scarcely bothered to train the most recent black-and-white collie mix, which Andy the Post had given him, choosing instead to dig a shallow hole at the eastern gable of the cottage, where he confined the pup beneath an old bicycle wheel, anchored by a large stone.

'Does he bite?' Jack Gara asked upon seeing the makeshift kennel. 'If you took up a stick and hit him,' replied Packy, 'he wouldn't do it again.' In fact Shep, as the boys christened him, did not bite, preferring, once he had outgrown his hole, to lock forelegs around and hump the bejesus out of the leg of any and all male visitors to the house. That said, the dog also proved a formidable ratter who'd deposit his broken-necked bounty by the front door, like an argument for his keep, one or two times most months.

As with dogs, what else Packy turned his hand to would often give him a kick in return. Short of a final fibreglass sheet for the loom-shed roof, he quickly mixed a load of cement to slap over the remaining thatch. 'Like icing on a feckin' cake,' Andy the Post remarked in Molly's, where earlier that night Packy had declared himself done footering with thatch forever. 'Like a dog's breakfast,' Andy offered again some six months later, after the cement had fallen through the rotten thatch.

*

'The back of beyond,' Fintan sometimes says when people in America ask what part of Ireland he grew up in. But fact is the wider world had washed in to Glenbay from time to time. Sometimes literally so, as with the three drowned

French sailors the sea spat onto the stony shingle at Pier back in 1879. Or the single seaman a decade or so later, with a fine gold ring on his finger, which came away when the parishioner who'd discovered his remains tried to prise the ring off with a bit of driftwood. Or the rusty, solid-iron sphere that beached itself like a gigantic globe on the Big Strand of a November morning in 1917.

'The 13th of November 1917,' Jack Gara told Fintan one afternoon after Mary had sent him over with a half-scone of soda bread. 'I'll not be long,' Jack's father, Dominic, had told his family that morning before heading down to the strand, as he did daily, to see what might've come in on the filling tide. But two other Glenbay men had already spotted the huge iron orb and, taking it for some class of buoy, were tentatively probing it with a longish bit of driftwood as Dominic Gara drew near. The subsequent blast from the naval mine was heard throughout the village, the remains of the three men found scattered along the beach. 'I'll not be long,' Jack said again now to Fintan – as if to underline how words you utter unawares might echo thereafter down the years.

A year later – the 11th of November 1918 to be precise – word from the wider world blew in on the wind to Glen. 'I was gathering spuds when we heard the bells,' Jack told Fintan, who'd been sent over to the neighbour this time by Packy, looking for the loan of a loom paddle from Jack, who no longer wove. First those of the coastguard station by Rossan Point, followed by the Glenbay chapel bell, and then far off to the east, the tiny chime of the Carrig church bell. 'We stood there puzzling,' Jack said, 'till my brother worked out it might have something to do with the war. The chapel bell cracked that day,' he added, an assertion Fintan never doubted, even after he came upon similar stories of the Liberty Bell years later in Philadelphia.

A few years later, a gang of English sappers arrived in the village to sink a shaft in the meadow below the Garas' cottage. The mining operation lasted only a fortnight, but a handful of strangers turned up at the entrance to the shaft over the next several years, including three men in well-weathered trench coats the following April, carrying a clock-like apparatus that they variously positioned on the ground around the shaft. Plus an Englishman another August, who divined what he called 'the vein' with a hazel rod, following its course down the meadow, until the rod suddenly flew back up with sufficient force to break in half against his face. Texarkana told Jack's widowed mother it was gold the sappers were after, but Montana later told Jack it was pyrites they had found; pyrites a sure sign of copper, the very metal Montana had mined in America.

In 1952 then, three years before Fintan's birth, the wider world had walked, not washed, into the parish of Glenbay. Arrived on foot from Killybegs in the person of Randall Hart, an American artist, adventurer and ardent socialist who sounded to Fintan far larger than life than the first American tourists who began to filter through southwest Donegal in his early teens. Struck by the sparseness of the locale, backdropped by majestic sea-cliffs and boundless ocean, Hart had stayed some two years in Glenelg, a tiny townland beyond Pier Hill that rose up behind Fintan's mother's home place on the far side of Glen Head from the village proper.

Mary Cunnea, then but a year back from Chicago, often saw the Yank, who walked over the hill to Pier most evenings, calling into one or more of its half-dozen cottages, including the Cunneas', where Mary lived with her ailing mother Kate, her Auntie Cassie and her older brother Condy, himself home from America but a year before his sister. She lived there until she wed Packy Doherty, leaving Pier for Packy's cottage on the north side a few months before Hart went back to America.

\*

Fintan turned eleven his last year at the village school. A kind of nowhere year it felt, too old for waving homemade wooden pistols up on Scrigg Mor, but too young to be allowed much more scope, nor old enough yet to truly care about girls. What few books the Master kept on the classroom window ledge Fintan had finished the previous year, likewise whatever exercises the Master set them, sometimes the very same sums as the previous week, while he chain-smoked at his desk in the front of the classroom, nose buried in the *Irish Press* that had reached the village on the midday bus. 'He wouldn't teach goats to climb!' Condy grunted, dismissing the Master in a half-dozen words after Fintan had grumbled about him – more easily done with his uncle than around Packy, who did not readily entertain complaints.

Players were what the Master smoked, whereas it was the odd Woodbine that Rory nicked from his father's pack to share with Fintan behind the Spink, the cigarette cupped against a November shower, or sheltering out of sight below the Minister's Bridge. Fintan wasn't gone at first on the acrid taste, and even less the bitter shock of smoke on lungs, though he took great pleasure from the cigarette they shared one Saturday afternoon outside Freddy Rua's cottage, taking turns to exhale into the keyhole in hopes Freddy might go mad upon his return from Molly's, thinking somebody had been in the cottage.

Not that Freddy wasn't half-mad already, unstrung by the same combination of isolation and alcohol that bachelors living alone in the west of Ireland often failed to finesse. It helped to have a brother at home – or, better yet, a sister – a quotient of companionship, provided the siblings got on. But Freddy's only brother, John James, was out in America, living on a disabled veteran's pension from the Korean conflict. 'He was badly affected by the war,' Freddy would tell any stranger, most of whom, as he described the poisonous snakes loosed by the Koreans, quickly sussed which brother the war had likely most affected. 'Big snakes, Freddy?' Rory chanced once for badness, to draw him out. 'Oh, aye,' Freddy trembled, 'nine-foot long some of them, capable of killing with their spit,' before recounting yet again how only the brother and another soldier had survived.

It was that same last year at the village school that Fintan first walked out over the hill to Pier, a forty-minute journey each way. 'I called over to Uncle Condy,' he told Packy, after his da asked where had he disappeared to. But Packy said nothing further after Mary, smiling broadly, inquired after news of her brother. Two weeks later Fintan chanced the journey again, only ensuring this time that the cow was foddered and the kitchen turf-creel filled before he struck off. The first part of the trek was hardest, climbing up past the radio mast on the brow of Glen Head, before the road began its gradual decline towards the five dwellings scattered in the lee of Pier Hill, which rose more steeply behind. He might not always find Condy at home and, half-scared of Great-Auntie Cassie, he wouldn't sit with her for long. But there was always something to forage for among the lobster traps scattered on the small shingled beach, or the sea to peer down into from a small concrete pier tucked into the rock face on the far side of the small harbour, its two sea stacks like roughly hewn twin towers of stone. Two other Glenbay men also fished out of Pier, but the Cunneas' was now the sole townland home place still inhabited.

Before that spring was out, Fintan would see his mother Mary everywhere he looked in Pier – imagining her as a child in that same house, or making the daily trek over the hill and back from the same school he and Frankie reached in five minutes flat. Or standing beside her older brother Condy atop Pier Hill, waving at their father in a boat below as it headed towards the herring shoals that shifted like red shadows on the sea. There would be several boats out after the herring, each with a spotter on the hill, and Condy might employ covert signals – wipe his face, say, to indicate that a shoal had been spotted – after which Mary would turn in its direction. And the men in the boats wouldn't always see the herrings even when directly over them, at which point Condy would take off his cap for them to drop their net. All of it an arcane code that Fintan marvelled at – then forgot, until watching his first baseball game in San Francisco's Candlestick Park years later, where Belinda, a die-hard Giants fan he was seeing, explained how the two base-coaches employed similar stratagems, possibly touching the peak of their caps for the batter to swing at the next pitch, or spitting over their left shoulder if a runner on first was to break for second.

But Mary had yet to weigh heavily upon his heart during those first autumnal forays, and so he simply took in the lay of the land, the play of light and cloud on heather, clay and rock. Or the flash of a red beak on a black-winged chough, or an occasional peregrine circling lazily on high. Taking with him in late October a jar of brambleberry jam his mother had sent over for her brother and aunt, out of the batch she made each year from berries gathered along the road, assisted by two sons who ate far more than they harvested, until the past year in which Fintan had grown old enough to truly lend a hand, while taking care to show Frankie that he had harvested far more berries before emptying them into the kettle Mary carried.

Smiling like a child, Auntie Cassie helped herself to spoonfuls of the jam straight from the jar that afternoon. Small, stout, and nearly ninety, she wore a kerchief over whatever hair she still had, though not low enough to cover a large black wen, which to her grand-nephew Fintan looked like a coat button affixed to her brow. Most any time Mary called out with the boys, Cassie read their cups, instructing them to upend the dregs of the tea leaves onto the saucer first. Yet Uncle Condy, were he about, would not allow Cassie to read his, taking care always to rinse his cup out at the sink.

Occasionally Auntie Cassie might read the cards for them too, foretelling of money, letters, weddings and visitors. One afternoon she turned up the knave of diamonds –

'Sandy-haired like Fintan!' Staring intently at the card, she had him shivering as she exclaimed with excited laughter: 'You've good news across deep water!' – as if she actually saw him elsewhere. On their way back home then over the hill, Mary had told him and Frankie how their grandfather, deceased from a stroke before they were born, had always insisted any deck of cards in the house go out into the byre during a lightning storm. On their August visit, however, Auntie Cassie had said nothing as she held her niece's saucer up to the window, had turned away, telling them later that she hadn't a notion as to where the cards had got.

The sense of a solitary adventure – of finally being old enough to take that road alone – saw Fintan dissemble the first few times Rory asked where he had been. 'Up after sheep,' he'd reply. Or 'fishing' – which he and Rory were now finally allowed to do together on their own, casting for glasán from the rocky shore – 'only there was nothing going'. But one November afternoon he relented and, calling for Rory, took his friend with him up over the hill. Daring each other to dip their bare feet into the small stream flowing down to the sea just before the townland of Pier, they eventually arrived at Uncle Condy's, where they paused to play a game with the electric fence, counting aloud to see who could hold on to the wire longest, wriggling in pain as the current laced their palms. 'Jaysus, a cow has more sense than ye!' Condy gave out when he caught them at it, but taking the sting out of it shortly after with a cup of tea and a heel each from a freshly baked pan loaf, the bread lathered with Stork and marmalade, the three of them seated at the kitchen table, and both lads feeling grown-up or just about.

Rory had never before been in Pier, so Fintan lorded his advantage over him that first visit. Pointed to where Glenelg lay beyond Pier Hill, and at three faint mounds in the green bank beside the descending path – not unlike abandoned potato lazy beds – where the trio of drowned French sailors had been buried the previous century. He also repeated for Rory what Condy had told him of that shipwreck, of so much timber strewn along the shore that you might walk like Jesus on the water from Pier to Glen, including the finest mahogany, which was subsequently fashioned into chairs throughout the parish. And of the two survivors who swam in, not a stitch on them. And of the ship's dog that also washed ashore, minus his head, shorn off by a piece of the jettisoned timber.

Fintan had heard at home from Mary how she and two neighbour girls used to feel lonely when they passed those unconsecrated graves at night, coming back over the hill from a dance in the Glen. Lonely in the Donegal sense of that other world that lies about us, and so they blessed themselves as they hurried past, an act of faith to counter any evil spirits, whether Christian or pagan. Indeed the prayers offered at the end of Mass against the fairies had only ceased when Father Boyle arrived as curate. Only Father Boyle himself had come down hugely since – had taken to using snuff on the altar, his vestments streaked yellow with the stuff – until the bishop had finally retired him the previous summer.

The new curate, a waspish priest named Father Mullane, not a speck on his black rig-out, was mad for card games, which he played with his favourites, all females, in the parish. But Mary

19

was not among those – nor did she join the Legion of Mary, which the new curate had introduced, her sojourn Stateside having given her the confidence to sidestep at least that much of the clerical control that clenched rural Ireland in its fist.

*

Packy too had little time for the new priest, concurring with his wife for a change. Not that he and Mary disagreed on everything – not openly anyhow. There were few enough angry rows during the twelve years of their marriage. The heated exchange after Fintan had fetched his father home from Molly's pub, the same night he'd heard Texarkana singing of Laredo, had been an exception, as were the pound notes to hand, which had afforded Packy a feed of pints earlier that evening, from a better-than-expected price for a calf sold the previous day in Dunkineely. Instead a kind of muted indifference marked the ground between their parents, whereon Packy generally managed to check his habitual truculence, if less successfully with his childer, although arguably easier on son Frankie than son Fintan.

And if Mary felt she'd made a poor match, chosen an ineffectual man, she never said as much in the cottage, at least not within earshot of her sons. Still it seemed on the surface a curious match, a younger, travelled, naturally inquisitive woman having settled for an older, largely uncurious man. Any wanderlust within the Doherty clan had likely expired along with Packy's gunshot-granda in Missouri, but even that chapter belonged amongst all that Packy chose not to speak of, nor was it a tale Fintan would hear from his mother, only getting it at age eighteen from Uncle Condy.

Instead, Packy often preferred to talk about what he scarcely, if at all, knew – of how a Jewish shopkeeper in America would never refuse the first money of a morning. 'Say you offer him two dollars,' he informed his sons, 'for something that costs three? Well, he won't say no! Bad luck to refuse the first offer!'

'You wouldn't get far trying that on Mr Stein,' Mary laughed when Fintan repeated it later that evening when his da was out, describing for her sons the small hunched shopkeeper with outsized spectacles on her Chicago street, who never failed to dole out free sweets to the doctor's two little daughters.

Something his parents did share though were their good looks – Mary retaining her strongly-featured beauty into her late thirties and Packy, for all his awkwardness, carrying a muted handsomeness into his early fifties. Who knows what initial spark there might have been, though marriages might also factor in the size of a man's farm – or what resources a wife might bring – as well as any manifest sexual magnetism. Yet such economics had not likely figured within their match, as Packy had but two acres of a rushes-filled north side meadow behind his cottage, and Mary, whose father had died the previous year, only the few dollars in savings that she'd managed to bring back from Chicago.

Both of course attended Mass, Mary's brother Condy being the sole parishioner who declined to darken the chapel door. That Packy left the cottage first of a Sunday, a few minutes ahead of Mary and the boys, also betokened little, as most Glenbay couples made their way so to Mass, wife trailing husband or vice versa. But whatever faith Packy had –

as apart from practised – was not as readily apparent. One of a half-dozen men who chose to loiter inside the chapel porch during Mass, he received no Communion bar when fulfilling his Easter duty. Whereas Mary, a regular communicant, took her sons several times a year up the hill behind their cottage to the Holy Well ascribed to St Colmcille, who was said to have visited Glenbay many centuries ago. A massive cairn of stones had formed over time beside the well, carried up by the faithful, and Fintan made sure each visit that his was a larger rock than Frankie's, while also making sure that his younger brother knew that too.

A small tranche of relics lay scattered across the flagstones that bordered the well: rosary beads, tiny crucifixes, a scapular half-rotted by rain, plus a jam jar, which Mary would fill with sea pinks or purple-flowered self-heal gathered on their climb up. Kneeling, she would bless herself with water from the small dark pool, followed in turn by Fintan and Frankie, after which they would pray silently together for a minute or two.

\*

On the morning of his eleventh birthday that February, Fintan noticed for the first time how tired his mother looked. Took in the dark circles under her eyes as he thanked her for his birthday jumper, an Aran knit with blackberry and diamond patterning, crafted over hours by the range after he had been sent to bed. Her weariness quickly gathered pace as well, and before long the simplest chores began to leave her breathless, her right hand pressed against her left side before she moved on to the next task. By mid-March she had taken to her bed, from where she instructed Fintan on how to begin the dinner if Packy were out digging lazy beds for the early spuds, or mending his traps for the lobstering that would resume in April, seas permitting.

By the end of March Father Mullane had begun to call to the house, accompanied by the Host, which he administered to Mary in her bedroom. Packy or Fintan would offer him a cup of tea, which the priest always refused, much to their shared, if unspoken, relief. His parents had never talked in front of them about Mullane, but Fintan could sense that his mother also had little time for the priest – who, with Mary confined to bed and subject to his ministrations, had her at a disadvantage now. And while she clearly welcomed the Eucharist, her spirits appeared to equally lift upon hearing its bearer go out the kitchen door.

One afternoon Packy retreated into the upper bedroom to fetch something before seeing Father Mullane off. Returning to the kitchen, he saw Shep locked around the priest's left leg, humping its black-trousered shin for all he was worth, while Fintan and Frankie looked on, horrified. Letting loose a roar, Packy swept a poker off the range and swung at the dog in a single, fluid motion – strangely graceful for an often ungainly man – and with such force that it might've taken the priest's leg off at the knee.

However Shep had uncoupled himself at Packy's bellow, and Mullane managed to jerk his leg back from the lethal trajectory of the iron rod. Fintan had the front door opened by then, through which Shep fled, followed directly by Father Mullane. Turning, he saw a rare smile on his father's face and so chanced a smile back. 'Sure, what harm?' chuckled Packy as he replaced the poker. 'It's not like he'd've known what the dog was at now, would he?'

Still Shep knew better than to try that on with Condy, who called in the following day, one of the few times Fintan could recall his uncle ever visiting the house. And had he been a year or two older, he might've been able to piece it all together – the priest and his uncle's visits, along with the pained, if awkward solicitude his father had latterly discovered for his mother. But such was the enormity of what was in play – larger by far than any storm cloud out to sea – that Fintan could no ways see nor imagine such a thing at all.

That Friday after school, Frankie and he found Mary out of bed and sitting in her nightdress beside the range, a cardigan over her shoulders against the early April chill that spilled through the door whenever it opened. Delighted to see their mother up, the boys took out their books and began the weekend lessons that they usually left till Sunday night, happily content with her company once more in the kitchen. Frankie, aged seven, was reading now, and Mary even had energy enough to sound out the longer words with him, as he sat beside her with his tale about a fox and a foolish hen.

Saturday she stayed in bed, only poking at the dinner Fintan brought into her. She brightened at bedtime, however, as he described for her the carry-on of the cattle rustlers in his current paperback Western. Yet rising for Mass the following morning, the boys found the kitchen freezing, its range stone cold, and Packy sitting at the empty table, his face in his hands. '*Fuair sí bás orm,*' he said, as both boys stared at their father, who seldom ever spoke Irish at home.

'*Fuair sí bás orm*,' he repeated: 'She died on me.' Getting up, he awkwardly embraced his sons, before leading them into the upper bedroom, where all three knelt and blessed themselves by the bed where Mary lay, for all the world, asleep.

When Fintan next saw her – after Packy had sent them off alone to Mass, both of them silently weeping – Agnes Curtin, a near neighbour, and one of his mother's few close friends, had Mary already laid out. Clothed in a brown shroud, hair combed, hands clasping her rosary beads, Mary in no ways now feigned sleep, her brow and the set of her mouth more like a waxen facsimile of their mother. Choosing his moment – after Agnes departed, his father finally out at his toilet, and Frankie crying in their bedroom – he took the black-and-white photograph of Mary, dressed up to the nines in America, from the floral-patterned tea caddy on the mantel, and slipped it into the *Riders of the Purple Sage* softback on the chair beside his bed. And only wondering, as he did so, had his father ever seen it?

Fintan had held Frankie's hand during the Prayers for the Dead at Mass two hours earlier; had returned Cáit McGlinchey's greeting outside the chapel afterwards like any other Sunday. 'Oh, feeling better yesterday,' he replied as Moira Byrne, another parishioner, asked after their mother, trusting Frankie would hold his whisht. And back now in the lower bedroom, he put his arms tentatively around his brother, as if trying to tend him as Mary used to tend them both. He went out then with a few cold boiled spuds to the turf shed where Packy had Shep tied up, lest the dog pay court to all the men of the parish who, with their wives if they were wed, would call in to the cottage over the two days and nights in which they would wake Mary, before her remains were taken to the chapel on Tuesday evening for the funeral Mass the following morning.

Late that Wednesday night he again managed to stem Frankie's bedtime tears with a never-ending story of how they'd meet Mary again in Heaven, only Heaven lay somewhere east of China, with all kinds of creatures – dragons, griffins and every class of adventure – before they reached the huge palace, and it only a Summer Palace, all clapboards and verandas, where their mother now resided. And only after his brother's breathing finally evened out had he heard his own grow suddenly ragged, his own hot tears once again spilling out.

He did not, however, take Frankie along up to the Holy Well the following week, carefully making his way alone up the wet, grassy bank, then down into the hollow where the huge cairn rose like a tiny beached whale above the small pool of water. A few faded primroses sat in the chipped mug on the wee stone shelf above the well, nor had Fintan thought to pick any cowslips or buttercups on the way up, much less a stone to place upon the cairn. Kneeling, he said a prayer for Mary, then another for Packy, Frankie and himself. Getting up, he spotted Johnny Jack's dog tracking a half-dozen sheep across the scree below Craig Beefan, on whose ridge line that morning's brief snow shower yet lay, like a scattering of chalk dust under the slate-grey sky.

Nor did he take his brother along out to Pier a fortnight later, though the day was better, a dry east wind, and the sky that clear shade of blue that can often be oddly harder on a heavy heart than dull clouds overhead. Condy was off somewhere, his door on the latch, but Fintan didn't let himself in, even though his Great-Aunt Cassie might've welcomed a visit. Wandering back down to the small strand with its large, round, white stones, he followed the shoreline for a bit, before turning and walking back up to the wee bridge, where he sat with his feet hanging over the stream as it rushed down to the mother ocean. New growth was showing green across the banks and rocky fields, the sky an even deeper blue now overhead, and the tide retreating harshly over stone shingle, sounding like it were tearing the shore apart.

# 2

One June afternoon a year after her death, a stranger comes looking for Mary Doherty. Arrives in a brand-new blue Cortina that Fintan, making his way home up the lane after school, spots parked outside their cottage. A remarkable sight to be sure, given that Father Mullane's three-year-old Vauxhall was the latest model among the small handful of cars in the Glen unless a visitor were passing through, or a returned Yank, home on holidays from America and putting on the Ritz with a rental.

Shep barks a greeting from the turf shed, but Fintan is too curious about the car to pay him any heed. While Packy had outright banished the dog from the kitchen after Mary's death, his sons let him in to lie by the range for an hour or two any night their father went down to the pub. Yet Packy's drinking was another thing that had changed with Mary's death. He still took a drink, surely, but had yet to go on the batter in the fourteen months since her death, the three or four days of straight swilling he had heretofore done once or twice a year, whenever a run of salmon, twin calves, or a decent price for a bolt of tweed had boosted the household budget. 'Ach, he's been hard on himself since the wife died,' the village might've excused him – had Packy started to drink more – but it was almost as if something else had been laid to rest along with Mary.

Not that Packy was happier – just a tad more temperate and, suddenly, somehow, older. Yet even as his temper had improved somewhat, he also now seemed to favour Frankie less. 'Butt in you when you're spoken to!' he might snap if his younger son piped up when Packy and Jack Gara were talking. Nor was he any less contrary either, occasionally declaring 'He's no idea in the wide world!' of Jack as soon as their neighbour went out the door, dismissing out of hand some notion Jack had, say of how the fertiliser that ran off the fields was poisoning the streams. 'No idea in the wide world!' – this from a man who had himself never left Donegal.

On that June afternoon, however, Fintan found his father at home, as he now endeavoured to be when his sons arrived back from school, only this time he was seated opposite someone who had flown all the way from America to meet their mother. 'Hired a brand-new Cortina at Shannon Airport to drive up to the arse end of Donegal,' as Packy put it after the stranger departed. The inevitable last word – as soon as someone closed the cottage door behind them – whether Jack Gara and his distrust of bagged phosphorus, or Father Mullane the night Shep had lovingly locked himself around the cleric's knee. 'The best ride he'll ever have,' opined Packy, once he'd heard the priest motor off.

The Yank struck Fintan as a bit odd-looking: a big, flat, bald head like someone had tamped it down with a shovel, his large ears sticking out like semaphores. Busying himself at the kitchen sink, Fintan quickly gathered that the visitor had come to Glenbay on the trail of Randall Hart, and was keen to talk to anyone who'd known the painter during his stay in the parish, not least Mary Cunnea Doherty who, per the stranger, is pictured lying on a hill above the sea at Pier in one of Hart's paintings.

Scarcely believing his ears, Fintan heard his father allow as how he had heard about such a painting all right. 'I suppose it's worth a fortune now?' Packy then asked the Yank, who, laughing, asked in turn whether Packy had also known the painter.

'Aye, I spoke once or twice to him,' Packy grunted. 'Bade him good day.' It seemed Hart too had died the previous year, and the Professor – for that's what their Yank caller was, an art professor from a university in Iowa, somewhere Fintan had yet to hear of – was writing what he described as 'catalogue notes for a major retrospective of Hart's paintings'. Explaining this in a nasal twang to Packy, who nodded back as if fine-art exhibitions were all in a day's work. And nodding again when the Yank said once more how sorry he was to hear of his wife Mary's death. Getting up to leave, the Professor, who'd spoken of being in France as a GI during World War II, offered Fintan a yellow pack of chewing gum. A flavour called 'Juicy Fruit', which Fintan had never seen and which, after glancing at his father, he shyly accepted, remembering just in time to thank the Yank.

Jack Gara had apparently not spotted the blue Cortina, as he said nothing about it when he called over that evening; nor did Packy volunteer anything about the visitor or his mission. However, Frankie, who'd been out playing, asked Fintan where he had got the gum, persisting until Fintan finally shared a stick.

Packy went down to Molly's then after Jack departed that evening, waking Fintan in the wee hours as he stumbled back in, drunk as a hatchet, from Montana's cottage, where the pair had gone after the pub closed. But it was as if his father had put the brakes on then. Had pulled up short, staying away from Molly's for a fortnight, and taking it handy the few nights he went back down to the pub that summer.

Your man from America had trekked out to Pier to see Condy too, who like his sister, had known the painter from when Hart had lived over the hill in Glenelg. Yet Condy said little to his nephew about his visit either. 'Ach, that man would paint anything, a stone ditch or a wet day,' he replied when Fintan asked about the painting with Mary lying on the hill, of which Packy too had said nothing further. It happened Condy had also been wild fond of Juicy Fruit gum in America, only Fintan had the last stick of it well chewed by the time he learned that.

The first months after Mary's death had been hardest, days when the pit of his stomach felt altogether AWOL, or other days when his grief was more a light-headed, almost giddy kind of sorrow. Meantime Frankie had begun to wet the bed, for which Packy, while trying to do his best, had neither patience nor understanding, and so Fintan began getting his younger brother up midway through the night for a month or so, until Frankie managed to stop altogether.

Yet in the fortnight following the American's visit, his mother's absence again seemed to overshadow all, draining Fintan once more from the inside out. A few nights later he awoke from a dream wherein Mary had made him affix a scarlet ribbon to Shep's tail, the pair of them laughing as she insisted he finish it off in a bow. Yet the dream made no sense to him whatsoever when he woke, no more than had her death. Worse still was how close she had felt – as if she were still alive – yet only as he slept. He rose then and went outside for a leak in the cool, dark air, staring over the fuchsia hedge at the distant red and green running lights of a lone trawler far out on the pitch-black sea.

*

School happily finished up a fortnight later, though not half as happily as when summer holidays had meant being shut of the village Master for two months. His first year at the Tech had been one of changes, beginning with the large yellow American-style school bus that took Fintan, Rory and the other Glen lads each morning out to Carrig, where they had been assigned different teachers for different subjects through the day, not least Miss Friel from Buncrana for Geography, whom the boys all shyly fancied, and who identified the long brown Caribbean carob bean that Fintan had found one afternoon on the Big Strand, yet another bit of that wider world washed in.

There was greater freedom at the Tech too, once you mastered the larger building and initially confusing timetable. And Fintan had made new pals readily enough among the Carrig lads, not so much gregarious as quietly confident. Jealous of his best friend's new-found popularity, Rory picked a fight back on the north side one November afternoon after school. 'Fuck you!' he shouted at Fintan, who had turned for home after their brief wrestling match ended in a draw. 'And if you've relations in America, fuck them too!'

Second year at the Tech was even better, thanks in large part to their English teacher, Mr McGarvey, who gave them an American novel about some half-eejit out West, who liked mice too much and got shot by his best pal with a Luger after he strangled a woman.

Third year was OK too – as far as books went anyhow – with Fintan for the first time truly interested in something written in Irish. Not *Peig*, which they had all hated the previous year – some old doll down in Kerry wittering on about the sorrows of the world – but *Rotha Mór an tSaoil/ The Big Wheel of Life* by Mící Mac Gabhann, which Mr Devlin, their Irish teacher, said had been written by a Donegal man who first travelled to Scotland, and then on to the States, where he'd worked in both Montana and the Klondike. There was great stuff in it too, somebody tearing his blanket in two, then stitching both halves together to make a proper length. Or the men on a dog sled, who running out of food, cut off, boiled and devoured the tails of their dogs – before feeding the poor beasts the soup. 'I didn't care for America,' your man also wrote, but Fintan paid less heed to that.

Nor was Mící Mac Gabhann's account of Montana mining life altogether new to Fintan, who had already heard several stories of Butte from Condy, whose own father, Cornelius, Fintan's granda, had told of prospecting for copper during his time over there. Of digging a mile underground, where the temperature and humidity were often jungle-like. 'A hot box,' Condy said Cornelius had called it – ten-hour shifts in which you drank gallons of water, yet sweated so much you seldom had to pee.

Or hoisted out of the shaft in winter, travelling from 90° Fahrenheit to 30° below in five minutes' time. 'You'd come up sweating,' Condy had told him, 'then vanish into a ball of steam when the cold air hit you. Your clothes freezing to you as you walked home!' After six months underground, where he saw two men blown to bits by a premature blast, and another with his back crushed by a rock fall, Cornelius Cunnea took to heart one of the omnipresent hand-painted signs – DON'T GET HURT: THERE ARE TEN MEN WAITING FOR YOUR JOB – and so left the hard-rock men below to work topside as a carpenter and rope man.

Fintan hadn't known whether to credit all that Condy claimed for Montana – little of which sounded much like the Wild West depicted on TV. Massive boarding houses that slept hundreds, six men to a small, fly-infested room, many rooms without a window; filthy toilets in the cellar and slops thrown out behind. Or pubs that stayed open twenty-four hours, 'saloons' as Condy called them, full of hurdy-gurdy men and faro dealers. Nor whether to believe there were truly 2,000 Irishmen in Butte in 1900 when Cornelius had landed there, some of whom had departed Donegal with BUTTE, MONTANA on a scrap of paper, pinned to their jacket like a baggage label. Or how once they found work there, the same men, or so his uncle said, wrote home for others to join them: DON'T STOP IN THE US COME STRAIGHT OUT TO BUTTE, AMERICA. 'Sure, there were plenty here in Glenbay who knew more about Butte from family who went out,' claimed Condy, 'than they knew about Dublin.'

Condy himself had only passed through Butte in 1944 – to see where his da, Cornelius, had toiled before returning to Donegal in 1909 – as any copper underground had been fairly played out by then, and open-pit mining yet to begin. There was other stuff too his uncle might mention of his years Stateside that likewise lodged with Fintan – like 'the wild noise in the bowling alleys', which puzzled his nephew, seeing how Condy had grown up but a hundred yards from the wind-whipped onslaught of stormy seas on rock and shingle.

'How so wild noise?' he asked, prompting his uncle to describe the acoustic effects of low ceilings, hardwood floors and massive black balls that scattered the tenpins, once you got the hang of it. 'There's fierce heat in the self-serve laundries,' he similarly recalled, apropos of nothing another afternoon, giving Fintan something else to puzzle as he made his way home over the hill. And thinking, as the track began its descent past the radio mast, how Condy's America sounded more like everything's up to date in Kansas City than the black-and-white six-gun West that had first beguiled him. More modern surely, yet mysterious all the same.

If less travelled than Dakota, Condy had nonetheless worked in several states – though exactly where and at what, Fintan had to press his uncle hard to hear – much as he used to pester his mother about Chicago. Like 'What's the best job you ever had over there?', which he asked on his next visit to Pier.

'Wheeling hair out of a barbershop,' Condy replied, declining any invitation to stroll down memory lane. But one afternoon, the week Fintan turned sixteen, his uncle told him a real story – taking him not so much down memory lane as a long-ago ride down Route 66. Of how stranded in a Californian town called, of all things, Needles, and needing to get back east, Condy had stood with his thumb out beneath a stand of tall palm trees, where nobody gave him a second look. After two hours in the heat, he approached a man with a wife and baby at a nearby filling station and asked whether he might ride with them. The man never said a word, just handed Condy the keys, before getting into the back seat with the wife and infant.

'You knew how to drive?' Fintan chanced, interjecting.

'Just about,' Condy said. 'There were only two lanes, so all I had to do was pretty much point and steer.'

Only Condy kept talking for a change: of how he had driven up onto the mesa and into the night with the family asleep in the back. Describing for his nephew how he met more traffic than you might think, night-time being best for crossing the Mojave Desert in summer. Reaching, an hour before dawn, the tiny town of Peach Springs, Arizona, where the man awoke and directed Condy to pull into a cabin court, which Condy had to decipher for his nephew, who'd already inquired 'Why Needles?'

'Sharp peaks on the mountains either side.'

'Why Peach Springs?' he queried again.

'You tell me and I'll tell you.'

But Condy carried on, telling how the family took a cabin, leaving him to sleep in the car for a few hours, until the sun on its roof made his neck sweat so it woke him up. Getting out of the car, he climbed the yellowish bluff behind the cabins, hiked past pinyon pines and juniper to where he could see for miles – desert, distant mountains, a few buzzards above in the pale-blue sky – and tiny railroad tracks down below, along which a freight train eventually came, rattling dimly in the distance.

'What happened next?'

'Nothing happened,' snorted Condy. 'Your man said they were stopping over as his wife was feeling poorly with the heat, so I stuck my thumb out again.'

'And who lifted you next?' Fintan asked, though he knew better.

'Would you stop?'

'I didn't know they had palm trees in America,' Fintan said, resigned now to raking over the coals of what'd already been related.

'Sure, they've palm trees in Dublin!' his uncle said, laughing again. More news to the nephew.

Putting on his coat to fetch a bucket of turf, Condy informed Fintan, as he went out the door, how the husband had taken a photograph that he later posted to Condy, though Fintan couldn't imagine what address in America his uncle might've had.

'Have you the picture still?' he asked, trying to mask his eagerness.

'Would you ever stop?' Condy said. But he laughed yet again and, better yet, he dug it out from a beat-up steamer trunk beneath his bed to show the nephew when Fintan called in a fortnight later. The photo was entirely unlike the portrait of Mary, taken close up against that clapboarded summer house. Instead, Condy's photo had foreground and background both, the latter a distant range of sun-bleached mountains beneath an empty sky. But foreground was what held Fintan's eye: wherein his uncle, not yet thirty, wearing dark trousers and a white shirt with sleeves rolled up, stood beside a dusty sedan with a battered holdall at his feet and a quizzical half-smile on his face – as if still trying to work out how the stranger behind the camera had divined he might entrust his wife, their infant child and automobile to another stranger, never mind the generosity inherent in said trust.

The sedan in the photo looked massive by Irish standards – if only half as long as the American cars that were soon to follow. Replete with whitewall tyres and hugely rounded at the back compared to the half-hearted hump on the Morris Minor Condy now kept garaged in a byre. 'A Buick,' Condy said, anticipating Fintan, who promptly filed it in his inner automotive lexicon, alongside Chevrolet, Pontiac and Oldsmobile.

He looked again at the image of his uncle, pondering the full head of hair and youthful leanness, along with the casual dress that looked like high fashion, given the tattered gansey and muddied trousers on the now grey-haired man who, taking the photo back, tossed it casually onto the kitchen table. Fact is, Fintan needed the algebra they were learning that year at the Tech – or something like it – to square the bloke in the picture with the uncle who would shortly after walk him part of the way back over the hill, itself another landscape surely, allowing how he needed to check on a ewe who'd come down with a case of the staggers.

*

No doubt Condy had helped fill a small portion of the gaping hole left by his mother's death – somebody grown with whom Fintan could converse, given how little father Packy spoke around the house. And if his uncle was away, to the hill after sheep say, Fintan could let himself in, throw a few sods of turf into the range and put on the kettle.

Jack Gara was another adult Fintan gravitated to in the years after Mary's death, calling over to their neighbour afternoons after school, much as the older man called in to Packy most evenings. Unlike Condy, Jack had not travelled beyond Donegal, but unlike Packy, he was keenly interested in the life around him, with all its minutiae.

'Will ye have a blue one?' he might greet Fintan, offering him an egg from the ducks he kept, and telling how the English, thinking a duck's egg poisonous, used it only for baking.

'Oh, a hen's egg's lovely!' Jack assured him, after Fintan asked did he eat hens' eggs too. 'But not the shop-bought ones,' he added, putting on a face that showed his teeth, or what was left of them, a few blackened stumps. 'Sure, you can taste the fishmeal fed to a battery hen in a shop-bought egg.'

A keen environmentalist too, though Fintan wouldn't know to call him that until years later in America. Nor had Jack needed to travel the world to know what was wrong with it. 'Making things better to make things worse!' was his mantra – whether decrying 'bag manure', as he called phosphorus, or the deep-sea trawlers that swept the ocean floor clean, spawn and all. 'You can't beat fresh fish!' he often enthused. 'It's all fertilised nowadays, bar the fish. Sheep, beef, oats – all fertilised.'

And Jack knew his fish surely, having gone out after cod, herring and salmon, until he got too old, too bad with arthritis. Although Fintan himself now went out with his father in the summer after lobster, it was Jack, not Packy, who gave him the life cycle of the conger eels they occasionally pulled up in the traps, thick as a man's forearm with an overhung upper jaw, slimy, scale-less skin, big, baleful eyes and razor-edge teeth. 'They breed thousands of miles from here,' Jack had informed Fintan of the eels, the same eels Packy carefully dumped into the bottom of the boat, before breaking their backs with a length of iron pipe he kept stowed under a seat and tossing them back into the ocean. 'Down in the Saragossa Sea,' Jack explained, giving Fintan another name for the atlas inside his head – though he had to guess several times at its spelling before eventually finding it in the tattered, blue-cover, hardback atlas at the Tech.

'The conger eel can live forever out of water,' Jack claimed. 'If you leave one atop the hill, all he wants is a wee stream to reach the sea – working his way towards water always. Tough!' he added. 'Oh, nothing tougher.'

It was this fund of knowledge, the degree to which Jack truly inhabited his world, always aware from which quarter the wind blew, and how the manner in which the cow stood in the meadow or the starlings gathered on a telephone line both presaged rain – a fund of knowledge that would play on Fintan years later, whenever he recalled the old man's Close Encounter of the Inexplicable Kind. This was a story Jack had told Fintan during his fifth year at the Tech, three days after his neighbour had seen whatever it was he saw. Recounting how he had reached for a pipe and matches he kept on the chair beside his bed, should he not be able to sleep with his arthritis. 'Maybe only once a week,' he explained to Fintan, 'but I fill the pipe each night before bed.' Only that night, before he could strike a match, there came suddenly through the bedroom window a light so bright that Jack first thought the hill behind was on fire. 'Or your house,' he told Fintan, 'or the Curtins' – something, anyhow!'

Throwing on his clothes, Jack went out to find no lights, much less flames anywhere in the townland. What he saw instead was a blazing orb over the north-side hill – 'the size of a massive football' – which then suddenly seemed to condense, the sky around it darkening as it churned against the clouds.

'How bright?' Fintan asked.

'So bright it took the water from my eyes out there in the lane.'

'It changed shape then,' Jack continued, animated now in his chair, rubbing the knees of his black trousers, whose sheen already shone like ebony. 'As if somebody had thrown a switch! Grew three times as big, like a barrel, rounded on one end and boxed on the other.'

It was the specificity of what Jack described that stayed with Fintan. How the shape had thrown out 'three prongs of light', the third tine shooting far up into the sky, 'where a thinner wire of light came out of it – like a cable just – twisting back down along the shaft'.

'What happened next?' – Fintan's favourite query since age three.

'Oh it just took off,' Jack said. 'Only it didn't skite like a shooting star. A satellite it was … Or so I thought, once nobody else remarked it.' He took down his fiddle then, as he occasionally might when Fintan called, opting to play a tune or two instead of another story, a reel or hornpipe with improbable-sounding names – like 'Pigeon on the Gate' or

'Upstairs in the Tent' – which Fintan, when younger, used to think Jack made up on the spot.

*Nor does a shooting star hang about either*, Fintan thought as he headed home that afternoon. Nor put on a light show for an old man who has looked out over that same hill every day and night of his life. A man without a telly, and like most countrymen, a canny, acute observer of the natural world. A pioneer too, whereas had Montana reported such a sighting, you might easily think it drink. 'But beautiful all the same,' had been Jack's last words on the subject, 'and I'd look at it again, surely.'

\*

Whatever it was Jack had seen, there followed further intimations aplenty of a wider world beyond Glenbay. Like the closed cottage Fintan and Rory came across later that summer far up the Glen, mouse dirt and bits of scraw from under the thatch above on the kitchen table, a tea chest stencilled PRODUCE OF INDIA in the upper bedroom, along with a London street-map spread out on a mildewed mattress – as if its occupants had double-checked their destination only moments before shutting the door behind them. 'You can sometimes find money in the walls,' Rory proposed, but there hung an air of inhabitation in the rooms yet, and neither he nor Fintan did more than look for signs of loosened stone.

According to Condy, Fintan's grandfather Cornelius had picked out the first currants ever he saw from a slice of bread and thrown them into the fire, whereas it seemed now as if a sluice gate had lately opened up somewhere east of Glenbay, through which the world's foodstuffs now flooded into the back of beyond. Or so Fintan mused the afternoon he caught a lift from Carrig in the back of a vegetable van, hunched down amid boxes of apples from Italy, Israeli oranges, bags of New Zealand onions and bananas from Panama.

It took him another year, however, to place on the map the Charlie calf he had helped Uncle Condy to deliver, after having found his uncle on his knees in the byre one afternoon that same May, talking in turns to Jesus, Mary and the cow, which lay with her head in the slurry trough. Grasping the calf's head, Condy instructed Fintan to take its forelegs, and together they had pulled it out, hefting it into a corner of the byre, where a greatly relieved Condy wiped it down with a handful of hay.

The Charlie was a new breed in the Glen, difficult to birth, according to Condy, 'and if it's a bull calf, forget it'. Later that same evening, Jack Gara in turn told Fintan how a cow went into labour – 'got sick' – with the tide. A filling tide were it a bull calf, or with a heifer calf like Condy's, as the tide turns. But it was his Geography teacher, Mr Devine, who eventually glossed the Donegal 'Charlie' as Charolais for Fintan, opening his atlas to the French county from whence the breed originated, then showing Fintan a classified ad from the *Donegal Democrat* two weeks later: 'For sale: two-year-old Charolais bull, guaranteed quiet and fruitful.'

Fintan himself was reading more now too. Mostly fiction, and most of it pulp, though he managed to lay hands on an odd classic like *White Fang* along with a collection of Hemingway stories. Mr McGarvey at the Tech also assigned an occasional poem that worked – worked for Fintan anyhow – like a key in a door or a torch shone suddenly into a darkened room. A poem about a soldier dying young, another comparing reincarnation to a railroad journey, or one that McGarvey read aloud from a book of his own, full of drunken tramps stumbling out of an New York subway. Yeats he could do less with, though the one about the swan and the girl with its line about loosened thighs had momentarily focused most of the Fifth Year lads. 'He gets a lot into a little?' Fintan offered when McGarvey asked him to describe the poet's technique, a comment that seemingly pleased the teacher, who nodded and laughed before calling on someone else.

Certainly the poems McGarvey assigned were better than the doggerel the Master in the Glen had drilled them on, apart from one about Sam Magee from Tennessee, who ended up cremated in Alaska. That poem was a favourite also of Freddy Rua's, only Freddy would get Sam mixed up halfway through with his own brother John James, the Korean vet, who Fintan had overheard Montana telling his father how Packy was actually in Fort Leavenworth for having burnt down his captain's quarters, not home and dry in Philadelphia with an army pension, as Freddy had it.

There was no knowing if Montana's claim were any truer than the tales Freddy Rua told – of how, say, the Koreans had cut the tongues off most of the Yank POWs – but Fintan was no longer interested in blowing cigarette smoke into the poor fecker's cottage either. 'Give us "Black Solider USA",' he coaxed instead of the old man seated one afternoon on the bench outside Molly's pub, thinking even Freddy Rua could distinguish between a Black brother and his own John

James. It worked a treat too, as Freddy settled himself before singing a few verses of your man:

*They used to call him lazybones in Harlem,*
*Lazy, good for nothing, all the day.*
*But now they're mighty proud of him in Harlem,*
*Since the day he first heard that bugle play.*

The same song had been popular during the war years, played as a slow foxtrot by dance bands at weddings in Donegal Town. Or so Andy the Post had told Fintan, who first saw a Black person at age nine on a shopping trip to Killybegs with brother Frankie and their mother. Only to recall the song then years later, when Jon Martell, head janitor at a Flagstaff, Arizona hospital where Fintan was working in maintenance – an older bloke with a faded, yellow forelock – spoke of the Allied-occupied German town during World War II where he'd seen three African Americans, fellow GIs, hanging from trees on the square. 'It sickened me then,' Jon said, 'and sickens me now telling it.' 'Nothing you could dance to, surely,' winced Fintan as Jon, stubbing out his cigarette, handed him a mop.

'Don't stare!' Mary had cautioned Frankie that Killybegs afternoon, who like Fintan, couldn't take his eyes off the tall, Black man with a shiny, shaved head, a crew member off one of the foreign factory ships that was visiting the fishing port. Yet on the bus back home she told them both of Mattie, the African American maid who had worked for the same Chicago doctor as herself. 'A lovely woman,' Mary said, describing how Mattie, same age as herself, had shown her how to hand-press her clothes still warm from the automatic dryer.

Any kind of first-hand experience of Black was rare in Glenbay, where most stories of 'the Darkies' carried a strong whiff of folktale. Like the returned Yank, Duffy, based in a cottage out on the Glen road to Carrig, whose rooster, according to Jack Gara, had one night set to crow and crow. 'There was nothing he could do to stop it,' or so the story went, 'only strike the head off it. But didn't a Black woman come on him as soon as he was back in his kitchen. From America, some woman he'd mistreated, maybe killed. And hadn't the rooster kept her off him all those years?'

Condy, who like his sister had worked alongside African Americans, had no opinions either way. But he too had a story, one his father Cornelius had told him, of a Gallagher from Carrig who'd had a saloon somewhere in Texas, until a Black barman seemingly murdered him. Only the way Condy told it, the murderer sounded to be Black in the same way he might've been a Cork or Kerryman.

Once sixteen, Fintan began to thumb into Killybegs the odd Saturday evening, savouring the same sense of solitary adventure as when he'd first gone over the hill alone to Pier. Buying a bag of chips in Melly's, he'd proceed then to the tiny cinema tucked up a narrow street if a film looked any good, else wander down to the harbour where the fishing trawlers lay tied up two or three deep along the pier.

One evening in Melly's, an American – or so your man described himself – sat down at the same table, though he struck Fintan as more likely a returned Yank, that strange hybrid that a good handful of years Stateside can make of an Irishman. Either way, the stranger told Fintan of having worked on the New York docks for years, unloading ships of everything from grain and gravel to bananas. He looked every inch the part too, navy peacoat and woollen watch cap, as he disappeared out the chipper door.

Finishing his chips, Fintan departed down to the harbour, picking his way past a tanker truck mired in the muddy ruts of the service road, and onto the street-lamp-lit concrete pier, which shone all pink-flecked from crushed fish underfoot, the orange, yellow and red fish-boxes a further riot of colour alongside pools of bloody water, plus a generator on the largest trawler pulsing like a soundtrack to it all, adding its diesel to the heady, aromatic mix of fish, money and the promise of somewhere else.

# 3

That next summer brings even more visitors to the Glen, even if most of them are day-trippers, English couples or Northerners who motor in, point a camera at Glen Head, drive past Andy the Post's wife's B&B sign, have a pint in Molly's, then motor off. The odd Continental has begun to turn up too, an occasional French family, but mostly Germans, including the Fräulein in a white bikini who walks out of the sea one afternoon as Fintan and Rory are lazing on the grass above the Wee Strand. Or so the two lads think, until your one draws near enough for them to see her untanned skin, which they'd mistaken for swimming togs. Their first-ever sight of a naked woman, albeit too fleeting for the extended study afforded by a copy of *Playboy* that Rory's uncle, a bus driver out in Buffalo, NY, brings over later that summer. The same uncle who used to post his nephew a large envelope stuffed with *The Lone Ranger* comic strips cut from his daily newspaper.

The entire question of the opposite sex continued to confound Fintan after he started at the Tech. School aside, there were fewer females in his life now since Mary died; no sisters, no girl cousins, never mind anything like a girlfriend. Even Great-Auntie Cassie no longer sat in her corner of

Uncle Condy's kitchen, having crossed over to the other side six months after her niece. Clueless but keen, he now found himself pausing over passages he might've skimmed or skipped in whatever he was reading a year or two ago, descriptions of women, say, while occasionally noting down the odd word – *nubile* or *cleavage* – to look up in the dictionary at the Tech. That it was invariably a girl's eyes that he noticed first also puzzled him, when set against Rory's 'great tits, nice arse' as their German bather disappeared from view, but he kept all such confusions – as if suspect – to himself.

Mass too was now of greater interest, an opportunity to further gauge the parish talent, to covertly stare at Maggie Cunningham in the catwalk of girls proceeding up and back from the Communion rail. Maggie, a year ahead of him at the Tech, with none of the skittishness that marked most of the Glen girls: a kind of tense, wide-eyed shyness – not unlike a sheep – as if waiting always to be startled. Not entirely unlike his own shyness, which left him stranded in the crush of lads at those first Halla Mhuire dances, unable to cross over to the far side of the floor to ask any girl, much less Maggie, for a dance.

Fintan would forsake Mass after he left for London, but he partook the odd time during his first years in America – more a kind of meditation, he told himself, than a religious pursuit. But not even his wildest daydreams in the Glenbay chapel had prepared him for the young, dark-haired woman beside him in a Cleveland pew one Sunday, muttering, 'Oh, shut the fuck up!' under her breath at the priest bemoaning the price of heating oil up on the altar, prompting Fintan to softly laugh aloud. 'Jo-Ann,' she said outside the church, offering him a hand to shake before inviting him back to her flat for a coffee, the same flat where they would go to bed a few weeks later, Jo-Ann handing him a condom in the same matter-of-fact manner with which she'd introduced herself after Mass.

\*

If his awkwardness on the dance floor likely came from Packy, there was as well an openness to his nature as likely bequeathed him by Mary Cunnea. A kind of tolerance, along with a capacity to suspend judgement, to consider facts, or what passed as fact concerning others – villagers, classmates, teachers – without necessarily reaching a conclusion. Jack Gara had possibly contributed to this too, being one of the few who Fintan felt did not keep a perpetual watch on his Glenbay neighbours, forever on the lookout for the untoward.

Either way, he was growing up reasonably open, not just to those around him, but open also to opinions, contradictions and anathemas. McGarvey at the Tech had a hand here too, giving him an occasional text like *1984* or *The Grapes of Wrath*, while also urging him to apply for a scholarship for third-level study. But Fintan was not pushed about university, happy enough just to jot down at home in an old school copy the odd new word he encountered – *svelte* or *supine*, say – and wanted to retain.

\*

By January of Fifth Year he was also tinkering beneath the bonnet of Condy's Morris Minor, having been taught to drive by his uncle the previous summer, Condy chiding him to *ease* the clutch out, as the car hopped and bucked like a big black rabbit down the long empty road out of Pier. Gears mastered, Fintan then set himself to understand its innards. 'How do you adjust the timing?' he began to pester, once his uncle had shown him how to change the spark plugs and oil, and tighten the fan belt. 'The man who made time,' Condy replied, 'made plenty of it. And you leave the timing belt alone.'

The talk between them had likewise shifted gears as Fintan matured. 'The poor feckers' was all Condy would say of the fourteen people shot dead by the British army in Derry, and he proved no less taciturn one Sunday afternoon after Fintan reported how Father Mullane had complained at Mass about sheep fouling the front of the church, the kind of thing that passed for local news that far from the border. 'You'd be as well off going to a cattle auction as to Mass,' Condy replied.

'You know the first money ever I earned?' he then inquired, his face brightening. 'A tuppence I took from the table just inside the chapel, where you gave a ha'penny on your way in. Only I lifted four ha'pennies instead, bought myself five Woodbine, and went off to a dance that night!'

If Condy sounded bitter about the Church, he wasn't at heart an embittered soul. Harsh, surely, on any number of scores, but often generous as well. 'Refuse nothing – only the blows!' he more than once counselled Fintan. 'Eat your fill, and pocket none,' he might likewise command, whenever they sat down to a cup of tea and a slice of bread. Or to a proper feed, had Fintan come over the hill to lend a hand, say, with the hay or turf, after which Condy might serve up a fry or a bit of meat with spuds and cabbage.

In March Condy told Fintan how Mary had been born with 'a weak heart'. How his only sibling had been told from the git-go she'd be unable to bear children, 'git-go' being some of the Texan-speak his uncle had brought back from over beyond. Seemingly the gentleman doctor in Chicago had advised her that – 'Only hadn't he got it wrong,' Condy said, 'seeing that she bore two fine sons?' Fintan in turn had puzzled over that one for a time; had wondered what exactly constituted a weak heart, given his mother had always seemed so much stronger, more whole-hearted, than his father.

*

One Saturday that May a slender, dark-skinned lad in a crimson turban struggled up Condy's lane, hauling a huge suitcase behind. 'Hello, how are you, my friend?' he sing-songed at them, 'Missus is at home?' Opening the case then, he began to display his brightly coloured wares: knitwear, wash 'n' wear, polyester and nylon garments.

'There's no woman here,' Condy had informed the pedlar, only to surprise Fintan then by stepping up for a closer look, before selecting, of all things, two pillowslips. After paying the man, he asked from where he hailed.

'Indiana,' your man from India said, making Condy laugh as he pocketed his change. As the pedlar began to lug his case back towards Glen, twice the journey by road as by over the hill, Condy smiled down at the pillowslips in his hand, 'Ach, I always buy from a traveller, if only a few coppers.' Adding something then about how Andy the Post claimed Indians carried the whooping cough, but he didn't give in to that at all.

Indeed Fintan already knew from his uncle and Jack Gara both how the old folks had always delighted in seeing a tramp wander into Glenbay, travelling folk who had all the news. Most of them carried their own bedding; if not, an armful of hay was thrown on a kitchen floor, with maybe a blanket over it. That evening neighbours would then call in, keen to hear old yarns and current events both. 'Sometimes a hat was passed, a few pennies or sixpence, whatever you wanted to give.' At harvest time a traveller might also go into a field to gather a few spuds lying on the ridges. 'Nothing would be said,' according to Condy, 'and your man could sell them in the next village, earn a few bob.'

One pedlar, who used to call when Condy was a child, had always carried a large wicker creel, from which he'd produce a penny biscuit large as a saucer, sprinkling it with sugar, and offering Condy half. 'How many holes in a biscuit?' your man once riddled Condy's father. 'Ach, how many holes in a badger's arse,' Cornelius had snarled back.

'Your great-grandfather was a pedlar in America,' Condy had remarked later that afternoon, as if reminded of the fact by the Indian lad.

'Your grandfather? Cornelius's da?'

'No – your father's grandfather.'

'He was in America too?'

'Did Packy never tell you?'

Packy had not, nor did Fintan learn anything further from Condy before he left, nor much more from his father later that evening.

'Sure, he died in America,' was all Packy said at tea, before telling Frankie to take some stale bread out to the hens.

It was Uncle Condy, two years later, who finally told Fintan how Paedar Doherty had died way out West. Had shared the story a few weeks only before Paedar's own great-grandson himself would leave the Glen. A story that Molly the Pub's grandfather, Charley McNelis, had brought back from America, where Charley too had worked for a time as a drummer. As chance had it, the two Glenbay men had separately sought lodging one night in the same Missouri boarding house, only to spot a familiar face not seen since Donegal. The house being nearly full, they were offered the remaining double bed, no bother to them.

Unable to sleep, however, Paedar had risen towards dawn, hopeful a stroll might help settle him. Charley, out for the count, awoke an hour later and went out to get some tobacco off his former schoolmate. Coming down the boarding-house steps, he suddenly heard a single pistol shot as a man on horseback disappeared into a stand of trees some thirty yards down the road. Moments later, he found Paedar lying dead on the ground, his pockets all turned out. 'Even the scapular around his neck torn open,' Condy said after a pause, 'its wee pouch probably mistaken for a purse' – like the final touch of a consummate painter's brush to a compelling, tragic tale.

Then, musing a minute or two later: 'Had Charley not met Paedar the night before, there'd be no knowing how he'd died.'

'When was that?' Fintan asked.

'Somewhere in the 1880s,' said Condy, having counted down the decades in his head.

Fintan tried to picture it all as he walked home over the hill – down to the boots on the dead man's feet. What images he conjured up were in full colour too – the crimson stitching on Paedar's boots, or the blue bandana on Charley's neck as he knelt beside the body of his old school chum – as if it needed something beyond the Westerns on Father Boyle's telly, something more that might square that black-and-white storyland with the more complex, multi-hued world he was growing into. Something more like the Western that had kept him awake for over an hour after he'd thumbed back from the Killybegs cinema a few weeks before, the story of a gambler with a hatbox, a demonic preacher, and Julie Christie as an opium-addicted brothel madam whose charges knifed their johns, set in a Washington state town that looked like it had been slashed out of the wilderness – all brown mud, green pines and red blood – yet another technicolour version of that long-ago West: only this time as it might have truly transpired.

While Fintan said nothing at supper that evening about his great-grandfather Paedar, he wondered whether it might explain why his own father had rarely set foot outside the parish. Later that night he told Frankie a bedtime story for the first time in several years, recounting nearly word for word what Condy had told him – as if that long-ago tale were his brother's birthright too. Then, just before sleep came, his transistor radio on low, he heard some ballad play, of a drifter robbed, shot and left for dead, 'somewhere way out West', an electric guitar fading in and out behind the lyrics like the bleed between a storied past and the here and now.

*

'Your one in red?' Rory indicated with his head at the Fintra disco outside Killybegs that September. 'With the big headlamps?'

'I don't think so,' Fintan said.

'For fuck's sake, do you want jam on it?'

'Fuck off – ask her yourself.'

The next Saturday he saw Noeleen there for the first time. Saw her faraway eyes and full mouth, not altogether unlike Julie Christie. And he asked her to dance – something he could manage now, provided he had a drink in him. Noeleen said yes but little else, and Fintan simply thanked her when the music stopped. But she said yes again the following week, and this time they had a cigarette outside, where Fintan learned she was from Donegal Town. Lived on the Diamond, above the Bank of Ireland, which her father managed. Like Fintan, in her last year of secondary school, which she absolutely loathed.

'Did you get tit?' Rory asked on their way back to Glen.

'Fuck off,' Fintan said.

Nor did he tell Rory of having thumbed to Donegal Town the following Friday after school, where Noeleen and he had talked for two hours over a coffee in a café on the Diamond, before Fintan hitched the thirty-five miles back home. Nor how she had no airs or graces – a bank manager's only daughter or not – just that quieter confidence the town girls often had. Confident enough anyhow to dress as she did – almost boyish, an old tweed jacket, baggy jumper, loose trousers and purple Docs. Yet nothing mannish about her head of massive brown curls, nor the soft lips that Fintan felt press hard against his own, the surprising warmth of her tongue with its metallic tobacco taste, outside the Fintra disco the following Saturday.

'Did you get bare tit?' Rory asked.

'Go play with yourself,' Fintan replied. 'Wanker.'

It was all so new, so heady, the way they kissed, how she might let him put his hand inside her shirt some Saturdays, other times grabbed his wrist and shook her head, never bothering to say why, nor did he ask. Their talk was heady too, the way Noeleen spoke so easily about stuff she felt, at times startling Fintan, who'd not heard someone do much of that before. How she still missed her mother, who had died when she turned twelve, a year after Fintan's Mary. Or how she loved her father even as he drove her mad, a mild-mannered man with a quietly sad smile when Fintan eventually met him. She too read a lot, though school drove her mad and always had. Even as a small child she had sneaked back home, to hide in a wardrobe, or on one occasion behind the sofa, where the painter decorating the sitting room had shouted aloud in fright later that morning, having pulled it out to find a wee body curled up there, asleep on the floor.

The notion you might actually interact with your father intrigued Fintan, who pretty much just co-existed back home with Packy. Whereas Noeleen often fought with hers, telling Fintan on another disco Saturday how she'd kicked out a glass panel in the kitchen door of their flat above the bank the night before in an argument over her school report. It happened she was more upset with a girlfriend who had lost her favourite Donovan tape, but her father forgave her anyhow, doing his best in what he knew at heart was an ongoing lament for her missing mother.

'Five mornings out of seven a single magpie's sitting on the back wall when I rise,' she told Fintan over a Nescafé in her tiny kitchen the following Friday night. 'Most mornings I don't even bother drawing the bedroom curtain.' A tiny ventilation fan on the wall behind added to the unfamiliarity of a spotless kitchen, its slowly revolving blades recalling the Tibetan prayer wheels he had recently read of, though he hadn't a clue as to what a prayer wheel actually looked like. There was the strangeness too of having a girl for a friend – never mind a girlfriend – who, if she almost always kept her own trousers buttoned, now sometimes touched him through his jeans on the same sitting-room sofa she'd once hidden behind.

The Tech finished up that May, followed by the Leaving Cert exams. Mr McGarvey said he was foolish not to try for third level, but Fintan had a job already waiting at the fish factory outside Carrig, unloading boxes of mackerel to be ground into fishmeal, or sorting crates of crabs by gender, following which the meatier females were boiled in huge vats, for shipment in vacuum-packed bags to France. The factory itself was a huge barn of corrugated iron, surrounded by smaller prefabs scattered about the yard, plus a pair of petrol pumps that serviced a constant stream of lorries, all of the enterprise brightly lit at night by tall arc lamps, like a kind of latter-day Gold Rush town knocked up against the higher green hills behind.

The job lasted some six months before Fintan got laid off – not that he'd minded, tired of breathing through his mouth so as not to smell fish, fish and more fish, not to mention the repetitive tasks, the tedium broken only by an occasional, satisfactory *pop* as a crab imploded inside its vacuum pack.

He spent the next fortnight looking for work, avoiding home, where Packy moaned of how machine-knits had ruined the weaving trade, or about the futility of salmon fishing now that the fisheries crowd had outlawed monofilament nets. That Montana had come down considerably in the past year hadn't helped either, no longer frequenting Molly's, where Packy only occasionally now showed up himself. And if Fintan were more often in the pub himself, a week or two still passed in which he did not take a drink.

Finally, in late January, he found work at a garage outside Killybegs, which saw him already halfway to Donegal Town those evenings he journeyed farther east to see Noeleen. Garrett, the garage owner, had him at first mostly pumping petrol and changing tyres – else doing the simple service tasks Fintan had already mastered on Uncle Condy's car – but he gradually began to show Fintan how to tune a carburettor or replace a water pump. 'First thing off is the last thing on,' he instructed, 'same as undressing a woman.' But Garrett wasn't largely given to that kind of chat, rarely if ever commenting on any female who pulled in for petrol.

'You get to stick it in?' Rory occasionally still asked, not that Fintan shared anything whatsoever. How Noeleen and he had finally made love on her sitting-room sofa one Friday evening after her da had left for a Donegal Historical Society meeting. Fintan unwrapping the foil from a condom bought off Dessie, a fellow mechanic two years Fintan's elder, whose brother had smuggled them over on the Stranraer-to-Larne ferry under his lorry seat. Nor was it a case of first off, last on either, as Noeleen only undid her shirt and lowered her trousers, having declared how much she hated herself naked.

Like most first sex it was fumbling and hurried, yet Fintan was aware too of what had long fed the urgency he now felt from the warm surprise of her skin as her clothing parted. Things like the light behind her green-grey eyes or the indented corners of her mouth, aspects apprehended by simply looking at her across a kitchen table. Plus the stuff they talked about – day-to-day happenings or hopes and dreams. And possibly that hidden, pre-teen wound that she too harboured – or so he would muse a few years later – which had similarly factored into what he had meant when, stretched over her, their hands interlocked behind the pillow at her head, each with an ear out for her father's footfall, he'd whispered that he loved her.

That said, it was often fraught between them – her mercurial temper flashing, or darker moods wherein she utterly rebuffed him, refusing to talk, only to hold him tightly before he headed off. Or the night they even seemed to go 'astray' in the little garden behind the bank, where Noeleen – still hiding from her father the fact that she did – always went to smoke. Only this night they couldn't make their way back, couldn't find the flagged path to the door, couldn't find their way to it anyhow. Fintan feeling the rain on his face as Noeleen, huddling against him, asked over and over: 'Do you *know* cold?'

*Seachráin* was what Jack Gara had called going astray, had informed Fintan some years before how it could come on you if ever you walked out with a deck of cards on your person. Or leave you befuddled, cards or no cards, in the same field you went into daily, unable to find the gate out. 'You have to drown the deck before you take it out of the house,' explained Jack, who knew more than a few charms. 'Place the five and ace of clubs face to face in the middle of the deck, and you're safe enough.' Turning the hat on your head was seemingly also good for countering the spell, only both of them had been bareheaded that evening.

It was Noeleen who left Donegal first, breaking the news in Fintra as they danced to a band called Bound for Boston, how she was bound for Spain as an au pair for a family in Seville. Suggesting that Fintan follow and find work, though they both knew deep down that wasn't going to happen. And so they wrote to each other for several months, until the letters lessened and eventually ceased. Still Fintan called into the tiny flat over the bank shortly before he too set off the following year. Took a cup of tea at the same kitchen table where he and Noeleen had plotted their escape, the small wall-extrusion fan spluttering above her father, who told him how Noeleen was working as a tour guide for an English holiday crowd, criss-crossing Spain in an big air-conditioned coach full of retired couples from Liverpool and Manchester. 'Here's her address,' he told Fintan with his habitual sad smile, tearing a sheet from a Bank of Ireland notepad on the table. 'She'd love to hear from you,' his voice rising slightly, like a played-out breeze briefly picking up.

It happened that Fintan had been treading water all that autumn, waiting for Frankie to settle into the Tech before striking off. He didn't bother with dances much, still thought about Noeleen a lot. Then, one late October afternoon, he took a rod down to Leach na Ronnach – Mackerel Rock – where the south side of the Glen fell away in a stony tumble to the sea. It was as much to be at eye level with the sea than any prospect of catching something for their tea, taking it all in as he cast repeatedly: the vapour trail from a westbound jet casting a momentary shadow across the sinking sun, the last of its light glancing off the black, craggy cliffs, until a rogue wave suddenly washed into his right boot, the shock of the freezing water bringing with it an urgent need to urinate, like some strange, internal confluence with the almighty Atlantic itself.

Later that night he rolled himself a joint, mixing tobacco with hash bought from Dessie, having lit up for the first time at the fish factory with Rory one Friday afternoon after work the previous year. Going outside, he took in the night sky, snatches of stars behind whitish clouds flying past on a southwesterly breeze, a scattering of trawler lights on the horizon, the moonlight bright on the whitewashed cottage gable wall whenever the cloud cover gave way. Blowing out smoke, he thought about how all of it – light, wind and sky – was perpetually quickening, unlike his static, home-anchored self.

Work meantime was the best of it, far easier than being on his own, plus the tinkering with motors, getting them to run right again. He had something of a gift for it, enough so that Garrett offered him another weekly fiver when Fintan handed in his notice that January, having caught yet another American film in Killybegs the previous night, a tale of some loner criss-crossing the States in a black Pontiac, running from the mob, the law, himself. And so it seemed all of a piece somehow, his low-key infatuation with the internal combustion engine simply the latest instalment in a long-standing, long-distance love affair with America, its current soundtrack a Boston band called the Cars, who he and

Dessie played non-stop at the garage until Garrett finally fecked the tape into the bin, after sending both lads home early one slow Friday.

*

'He's off to America,' Rory announced to the general assembly in Molly's the following week, 'looking for a soft hand to give his cock a pull.' But Fintan scarcely heard Rory anymore, had left most of their diminishing friendship back at the fish factory, where Rory still worked a few months in the summer high season. Nor was it to America that Fintan was headed either, a straight line towards goal something he had yet to manage. Having counselled Frankie to stick at his school studies in the lower bedroom the next night, followed by a quick hug upon awakening, he shook hands awkwardly with Packy after breakfast, then headed for London via the bus to Belfast and a ferry to Liverpool. 'Write when you find work,' Uncle Condy had said on his last visit to Pier. 'Better yet, get yourself a large widow with a small pub.'

He found work within days as a mechanic with a large Camden hackney company, kept his head down, eyes open, mouth shut, calculating the myriad differences on the job and nearly all else to what he'd known back home. He knew too within a month that he would not stick London – its sheer size, non-stop traffic, bad air and his dreary digs – the city more like a state of mind than a place you could actually inhabit. Drinking more nights than he cared to, albeit reading on his bed for a few hours first, there being feck-all else to do, apart from the pictures. 'England won't let you in,'

Gerry, a Mayo man, explained from a high stool one cold, overcast Saturday afternoon. 'And it's too near to Ireland to let you out.'

It was true enough too, the way the Irish around him gave out about the bad year back home for the turf, as the London sleet slid down a pub window. And so when spring finally arrived four months on, Fintan hopped the ferry from Dover to Le Havre. '*Ou est la guerre?*' he asked the first Frenchman he encountered outside the terminal. Initially puzzled, your man had suddenly laughed. '*La gare!*' he'd exclaimed, before pointing in the general direction of '*le train pour Paris*'.

Paris proved as splendid as his mother Mary's postcards promised: tree-lined avenues, grand, nay stunning buildings lit up at night. Its women too with ample make-up and hair pulled back over their ears, plus plentiful moustaches on the blokes. A city that both looked and felt far better than London, and had he paid more heed to Miss McEvoy at the Tech, he might've in time got a handle on the *parlez-vous*. But the work was in Germany – or so a Limerick man at the hostel had informed him – even if Fintan had feck-all German to go with his *quinze* words of French.

And so two nights later, *aprés un café* in the station, he hopped aboard a night train from Gare du Nord to Düsseldorf, where he boarded a city bus that dropped him beside the autobahn. Sticking out his thumb, he eventually caught a lift to Hanover – the driver a judge who'd learned his English on a World War II British prison ship – followed by a ride with a heavy-set schoolteacher to Hamburg, where the Limerick bloke had given him the name of a subbie, Stefan, at a large construction project. He got a start too, but after six weeks of digging trenches and wheeling barrows of wet cement across the building site, he quoted Uncle Condy back to the ganger: 'We want jobs, not work!' before packing it in.

There was scant chance, he knew, of finding either in a garage full of Audis and Mercs without the lingo, but he had the name of a deputy manager at a UK-owned Munich hotel with a large English clientele, where he was taken on as a kitchen porter. It too was more work than job – shite pay, plus tedious beyond belief – but it came with a bed in a tiny closet-like room, and two daily meals in the staff canteen, such that he began to save a few bob each week, despite the gorgeous dark-brown beer. He even wrote to Noeleen at the address her father had given him, saying he'd look her up when he got to Spain, but only got his own letter back, stamped *Destinatario Desconocido*.

Then, one September night, he heard a song on the tiny transistor radio he'd brought from Donegal: a woman singing of how Boston wasn't the 'kinda town' of some 'man from Tennessee'. Lying in bed, he felt suddenly hugely homesick, a palpable ache stabbing at the pit of his stomach. Only it was hardly home he missed – a north-side cottage with a hole at its heart, his father all but MIA too. Rather a familiar, keen-edged longing for where he'd never been, yet what had seemed always lying in wait west of Glenbay: those fabled, wide-open spaces in that storied land of plenty.

It happened too that additional kitchen shifts were on offer as the hotel geared up for Oktoberfest, so the following morning he signed up for all the hours he could get. He swore off the brown beer too, had the payroll lass keep his wages on the books, and four weeks later he rose at 5 a.m. to take the S-Bahn out to Flughafen München-Riem to queue for a cheap stand-by flight. It took three mornings of that routine to get a ticket, but later that afternoon he was finally, truly, headed West.

# II

## 4

It's not the fabled Far West that Fintan makes for however
– not straight off anyhow. Nor one of those storied cities
that proved first port of call for so many of the Irish in
America – New York, Boston or Chicago. He flies into JFK
all right, but only in order to hop a city bus into the Port
Authority, squeezing in next to a Black guy in dungarees and
red bandana and staring, along with half the bus, at a woman
getting on just as the doors are closing, herself kitted out in
a blue shirt and matching skirt, red leather gloves and red
cowboy boots, platinum-blonde hair spilling out from under
a white Stetson, as she loudly directs her ten-year-old son,
skateboard under his arm, to the last two remaining seats.

Four hours later he's on a Greyhound bus to Ohio.
Asleep within minutes, he wakes to find a husky bloke
around his own age in a baseball cap and purple runners
beside him on the aisle seat, nose buried in the *Bhagavad
Gita*. The bus shortly stops then for twenty minutes to assist
a woman whose car had skidded off into a cornfield beside
the highway, whereupon Fintan joins a half-dozen fellow
passengers who help the driver push her Nash Rambler
back onto the road. He then quickly walks ten yards farther
into the field, standing there on the cracked, dry earth, and

thinking he's never heard anything so alive, the wind on the endless rows of stalks shooting up above his head, the skittering of myriad grasshoppers, themselves easily twice the size of those at home.

Back on the bus, he wakes again an hour later from a mad, fantastical dream to find his Dharma-bum seatmate gone. Out the window a dark purple sky deepens the last of the late-afternoon golden sun, shimmering on farmhouse windows and gilding the rolling fields. What else he takes in awake does not all appear entirely real either, like the dead spit of Henry Fonda in a denim jacket, carrying his eggs and hash browns past a pinball machine to an adjoining table at a prolonged rest stop outside Erie, Pennsylvania, the same Erie he'd first heard of in mother Mary's litany of the Great Lakes back in Glenbay.

No less surreal are the oddly two-dimensional silhouettes of trucks on an overpass above the turnpike just before nightfall, moving across his line of vision like the wooden ducks he'd seen at a shooting gallery in a funfair outside Hamburg. Or the early dawn, which startles him when it breaks behind the bus, another golden splash streaked with carmine, given that he'd been mistakenly scanning the sky ahead for the first signs of light.

Shortly after, Cleveland appears out the bus window, massive factories with tall, smoking chimneys left of the fabled Interstate 90, with his mother's Lake Erie on the right. 'Check your watch, Mac,' the older fellow now on the aisle seat says, as Fintan gets his first look at the Midwest. 'That's still Eastern Standard Time.' But Fintan has all that yet to learn – how many Clevelanders fancy themselves Easterners, like John D. Rockefeller, say, who his now chatty seatmate says made his first millions here. All Fintan knows about Cleveland is the phone number given to him in Munich by a Galway man whose brother manages a bar there, O'Connell's, and would take him on, no bother.

*

In fact, it proved all kinds of bother. The number, which he rang repeatedly from the YMCA where he'd taken a room, never picked up, and when he managed a day later to track down the place, he learned that the Galway man had departed the week before, and no, thanks, they weren't hiring. But he got a break then in a nearby corner store, spying an index card with spidery handwriting pinned to a cork noticeboard: APT FOR RENT, $90 A MONTH. The finely threaded penmanship belonging to Miss Morris, eighty years old if a day, who answered his knock at the small two-storey wooden house on a quiet tree-lined street, pausing twice to catch her breath on the stairs up to the flat.

'It's a small apartment,' she said, but the sitting room, large bedroom, fair-sized kitchenette and toilet were roughly the same square footage as the cottage in Glenbay. Better still, the previous tenant had left behind a double bed, a beat-up sofa and a kitchen table and chairs.

'Eighty bucks a month if you'll put the barrels out on Wednesdays,' Miss Morris added. 'And shovel the porch steps and sidewalk when it snows.'

'Right you are,' said Fintan, though not at all sure he'd still be there when the first snow fell.

Digs sorted, all he needed now was work. A flyer on the same shop-noticeboard had promised BIG MONEY SELLING DOOR TO DOOR! – so he rang its number from the payphone at the Y after collecting his two bags. It made sense in a way, all those tales in the Glen – not his great-grandfather Paedar's sorry end in Missouri, surely – but all the dollars Dakota and Texarkana had reportedly made, peddling out West. Or the crimson-turbaned Indian walking all the way into Pier, to find but a 55-year-old bachelor, who nonetheless bought two pillowslips off him.

Or maybe Fintan was just keen to find something fast, having counted out $160 in ten-dollar bills into Miss Morris's hand, first and last months' rent in advance. As it happened he lasted but three weeks on the job, lugging a heavy case of glossy pamphlets and cheaply bound novels for a Book of the Month Club, which interested few of the mostly housewives who answered their bell. What more often interested them was his accent, and he tired quickly of being asked 'Do you like America?' – as if there were anything much yet to like.

'Doughnuts,' he told one of them. 'The gorgeous smell.' He meant it too, having puzzled over the unfamiliar, doughy scent, laced with coffee, which had all but sung 'Welcome to America' up his nose at the Arrivals Hall in JFK. Only to find 600 miles farther west the same pink-themed Dunkin' Donuts shops, a first lesson in how many enterprises are generally to be found across America, in this instance a franchise devoted entirely to doughnuts – sugar, raised, jelly, honey-dip, coconut, lemon custard – each shop with that same heavenly, heady aroma. 'Enough!' he could imagine

Condy saying, twenty-five years back home, and still shaking his head at America.

He thought of Condy again the morning a black Labrador charged out from behind a hedge, taking him unaware as he made his way up the path to yet another front door. Pivoting neatly, he caught the dog flush under its chops with the heavy book bag, then turned and retreated back down to the footpath – what the Yanks call a *sidewalk* – conceding the field of battle cum slim likelihood of a sale to the poor dog, who had in turn retreated back under the hedge.

But fact is Fintan was momentarily all the way back at Pier inside his head – back where Uncle Condy, standing outside his cottage, had told his twelve-year-old nephew of the pedlar who turned up every year with a large creel on his back, back when Condy himself was a boy, and back when there were four families going in the townland. And Condy describing how his father had warned the pedlar the first time he'd appeared in Pier of a fierce dog at the Maguires' cottage nearest the hill behind. 'No dog ever came at me twice,' the pedlar replied, taking an old rag from his pocket.

Condy and his daddy then watched as the pedlar neared the neighbour's door, where the snarling canine rushed out right on cue and, when your man didn't stop, had sprung for his throat – only to catch his own open jaws on the rag tautly stretched between the pedlar's hands, who threw him back with a force that all but snapped the dog's neck, tumbling him arse-over-tea-kettle onto the dusty lane, never to bark at a stranger again. 'Well, now!' was all Condy's father had said, well pleased with the show.

Yet Fintan himself loved dogs, most of whom he could settle even in Ohio with a few words, unfamiliar Irish accent notwithstanding. Nor did he mind all the walking that selling door to door entailed, there being far more to look at than you got peering into a car engine, or unloading a dishwasher. Tall trees up and down the streets, and tall trees in yards as if the houses had been planted around them, not vice versa. The last of the fall colours were another mighty thing – bright orange, sweet yellow and red as red gets – before the boughs shed their leaves.

A towering blue spruce claimed pride of place back at his own digs, beside a front porch with its two green-cushioned wicker rockers. Behind the house, an old apple tree and the remains of a lopsided trellis presided over the tangled underbrush where Johnson, Miss Morris's cat, played hide-and-seek with Fintan as he walked through the matted grass, feeling the windfalls underfoot as he made his way to a rusty yard chair, where he often sat for a few minutes on a weekend, as if he needed to be entirely quit of streets, cars and pavement.

'Flat, flat, flat!' he told the bald man in a purple terry-cloth bathrobe who'd inquired on his last day selling as to how he found America. 'Flattest place I've ever been.' Its roads were something he'd also noted: white concrete everywhere in lieu of black tarmac, with a bright yellow line often down the middle. But Fintan didn't say anything about the roads to the baldy bloke, who had scoffed at the idea Ohio was especially flat, before signing his wife up for the Cookery Books Club.

Nor did he remark on how low to the ground everything in Cleveland was, its boxy buildings, like the squat, window-less Kmart, which looked as if it had been plonked down in its shopping plaza like an oversized piece in a board game. Or how rectilinear – as if the entire city had been laid out with a rule and T-square, all at right angles, a million miles from the irregular bends, folds and jagged cliff-falls of Glenbay. And the numbers on everything, not just Interstate 90 but addresses like 647 East 105th Street, as though the city fathers had run out of names, even after those they'd stolen from Native Americans, like the Cuyahoga river or Josephatowa, though he'd later learn the latter neighbourhood had in fact been named after a Polish saint.

The following day he called into that anonymous Kmart and was hired on the spot as a retail assistant, which sounded a half-step up from clerk anyhow. He felt foolish having to show up to work in a white shirt and tie, but reasoned nobody he knew would see him togged out like that, and after a week he scarcely noticed himself. The work meantime was a doddle, tending a till, stocking shelves – or sometimes just patrolling the aisles, pointing out stuff to customers who seemed seldom able to find what they were looking for. He couldn't blame them either, given how shoddy much of the merchandise was, plastic flower pots, plastic kitchenware, plastic toys, all packaged in more plastic – enough so that a humongous, glistening globe of the stuff would be all that remained if ever a Kmart burnt to the ground. Or so he conjectured one afternoon after he and Oliver, a fellow retail assistant, skinny with bad acne, shared a joint on their lunch break behind the loading dock out back.

A lot of the customers were seriously overweight – men, women and kids – and after a few weeks of watching them waddle the aisles, Fintan began to walk past the Dunkin'

Donuts between home and work, eschewing the daily cruller he'd been ordering after hearing another customer pronounce it. And if it looked like a lonely time, he didn't find it so at first. Much of his two days off he would spend walking, discovering where the city centre, surprisingly small after London and Munich, eased into suburban neighbourhoods both east and west. He explored the shoreline too, marvelling that a lake had waves, which washed against ugly concrete slabs like battlements, wherever an apartment block had been built down to the water's edge.

Evenings he mostly spent back at the flat, which he too had now begun to call an apartment, finishing only *Shōgun* and *Ragtime* of the half-dozen novels he'd fecked from its Book Club case, after discovering a local library that astounded him. Shelves upon shelves of books, of which he also checked out an armful weekly – fiction and non-fiction both – whatever grabbed his eye, reading voraciously and indiscriminately: everything from Hemingway and US history to a Zen manual on motorcycles.

He started to visit the library several evenings a week too, just to get out of the house, reading for a couple of hours in the overstuffed library chairs, which were far more comfortable than the three folding chairs he'd beaten the binmen to on a Wednesday trash day. Kmart gave him 10 per cent off as an employee, but most of what he bought for the flat – plates, cutlery, a cheap chest of drawers – he had found at Goodwill or the Salvation Army. 'Charity shops stink of poverty,' Wesley would inform him later in Laredo, but Fintan preferred their second-hand smell to the recycled, air-conditioned aridity of whichever bank, drugstore or supermarket he frequented. America didn't do second-hand bedding though, so he used his 10 per cent discount at work on an electric blanket, once the early December nights grew even colder. Plus new – mostly polyester plastic – bedlinen, which sharply reflected the unshaded lightbulb over his bed, nor was it anywhere as soft as the worn flannelette sheets his mother Mary used to wash and drape over the fuchsia hedge to dry.

Winter arrived in earnest then, dumping vast quantities of snow onto the sidewalk, which Fintan cleared with the widest shovel he'd ever seen, a broad blade of lightweight aluminium ill-suited for shovelling anything else. That said, he welcomed the manual labour, taking care to sprinkle rock salt on the steps and path, though he seldom saw old Miss Morris venture out.

By January Lake Erie too had frozen solid, the waves that had initially surprised him in autumn now throwing up sloppy formations of ice that he clambered over in order to gain access to its flatly frozen surface. The snow itself he loved, the way it fell for hours on end, the street lamps backlighting its flaky fall at night, but the Arctic air sweeping down from Canada saw him buy his first cap ever, plus a pair of woollen gloves.

He went out a few times with Oliver after work, for a beer and another time bowling, which he wrote to Uncle Condy on a postcard afterwards 'was noisy but not that much'. They smoked a joint in the parking lot first, which had Fintan once inside doubling over with laughter each time his ball went down the gutter. And if Oliver was a tad morose, at least he talked less than most of his compatriots.

Otherwise Fintan did not venture out much those first few months, not so much retreating from America as needing to regroup from its overblown excesses – TV chat shows, sprawling shopping malls, or supermarket aisles festooned with foodstuffs.

Work was proving increasingly tedious as well, and after his second 'counselling session' – what management called the lecture you got if your cash register was five or more dollars out – Fintan handed in his notice.

'I'm not dipping into the till,' he told the assistant manager, a baldy fecker who seldom smiled. 'Nor taking any more of your shite either.' That said, he still managed to use his employee discount card on his last day to buy himself a warmer coat.

Two days later he was behind the bar at O'Connell's, retailing alcohol instead of plastic, which had been the Cleveland plan from the git-go. Its name aside, the place was not especially Irish. Or more accurately, especially Irish-American, which better described the James Boyle O'Reilly Social Club, perched like an afterthought on the edge of a south-side industrial estate, in a white stucco building you might easily mistake for a steak house or Holiday Inn, were it not for the huge tricolour hanging above the door. The Boyle main bar itself sat in the basement beneath the ground-floor meeting room, a large, dark bunker whose big black-and-white photographs of the deserted Great Blasket Island added to an overall funereal air. A padded-leather cushion ran the length of the bar, above which odd bits of Irish bric-a-brac were scattered about: shillelaghs, pieces of old delft and GOD SAVE IRELAND embroidered on a bit of tattered cloth. Nor did there look to be anybody Irish about the first Saturday afternoon Fintan had called in. No Irish accents anyhow from a table where three lads his age were sharing, if he could believe his eyes, a large glass pitcher of draught Guinness.

Meantime his new workplace, O'Connell's, was not much to write home about either, though he eventually dropped Packy and Frankie another postcard, saying he'd found more work and hoped they were keeping well. Yet sparing them any details of his workplace's interior decoration: red and blue jukebox lights winking in a corner of the sawdust-scattered floor, or the large jagged shard of glass that did for a mirror on a black wall over the washbasin in the men's toilet. No padded cushion either to spare the punters' elbows along the bar rail, which sported a curve of white caulking where Jim O'Connell had reattached a short span of the dark-grained oak, hammered off by someone with his fist in a long-forgotten argument. The black walls in the toilet were also Jim's handiwork – 'better than feckin' graffiti', he told Fintan. It worked well too, apart from whichever wag had stood on the toilet one night in order to write in Tipp-Ex: IF YOU CAN PISS ABOVE THIS LINE, THE CLEVELAND FIRE DEPT WANTS YOU!

The owner, Jim, a second-generation Irish American, had gone over to Kerry twice with the wife, but didn't seem especially pushed about the auld sod. He stocked bottled Guinness only, and the sole Irish ornament was a small Irish flag above the register. One night a diminutive Northerner, Ciarán from Armagh, came in with a collection tin on behalf of NORAID, but the take was scarcely worth his while, and he left after inviting Fintan to a meeting on the Six

Counties. He looked the hard man out of any film about the Troubles – clean-shaven, black T-shirt, denim jacket and half a forefinger missing on his left hand.

But Ciarán at least had a past in Ireland, Fintan reckoned, unlike those Irish Americans who avidly stuffed a dollar or three into said collection tins. He'd meet them across America in years to come too: most of them clueless about Ireland and quick to curse the Brits, though truth be told many Irish in the US would find more to talk of – if football only – with most English they encountered than with the majority of their American second cousins.

A few lasses came into O'Connell's after work or with boyfriends at night, but Fintan figured it unlikely he'd meet a woman there. But then again, he hadn't expected to meet Jo-Ann at that Mass either, after wandering into St Peter's a few streets over from his flat one Saturday evening. A student art teacher at a nearby primary school, she made Fintan laugh back at her apartment, describing over a coffee how her Fifth-Grade students had run out of the classroom her first day there, only to swerve round and fly back to their seats when the principal suddenly appeared at the far end of the corridor. Jo-Ann's own laugh was a sudden, sharp sound, like a bird taking flight, and she looked something like a bird of prey herself: short, raven-black hair, aquiline nose and large brown eyes.

They saw each other over the next several months, went out to the pictures and to the Museum of Art on several Sundays. For Fintan the museum was a revelation – almost too much to look at, not just pictures, but pottery, African fabrics, medieval armour. If he failed to see the point of a still life – why would anyone want to paint a dead hare or a leg of lamb? – he listened keenly as Jo-Ann spoke about colour and composition, noted her language, the way she pointed out the counterpoise of two boxers frozen in the centre of a ring, or the play of light on two peasants playing cards in an inn, its dark interior reminding him of Molly's pub, even if their gear was all wrong, never mind jugs for glasses, and white clay pipes with stems twice as long as those on the odd clay pipe you might unearth yet while putting in a row of spuds back in Glenbay.

They eventually went to bed one night back at her apartment, after finishing a bottle of cheap Californian red. Not the first time they'd talked over a glass of wine, nor had their friendship been necessarily heading bedward either. They made love again a week later, if only to persuade themselves the first time had not been a mistake. But the possibility of sex now seemed to get in the way of their formerly easy chat – Jo-Ann describing her school day, her impossible sisters, or listening as Fintan spoke of what sounded to her like another world altogether back in Donegal. They took in the St Patrick's Day parade together too – Fintan puzzling over the Scottish bagpipers, and downright refusing to believe how some years they even dyed the Cuyahoga river green – but by April they had fallen out of touch, leaving Fintan to later wonder, had they not become lovers, might they've remained friends instead?

*

Meantime the night shift at O'Connell's was generally jammers, and Fintan mostly enjoyed the talk and banter up and down the bar. But even better was the initial, quieter hour upon taking over from the day man, Paul: topping up the cache of orange, lime and lemon wedges, filling their plastic tubs with the soda-water hose to keep the fruit fresh till last call, and ensuring the ice tub was full. The regulars were largely a decent lot, a motley collection of postal workers, cabbies and one or two ex-cops. Most of the men still held jobs, and nearly all drank heavily, night after night on the same stool, like an assigned seat back in school.

Fintan didn't drink on the job, but once the door was locked at closing time, he'd fix himself a cocktail as Jim tallied the night's take behind the bar, invariably bitching about how bad business was. At first a different cocktail, sampling his way through the medley he'd already mastered mixing: Stingers, Blizzards, Bloody Marys, Tom Collinses, Black Russians or Rusty Nails. He loved the names more than the often too-sweet concoctions, which brought to mind Jack Gara next door back home, noting the sugar he tasted straight away in almost anything store-bought. Settling finally on a nightly Sombrero, he'd sit across from Jim, staring at the booze stacked up either side of the cash register, where the neon shelving-light, filtering through amber, green and golden bottles, seemed somehow less electric, more like sunlight underwater.

The bitter winter weather gradually gave way to spring, which arrived with far more of a flourish than in Ireland, while back at the house Miss Morris reappeared like an old bear out of her cave. He knew little of her habits, given his own irregular hours, noted only a front-room light that burnt all night long, illuminating small china figurines on a mantle below a mirror. His rent he handed over monthly to her nephew Simon, a bemused, pudgy man in his forties who lived across the city.

Then, one Saturday in late April, she and Johnson the cat appeared out back, where Fintan was replacing the brake pads on a second-hand racing bike he'd bought for $15 at a nearby yard sale. Showed up with an old rake in her hand, though it was mostly last year's grass still scraggly across the lawn. But it wasn't yard work on her mind. Instead, she told Fintan he needed to vacate by four that afternoon, as she expected callers who were coming by to see the apartment. After she left, Fintan cycled round to the same phone booth on the adjoining avenue from which he used to set up dates with Jo-Ann.

'Just ignore her,' Simon told Fintan down the phone. 'She gets an idea sometimes, that's all.'

He ignored her so, but she kept at him for another week.

'You'll have to leave by four, Mr Doherty, I'm expecting callers.'

'They'll have to look elsewhere, Miss Morris. I'm here to stay!'

'Well, have your things out by four, please,' she'd say, before moving off with her rake or Johnson, if not both, trailing along behind.

'Her mind wanders off,' the nephew explained when he called for the rent at the end of the month. 'She's nearly ninety, for Chrissake.'

'Do you need a torch?' Fintan asked as Simon started down the cellar steps to check on the water heater, only for the nephew to shoot him a puzzled look. Upon reappearing, Fintan offered him a beer instead.

He also clarified 'torch as in flashlight' once Simon had settled into the other wicker rocker on the front porch.

'Ah, gotcha!'

'She was born in this house,' Simon told him. 'Her older brother, my uncle Larry, lived here too, but he passed away fifteen years ago. Anyhow, she's had no problems for a while, except for the snakes.'

'Snakes?' Fintan asked.

'Small brown ones,' Simon said, spreading his hands some seven inches apart, while holding on to his longneck bottle of Schlitz. 'What we called garden snakes. She hates the sight of 'em, used to holler for her brother – "Larry, bring the shovel!"'

'We've no snakes back home,' Fintan said.

'Is that a fact?' the nephew asked, his broad brow wrinkling again.

It seems his aunt had lit a fire as well, the year before, in an old trash burner beside the back porch. 'A metal barrel with small holes in the sides,' Simon explained. 'Where you'd burn your rubbish before there was pollution.' Only the flames darting out its rusted side had ignited a sheet hanging on her laundry line. The fire department arrived in time to save the porch, but afterwards several neighbours started mentioning nursing homes to the nephew.

'When I told them she already had a home, one of them tried to get the city to move her.'

Over a second beer he told of the social worker from the Office of Human Services, who called out one afternoon.

'She told him they'd move her out over her dead body. "Over my dead body!" she kept repeating – pretty strong language for her, and the city guy must've copped as much, cuz he never came back.'

'Whatever you do, don't give her a torch,' he laughed at Fintan before he left.

\*

'Do you mind if I read on the porch?' Fintan asked the following week. 'Read wherever you like,' Miss Morris said, no longer bothered about her four o'clock appointment. Better still, she occasionally joined him for evenings on the porch, the pair of them like an old couple side by side, watching the neighbours' kids on their bikes, or Johnson stalking a starling under the blue spruce. One evening two teenage girls, sun-brown skin against white prom gowns, posed for photographs on a front stoop across the street, as if to highlight for Fintan the lack of a younger woman in his life. But mostly he just read while Miss Morris, in a checked gingham dress and worn-out tennis shoes, grey hair drawn back into a small bun, slowly rocked in the gathering dark.

Her mind worked enough well most evenings when she chose to speak, though she sometimes slowed at a wrong word – cafeteria for caffeine, say – like a trickle of water might upon encountering a twig or stone, before going on to assert: 'I still drink coffee, mind you, despite the doctor's orders.'

Her company also evoked something of home for Fintan, where old folks were more a fact of daily life, like Jack Gara next door, or under the same roof like Condy's Aunt Cassie or Rory's granny. As it happened he generally got on well with the elderly. 'You're an old soul yourself,' Marianne would inform him some years later in California, but Fintan had no interest in that – one life at a time being more than enough, thanks very much. Yet he'd been struck straight away by how many of those his own age he'd encountered in Cleveland seemed themselves far younger, as if America granted you more years in which to grow up – or not.

There were exceptions of course, like Charlie, a tall, skinny Vietnam vet with a nicotine-yellowed moustache, who drank in O'Connell's. Surely nothing like war to put years on you, Fintan figured, and it likely hadn't helped being called Charlie over there. Taciturn to begin with, he'd proceed to drink himself into an even profounder silence most nights. 'You know about bombs, Irish?' he nevertheless asked Fintan one Friday night, holding up a shot glass of bourbon.

'All of that was a hundred miles from us,' Fintan said. 'And if my luck holds, I'll never see Belfast again.'

His own favourite of the two or three irregulars at the bar was Roddy, whose salt-and-pepper hair ascended his head in receding waves like a 1940s film star. Roddy, who invariably showed up in the same white shirt and dark tie he wore to some desk job, and who still lived at home with the mother, though little else about him seemed to follow from any of that. Like the two rings, for instance – one on either hand, a silver snake's head and a turquoise oval – which put Fintan in mind of a What's Wrong with This Picture? puzzle, where you circle the bits that don't fit.

Then, one May Saturday by the shore, where he'd gone to test the tepid waters of Lake Erie for the first time, he heard his name called, and turned to see Roddy, sitting on a big red beach towel and wearing an old-fashioned pair of black swimming trunks with a button-up fly. But it was the skinny Botticelli blonde, half Roddy's age, in a pale-blue two-piece swimsuit on a towel beside him, who all but cried out for a puzzle circle drawn round herself. This was Clara, who brushed back her blonde curls and smiled brightly when introduced, but whose eyes, lashes thick with mascara, repeatedly returned to Roddy, as the three of them made small talk. A few weeks later Fintan again spotted the pair of them across a street *downtown*, as he was learning to call the city centre, along with a second young woman: another looker, dark-haired, in a red-and-black miniskirt.

'Oh, that was Angie,' Roddy said the following night in O'Connell's, after Fintan mentioned having seen the three of them. 'You should've come over and said hello.'

What else didn't fit was how Roddy preferred dope to drink, generally at the bar ordering a single rum & coke, which he nursed for an hour. Never having met anybody Roddy's age who smoked grass, Fintan said as much one night.

'Jazz,' Roddy replied. 'I knew these jazz musicians years back, who turned me on.'

Fintan kept adjusting the picture, like a TV on the blink, but still could not work out Roddy and his present coterie. Dope-dealing or witchcraft, maybe? Not that he gave in to the latter, any more than he would later on to Marianne's talk of previous lives.

On another slow night he might join Florence for a few minutes in one of the booths across from the bar where most couples generally sat, though Florence had remained single ever since her US Air Force husband, Walter, died in a plane crash over Guam back in 1945. 'Something to do with testing the H-Bomb,' she recounted, as if speaking of a previous life, and telling Fintan another night how Walter had been stationed for a time in a small town out west with a 'state-line' hotel, its clientele moving happily between the bar in Utah with its tax-free liquor and the adjoining casino room in Nevada, where gaming was legal.

'Every Saturday I took $5 up to play 22 and 27 on the roulette wheel.'

'Your lucky numbers?'

'Birthday and wedding anniversary.' Florence laughed. 'I'd win, too, sometimes as much as fifty bucks.'

Other evenings she spoke of Texas, of an endless night in the San Antonio train station, unable to close her eyes after a rat ran across her foot in the toilet. And how at dawn she and Walter had finally boarded a train south to Laredo. They found a hotel then on a street not far from the station, where a few hours later Florence awoke to find herself covered in welts.

'I thought I was ill,' she told Fintan. 'Until Walter held the bedside lamp over me. Bedbugs, he announced, so we checked out straight away.'

The tales reminded Fintan of Uncle Condy's, reminded him of that wide-open America, west of the Mississippi, which he had longed to see since childhood. Nor did it help how work was once more beginning to wear him down, serving the occasional free drink when O'Connell wasn't looking to the alcoholic regulars, who gave it back in tips at closing time. He too was drinking more, riding his bike for a laugh one night through a drive-in liquor store designed like a car-wash-cum-McDonald's, automated doors at either end, and an attendant who handed your order through your car window like it were a burger and fries. Only in Fintan's case, a twelve-pack of Old Milwaukee, which he secured with two bungee cords to his bike's carrier rack. But he wasn't overly worried about the drink, having previously pulled back from it in London and Munich, more just pissed off with himself. But that didn't stop him, though, from pouring a fair-sized ration of vodka & tonic into a two-quart plastic water bottle – to get around the public-drinking laws – on any day off he went down to the shore for a swim.

One overcast August Saturday he opted to visit the Museum of Art instead of the lake, and so rang Jo-Ann for the first time in months, hoping she might come along to talk again about what they saw. He rolled a joint after she didn't answer, thinking to have a conversation within his head at least. The museum was crowded but he hardly noticed, beguiled once more by the very idea of a building full of paintings. He could do little with the contemporary art – what seemed like arbitrary, random splashes of colour – but he double-backed through several rooms to look again at a single landscape: a dirt crossroads bordered on all sides by an enormous field planted with a luminescent, golden crop he guessed was wheat, the sky above filled with dark storm clouds. Simple yet haunting, he stared intently at it, determined to fathom how it worked that way. Its title, *Gray and Gold*, 1942, offered little help, not even telling where in America it were. Had Jo-Ann been there, she might've pointed out how the crossroads themselves were *off-centre*; might've termed the single line of oddly wireless telegraph poles disappearing into the distance as *surreal*.

He could still see its road, field and sky in bed that night, a further reminder of the America he had yet to find. Took him a moment or two to recall the name of the Yank painter who'd visited Glenbay before he was born, and wondering whether Randall Hart had anything in the Cleveland Museum of Art. A breeze then struck the wind chimes on the porch below, moving over him a half-second later on the bed. An onshore breeze, he reckoned, courtesy of Lake Erie, which the newspaper said was slowly coming back to life after years of pollution. A while later he heard Mrs Morris calling for Johnson, who'd succumbed to a late June heat-spell, only she hadn't always a grasp of that fact after the sun went down. Heard too the sound of her rake – protection against any marauding garden snakes, he figured – rattling along behind her on the concrete path that encircled the house.

He caught a glimpse of her through her open front door the following evening as he headed out, carrying her unplugged, still-steaming clothes-iron down the darkened hallway, like a benign, elderly dragon making its tired way home. Noting the next morning that she hadn't taken in her post, he knocked and got no reply. He rang Simon then – who came straight over, let himself in, tripping over the rake in the hall, before finding his aunt upstairs in her bed.

The police arrived next, two officers in a station-wagon cruiser that doubled as an ambulance – or, in this instance, a hearse. The cops carried her carefully downstairs on a stretcher, out of the house past the blue spruce, and down the concrete path. Back on the porch they handed her nephew a form to sign, like a shipping invoice, Fintan thought, the way everything – even dying – is done by the book in America. No messing about, 'no shilly-shallying', as Miss Morris herself had liked to say.

Only there was messing about, after the cops failed to find their keys when they returned to the wagon. After searching the house, front yard and vehicle, they finally radioed for a duplicate set. As he stood waiting with the others beside the two wicker rocking chairs on the porch, Fintan noted how they were all trying their hardest not to look at her remains in the wagon window, its gold-lettered legend CLEVELAND POLICE DEPT over her dead body, just as she had promised it would be.

*

Nephew Simon told Fintan he could stay on indefinitely, but indefinite was too much like what he was already feeling. Sitting behind the house beneath the apple tree a few nights later, he watched the full moon rise, every bit as big as the huge American moon he used to see in the Killybegs cinema. 'Wait till you see the Hunter's moon,' O'Connell said the following day, when Fintan mentioned it at work. O'Connell, who himself hunted deer with a bow and arrow, sitting in a tree for hours on a chair-like contraption affixed to the branches. He invited Fintan to come try his hand at an archery range that weekend, but Fintan passed, opting for the pictures instead, another Western about a drifter with more than his share of family trouble.

When Roddy came into the bar that Monday, Fintan decided to reprise the cinematic scene in which Jack Nicholson puts a compressed paper soda-straw wrapper into his nostril. It worked a treat too, as Roddy uneasily informed Fintan, 'You've something at your nose?' 'Thanks, Rod,' said Fintan, who proceeded to slowly extract what looked like a long white string of ectoplasm, prompting Roddy to blow a mouthful of rum & coke through his own nose, onto the bar, before running out the door. 'Yeah, I know,' Fintan told O'Connell, who was not impressed, though he again tried to talk Fintan out of quitting as they closed up that night. But Fintan stayed on another fortnight only, just long enough to give Roddy a rum & coke on the house when he finally showed his face again.

# 5

And so, nearly a year after he landed in Cleveland, Fintan finally gets farther west. Farther southwest, to be precise, 560 miles down I-71 and onto I-70 as far as St Louis. Picture him there some nine months later, on a June afternoon in 1977, within a stone's throw of the Mississippi. He stands at the southern end of the Gateway Arch, his cheek pressed against its slight chill as he tracks its parabola of shimmering steel with an upcast eye. It was the Arch that had first caught his eye last September – like a spout of silvery water shooting up from a hose behind a tall office block before pouring down onto the golden dome of the state capitol. The shirt salesman, Hank, who'd given him a lift outside Indianapolis, was heading for Tulsa, Oklahoma, but Fintan, unable to take his eyes off the massive metal sculpture, hopped out two red lights later, thinking to spend a day or two looking round.

What he saw quickly slowed his gallop west. Not just the Arch, nor the steamboats moored along a storied river he'd first encountered in a tattered paperback of *The Portable Mark Twain* that his mother Mary had bought back in Donegal, but the city itself – entire neighbourhoods of grand houses and cobblestone streets, jazz clubs, a baseball stadium and towering brick brewery – its vibe utterly unlike

Cleveland, not exactly Southern, but far funkier than what he'd so far seen of the corn-fed Midwest.

'Check this out, Chet,' he says, waving at a skinny Black guy with a wispy goatee, who wanders over to lean his head against the Arch and eyeball it too. Chet is now one of his clients, an ex-mental patient whom Fintan is helping to get housed as part of his current gig with the City Social Services Department. It's a new job, one he largely likes, driving around to Goodwill or Salvation Army shops where he helps a client pick out a bed or a kitchen table, which they trundle together into the green van with its SSD crest, to unload at whatever rented accommodation the client has secured, usually a single-room occupancy – or SRO, as Will, his boss, calls them.

The clients are largely OK too, a good few of them, like Chet, Vietnam vets. A lot of them drink, which he is supposed to take note of, but it's really none of his business, he figures, so he draws the line at not taking a swig from the bottle those who imbibe invariably proffer. St Louis differs from Cleveland in that way too, in that Fintan himself is drinking less.

'Uh-uh,' Chet says, jerking his head back from the steel base of the Arch. 'I don't dig heights.' They head back then to the van, Fintan not minding that the Arch hasn't worked for Chet like it does for most of the clients he brings down here. 'Holy shit!' they shout – or something similar – after he gets them to look up along the shaft, thinking it might startle them out of their heads, if only for a moment.

'I don't sleep in a bed,' Chet says in the Salvation Army shop on Union Road. 'Sleep on the floor, man.'

'What if you meet a woman?' Fintan counters.

'She can take *me* home!' Chet grunts. But when Fintan explains how they can't use the bed allowance on a tiny black-and-white TV, Chet finally agrees to a bed. He then tells Fintan, en route to his new abode, of a Marine buddy who went AWOL from a German military hospital only to end up in Ireland, where some guy with six kids whom he met in a Dublin pub took him home. Kept him for three months in a small shed at the bottom of his garden, the same shed, Chet says, where an aunt with TB had lived when the Irish guy was growing up.

\*

That too was something different about America that Fintan had noted, the way you weren't necessarily squirrelled away somewhere if you weren't entirely sound, body or mind. Not confined to a kitchen loft, like the mad brother in a house up the Glen, who according to Uncle Condy called out from on high 'More bread or I'll appear!' whenever his two spinster sisters entertained a caller. Nor packed off to a 'hospital' like Rory's simple younger sister, nor sent to any one of the grim and grimy institutions scattered around the country, if you suffered from epilepsy or cerebral palsy.

Take, for example, his boss Will, whom he'd met at his interview two months before. The advertised position of 'Care worker/van driver' was the first people-oriented job he'd ever gone for, from bartending, and he had waited nervously on a folding chair outside the interview room. Nor did it settle his nerves, once within, to see, at the head of the table, this bloke – with a head of shoulder-length, Wild

Bill Hickok hair and wearing a smashing pair of tan cowboy boots – sitting in a high-backed wheelchair, complete with a respirator tube tucked, hookah-smoking style, into a corner of his mouth.

'Take a seat,' Will had instructed him from the opposite corner, 'and draw a breath.' Said it as if the shoe were on the other foot, the way a guy looking for work is the fellow with the handicap, and he wanted to set Fintan at ease.

The woman on the three-member interview panel asked about his present position, so Fintan described the People's Food Co-op off Market Street, which had been happy to hire as Produce Manager someone with actual experience of planting cabbage, spuds, carrots and onions, albeit across the Atlantic. Though Produce Manager was a bit trumped up for a general dogsbody position, one of a half-dozen full-time staff at the Co-op, who oversaw the five hundred or so members, whose three hours of labour each month enabled them to buy at cost pretty much the same dry goods and fresh produce which the supermarkets sold.

Two weeks after he started at the Co-op, Fintan moved from the St Louis YMCA to 127 Lenox Place, a large Victorian sandstone townhouse with a spacious front porch in the Central West End. His room, a small single, was tucked up on the third floor under a mansard roof that crowned the two larger storeys below. His housemates, who numbered from six to eight depending on the ebb and flow of the various tenancies, along with the often mercurial sleeping arrangements, might've constituted a commune a few years before, but the 1970s were beginning to wind down, and so the household ran itself along less self-conscious lines: its cleaning rota stuck under a Mickey Mouse fridge magnet, and a weekly contribution to the food kitty about as doctrinaire as it got.

As it happened, a fellow Co-op member, Shelly, had mentioned a vacancy in the house one afternoon as she and Fintan worked side by side, cutting up blocks of Vermont cheddar and Monterey Jack before parcelling them up in what he called *cling film* and Shelly *Saran wrap*. That evening Fintan was more or less interviewed by some of the others in the house: Court, a tall sculptor with a bushy grey beard, and Simon, one of two brothers, both Scientologists, who shared a bedroom with pitch-black walls. Plus Joyce, a grad student in anthropology at Washington University, who, having joined them later, asked Fintan about the high incidence of schizophrenia in rural Ireland. 'I'd actually be of two minds about that,' he'd replied, prompting a laugh around the long wooden-plank table in the kitchen, with its spider plants, a poster, over an old enamel sink, of Jimi Hendrix brandishing his Stratocaster, and shelves of large glass jars containing pinto beans, chickpeas and the like, which Fintan had only begun to recognise at work.

In some ways moving to St Louis felt like immigrating to America all over again – both his digs in what felt like a mansion of sorts, and a new day job utterly unlike tending a Cleveland bar. Disposed by nature to try most things twice, he grew quickly fond of the sassafras tea Shelly made from the small bundle of twigs and bark picked up from a corner shop and brewed in a small saucepan. Before long he had also sampled most of the contents of those large glass jars – soybeans, pinto beans, black-eyed peas, red and green lentils.

Had even taken to miso, a Japanese seaweed-based soup that half the household hated, while also managing to make Simon the Scientologist gag one evening as he described the dillisk that Jack Gara had chewed back in Donegal, harvested from Leach na Ronnach at low tide, then left outside his door in the sun to dry.

*

One night in his second week in the house, Shelly invited him into her room, furnished with a queen-sized bed, an old-fashioned armoire and a large dentist's chair, behind which three shelves of dentures grinned back at him like a litter of Cheshire Cats atop a wall.

'Let me guess,' he said, not having sussed out yet exactly what Shelly did. 'You're a dental hygienist?'

'Close!' she laughed. 'A photographer, actually.' The dental chair and dentures were simply stuff she had salvaged from the kerbside trash downtown to decorate her room, like a tooth fairy gone bad. There were no photographs on view, oddly enough, but she showed him several a few weeks later, a selection depicting a cluster of secondary-school girls sitting in drugstore booths and soda shops, smiling past the camera. As with many Americans, Shelly came from somewhere else, in her case New Hampshire, where she had gone to boarding school with the film star Sigourney Weaver. In fact she didn't look unlike her classmate, tall and rangy, with long, dark, curly hair.

'Did yous get on?' he asked.

'Bosom buddies. Seriously. We even swore whoever got famous first would always keep in touch.'

'So you get a Christmas card each year?'

'Not so far,' Shelly grinned. 'She probably thinks I'll outdo her yet!'

'Do give her my best if she calls,' Fintan said with a laugh. Fact is he'd have taken a call from Shelly herself, only she already had a pony-tailed boyfriend, whose bright-blue 1000cc Harley-Davidson had more than once awakened Fintan as your man dropped her home at night.

\*

Work started at 4 a.m. six mornings a week, so Fintan was early to bed most nights. 'No bother,' he assured Margo, the Co-op manager, who had asked at his interview if he could drive the two-ton truck which he and a helper took two miles north of the Arch each morning to a wholesale fruit and veg market. The first week or two were nervy, not so much the extra gears on the truck as gauging clearances on a tight corner, or having to reverse into a loading bay at the market. He had applied straight away for a driver's licence too, trusting a cop wouldn't pull him over before he passed the test – which he did, no bother, a few weeks later, in housemate Court's beat-up 1967 Falcon. His luck then held for another month, and so one Friday morning, after collecting four boxes of plantains off a boat from Panama, he drove straight from the market to the Department of Motor Vehicles for a successful commercial Class B licence exam that would sanction his driving a truck on Missouri roads.

The early-morning market itself had produce far beyond what reached Donegal in any vegetable van. Artichokes from California, mangoes from Mexico or Puerto Rican avocado pears, which seemed as much a misnomer as the eggplant, whose royal purple caught his eye straight off. Any veg past its sell-by date at the Co-op he brought back to the house, hoping one of the others might cook it up for him to sample, including the eggplant, which anthropologist Joyce informed him was 'the most yin of all vegetables' as she sliced, salted and left it to leech on a baking tray.

\*

Sigourney Weaver had yet to ring, but one Sunday Shelly introduced Fintan to another of her pals, cropped and tousled blonde-haired Carla in a red sweatshirt and blue jeans – shorter at five foot four than both Shelly or Sigourney – along with an air of compacted energy in contrast to Shelly's lanky languor.

'Where are you from?' she asked straight away upon hearing Fintan speak.

'Ireland.'

'Cool!'

'And wet.'

She flashed a broad, blue-eyed smile then, showing the mouthful of perfect white teeth that so many Americans sported. He waited, hoping she wouldn't say she was Irish too. Nor did she, rather just picked at the label on her longneck bottle of Pabst.

'Yourself?'

'Oh, I grew up down the road.'

The road being Highway 40, he subsequently learned, which lay a few blocks south of their Lenox Place, and did in fact run some seventy-five miles farther east through

Terre Haute, Indiana, from whence Carla hailed. He saw her occasionally around the house then, over the winter, learned how she had studied history at college, but currently worked as a cleaner for a handful of upper-class households in the Clayton neighbourhood.

He puzzled about that for a while, even if she wasn't the first under-employed Yank he'd met with a third-level degree. The idea of going to college simply to read books still struck him as strange – even if that was pretty much what McGarvey at the Tech had encouraged him to do. He was still reading anyhow, poetry even, making his way slowly though 'The Love Song of J. Alfred Prufrock' in an anthology someone had left in the sitting room, having come upon it a day or two after Court had pointed out the house a few blocks east where T. S. Eliot himself had lived for a time.

And speaking of love songs, he learned too how Carla, like Shelly, already had a boyfriend, whose beat-up red Porsche he occasionally glimpsed as it dropped her off at Lenox Place to visit Shelly. He puzzled too the lack of a woman in his own life, but figured that too might happen in time. Yet he marvelled at how his workmate Peter, in charge of the Food Co-op meat counter – an acne-scarred Armenian American with a hooked nose, black curly hair and a blood-stained white apron – had to fend off the female staff members with a stick, blondes and brunettes whom Fintan would see hugging him at the start of their three-hour shifts, before donning their own spotless white coats and proceeding to chop up chicken parts.

'C'mere, man,' Peter had said, calling him over one afternoon and pointing to an intrusion of cockroaches swarming around a wall clock next to the walk-in cooler. Swatting as many as they could with rolled-up newspaper batons, Peter then sprayed the clock with a can of Raid, only for the clock to explode two minutes later with a loud bang and puff of white smoke, prompting the lovely redhead helping Peter to scream so loudly that manager Margo exited her small office beside the grains and cereals to investigate.

*

However most workdays were duller than not, and by early spring Fintan was looking for something else. What's more, when Will Woodward asked during his Department of Social Services interview whether he had a Class B driving licence, he could this time honestly answer yes. He got the job too, gave two weeks' notice at the Co-op, and reported the following Monday. Sitting in the office, he tried not to stare as Will, clenching a thin stick between his teeth, proceeded to type Fintan's details onto a payroll form on the typewriter vertically mounted above his head. He then shadowed the departing driver over the next two days on a series of runs, after which he was given the van and a first client of his own.

It would prove a different clientele to the Co-op too, as he quickly discovered when, after paying for a fill-up of gas, he returned to find Paquito, a skinny Latino he was moving into a room off Lafayette Square, passed out cold in the front seat. 'Try placing ice on his groin, sir,' the woman dispatcher at the St Louis Fire Department suggested when he rang 911 on the gas-station phone. 'Therapeutic hypothermia, sir,' she explained after he'd asked her to repeat herself. And wasn't America just that kind of place, with big ice machines right there in petrol stations, where the cubes-down-the-front-of-the-pants trick worked a treat, bringing Paquito sufficiently around to get all kinds of pissed off over his suddenly sopping crotch. 'Plenty of stimulus response!' Will said with a laugh back at the office, telling Fintan he'd done well.

Before long he himself was buying ice for back at the house, taken by how everyone put it into both coffee and tea. Fact was St Louis in May already felt hotter than Cleveland had in July, though 'It's not the heat,' housemate Court repeatedly intoned, 'it's the humidity!' 'Muggy, muggy, muggy,' Shelly would then moan in turn, another of those American words that Fintan loved. And taken too with Court's description of the huge masses of moist, warm air that blew up from the Gulf of Mexico, picturing them on the map inside his head, same as he had when his Cleveland landlady Miss Morris had spoken of the cold winds sweeping down from Canada.

Yet hot or humid, he still hated everything about air conditioning, and had only an old electric fan to move the stifling air in his room up under the roof, and so spent little time awake up there, preferring to be out of the house than in. Forest Park lay just a few blocks west, and by June he had traversed most of it on the bike that Simon's brother Seth, the other resident Scientologist, had sold him for seven dollars. He didn't bother much with its zoo, but cycled back a second time to the open-air World Fair Pavilion, set like a massive bus shelter on a hill overlooking acres of green space. Rereading the plaque that told how 20 million visitors had visited the white exhibit palaces, the working coal mine and a giant Ferris wheel at the fair in 1904, the very year, he thinks cycling home, that his grandfather Cornelius had spent up in Montana working in a mine.

On the Fourth of July Carla talked at the kitchen table about how her horse, Flapper, had broken out of their barn and run down the hill to join the other horses it had heard parading along Highway 40, formerly the Cumberland Road, which closed to traffic each Independence Day in Terre Haute.

'The Cumberland Road?'

'One of the first routes settlers took west.'

'You grew up on it?'

'Sure 'nuf,' she smiled. 'Couldn't sleep at night for those covered wagons rattlin' by.'

And then he asked, 'Terre Haute?'

'The French owned it first,' Carla said, giving him a crash course on the Louisiana Purchase as Court rolled another joint, opining how they were all on *terre haute* now.

'It was also known for a time as Sin City, given a host of brothels and gambling houses along the Wabash river,' she added, causing Court to half-choke as he exhaled.

Her sense of a historical past was some of what he admired about Carla; something the Irish had in their DNA, but of which many of the Yanks he'd so far met seemed oblivious. There was also a shade of melancholy behind her habitual American sunniness, which interested him, and he noted how he was always hoping she might hang around. But she departed shortly after that night too, following which the rest of the table headed down to the Mississippi river for a fireworks display, which struck Fintan, now seriously stoned, like a technicolour movie trailer for the apocalypse – a preview, framed by the Arch, of a final fire and brimstone light show yet to come.

*

The rest of the summer flew by. Work was seldom less than lively too, as Fintan had his own weekly caseload now of those he'd helped house, most of whom were decent skins, if fucked over by alcohol, drugs or family – though with some, like Walt Shea, the trajectory downhill had happened after an admirable ascent of several decades. A bearded redhead under a blue bandana, he told of a singular childhood as he sipped from a can of Knickerbocker beer, which Fintan had him conceal in a brown paper bag from St Louis's finest as they drove down Union Road to the Salvation Army store. Told how his mother had birthed five children in four years before she too flipped, locking her brood in a bedroom one Friday night while their dad was AWOL on a bender, before leaving Kansas City for Canada. Walt, at five the eldest – if only by five minutes to his twin brother Richie – managed to get out the bedroom window on the Sunday, hailing a neighbour en route to church who promptly called the police. The Missouri social services divvied up the siblings among five widespread foster families, and that was that until Walt joined the army at age eighteen. Where on his second day of basic training, the sergeant shouted, 'Shea for detail!' only for Walt to see another recruit step forward along with himself.

'Is that you, Walt?'

'Richie, how you doing?' said Walt, scarcely believing his eyes.

Fintan also called in to Chet in his SRO the following afternoon, who was watching the home-town Cardinals lose to the Cincinnati Reds on an old colour TV.

'Where's that bed we bought?' he asked with a laugh.

'Swapped it for the Zenith,' Chet smiled. 'Sleep like a baby over there,' gesturing at a pile of quilts on the floor. 'Japanese style.'

'You'll want to meet a Japanese woman so?'

'Shit,' said Chet, only it sounded like *shee-it*. Watching the end of the ball game with the first client he had befriended, Fintan finds himself thinking that here is one of his charges who, with a bit of luck, is going to manage OK.

Meantime Will seemed less like a boss as the weeks went by. 'Do you want the Mayor's number?' the office secretary Janet asked Will the day before a ribbon-cutting ceremony on a new block of subsidised housing. 'All I want from that bastard is his black heart on a plate,' replied Will, to which Janet hadn't batted an eye. Will had an interesting circle of friends too, including drop-dead-gorgeous Louise, who called by the office a couple of times. 'She's a David Bailey model,' Janet informed Fintan, who nodded back, though he hadn't a notion who David Bailey was.

Any idea he'd harboured of Will as handicapped had likewise begun to shift, his respirator, wheelchair and vertically suspended typewriter seeming more like just part of what it took to keep him on the move. 'What happened to your head?' Fintan chanced asking one Monday, pointing to a gash across the large bald patch that crowned Will's shoulder-length Wild West hair.

'Manny hit a pothole,' Will replied, describing how he had shot straight up from his wheelchair and hit the roof of Manny's van. Fintan had no idea who Manny was either, until the following Sunday, when he saw a Latino-looking guy pushing Will's chair along the Grand Basin in Forest Park, where Will had suggested the three of them meet up for a walk.

'Have you matches?' Manny asked as they made their way past a thicket of hawthorns to a smaller pond with a pagoda at its far end. Fintan hadn't, but when he started to ask a woman passer-by for a light, Manny shook his head. It began to spit rain then, so they made for the pagoda, where Manny spotted a book of matches on a bench within. '*Gracias á Dios!*' he marvelled, holding it out for them to see GIVE THANKS TO THE LORD! in gold lettering across the matchbook cover.

'Inside the bag,' Will in turn instructed Manny, pointing with his chin at the small backpack on his lap, then smiling up at Fintan as if to say *We're not on the city payroll Sundays* as Manny took out a small plastic baggie of grass.

And so Fintan cycled slowly home two hours later, marvelling yet again at ready-to-go America, where gas stations sell you ice, and churches, if not the Lord himself, lay on matches, should you feel like getting high. A Land of Opportunity where you get to doss about, stoned of a summer Sunday, in the company of what in Donegal you might've described as a coloured guy and a cripple. Only thinking how such words no longer suit, the same way *black* seemed less and less to do with Chet.

And so he cycled slowly home, or back to the house anyhow – as if increasingly unsure of exactly where home lay anymore. He still thought about Glenbay a great deal, missed the sea hugely, the ever-changing light on the hills, along with a myriad other aspects of the village. He also wrote a postcard to Packy and Frankie every month or so, and managed to finally send his brother a $10 bill for his birthday back in February, advising him to get a decent exchange rate off your man at the mobile bank, a large blue horse-van-like affair, which drove into Glenbay and parked outside Molly's pub every Monday. But Donegal lay light years away from this 'hot town, summer in the city', where America clearly had him in its thrall.

*

What's more, a month later Fintan was no longer sleeping alone, having taken up with Linda Sue after chatting her up behind a Dunkin' Donuts counter on Washington Avenue, felled by the frosted streaks in her strawberry-blonde hair, which had put him in mind of an ice-cream cone. Better yet was the faint scent of doughnuts that clung to her pink-and-white uniform the first evening he'd picked her up after work. Standing together at the bus stop, he saw where the summer sun had turned her scalp pink beneath her hair. On the bus she told him how she was saving her wages for both flying lessons and a hairdressing course. Not yet twenty, she lived with her folks and a younger brother, so it's not so much sleeping together when they eventually get there three weeks later, as fooling around in his single bed up under the eaves for an hour maybe before he sees her home. Linda Sue was both sweet-smelling and sweet, but what they shared was not really serious – not serious the way it might be with Carla, or so he thinks the odd time she calls by the house.

*

By October Fintan had become a regular caller at Will Woodward's house, where Will's 72-year-old father, Woody, who looked after Will, turned out to be every bit as droll as his son. Manny and he were pals by this point, and Fintan met a few others there, though not Louise the Model, who had departed to NYC. One Sunday Manny, Will and he returned to Forest Park to look at the last burst of autumnal colours on the trees before the winter arrived and stripped them bare, Manny remarking as they trundled back towards the van how the little round screen over the intake valve on the respirator affixed to Will's wheelchair was not unlike the bowl of a water pipe.

'Let's give it a go so!' Will said, smiling, so Fintan took the last of the grass he just happened to be carrying and struck a match as Manny turned on the respirator. It worked all right – worked too well, in fact, as the dope instantly combusted, giving Will a mighty hit and leaving Manny and Fintan but a few charred crumbs.

'Polio,' Will told him another evening at his house, describing how he had awakened one morning at age sixteen with pains in his legs, little knowing how his life was about to change. 'It could've been worse. I could've bought the farm altogether.' And Fintan telling him in turn as he left – nor for the first time – how Will should lend him his cowboy boots for a week, 'so as I can scuff them up for you'.

And as the year wound down, he realised he wasn't cut out to be a care worker, much as he liked many of the clientele. He wondered, too, would it be any easier to watch so many fighting a losing battle – not least the Vietnam vets – had he liked them less? Then, two weeks before Christmas, following his father's death, Walt Shea went AWOL. It took Fintan a week to track him down, eventually finding him back in his SRO, eyes bleary and bloodshot, no sign of his blue bandana, his red curls plastered across his scalp.

'My dad told me he was gonna croak. "You said that last night," I told him, only this time it was true.'

'What took him?' Fintan asked, after offering condolences.

'Vodka,' Walt said with a half-laugh. 'Alcohol poisoning, according to the hospital. "A drunk," I said when they asked me for his occupation – "same as myself."'

'Did you reach your brother Richie?'

'Can't find the fucker,' Walt said, shaking his head. 'Thought he'd signed up as a lifer, but the army says he was discharged last June.'

Chet meantime was one of the few in Fintan's caseload who seemed to be gaining any kind of foothold. Hired as a trash collector for the Public Works Department, he showed Fintan a large colour TV he found on the kerbside. 'Works fine,' he said, 'so I swapped the Zenith for an easy chair.'

'Keep an eye out for a bed so?' Fintan replied, to which Chet just smiled and shook his head.

Sundays grew to be too cold for cycling around Forest Park, so Fintan finally checked out the Art Museum there, overlooking the Grand Basin waterway. Thinking of Randall

Hart on the way in, he wondered again whether this museum might have him. The woman at the catalogue desk knew of Hart all right, but doubted they had a painting, nor did they. Wandering from one room to another, he came upon a colourful-looking harvest scene, wherein two men bind sheaves of wheat cropped by a third harvest-hand wielding a six-bladed scythe. It was the agricultural implement which drew Fintan in, nothing like the single-bladed scythe used to save the hay for the cows back in Donegal, plus how the elongated farm workers looked all but cartoon-like in their floppy straw hats; nor had he Jo-Ann there to explain why the meadow and trees should also look entirely unreal, so after a half-hour meander through another half-dozen rooms, he eventually buggered off.

One night in mid-January the phone on the hall table at Lenox Place rang around 8 p.m. 'For you, Fintan,' Shelly shouted up from the second-floor landing. It was Will, who said that he wouldn't be at the office in the morning, but that if Fintan would swing by on his way to work, he could have his boots for the day. They chatted for a minute or two before ringing off. Two hours later the phone rang again, only this time it was Woody, telling through tears how his son had died of a heart attack, an hour or so after he'd rung Fintan.

He called over to Woody the next morning on his way to work, spent a half-hour in the tiny kitchen, hearing how Will had helped Woody into bed, same as he had done nightly for the past twenty years. 'Took his leave with nary a word,' was how Woody summed it up. As Fintan rose to go, Woody signalled for him to follow back into the empty bedroom on the ground floor, Will's remains already at the funeral home.

'That machine was always loudest when it was off,' Woody said, nodding at the respirator in the corner.

'You were to collect these,' he then said, picking up Will's cowboy boots. 'No way can I take them,' protested Fintan, but Woody insisted, putting the boots into a plastic bag and onto Fintan's handlebars for the cycle into work.

# 6

As it happens, Fintan won't don a dead man's boots until later that summer, which finds him working on a lakeside carnival in Wisconsin. The Department of Social Services job doesn't take long to unravel after Will's death. Will's replacement, Judith, a middle-aged woman with abundant henna in her hair, seems a pencil-pushing paper-shuffler at heart, though truth be told, Fintan had been tiring of the gig. Linda Sue and he had stopped seeing each other too, not long after Will died, and as winter inches into spring Carla also turns up at the house on Lenox Place less and less.

Nor is Wisconsin the West he's had in his sights from an early age across the Atlantic, more like 'too long in the lowlands', as a song suggests one morning on the breakfast radio. As it happens, housemate Court's brother, Bobby, on a weekend visit from the Badger State, mentions how there's a groundskeeper's job going at the lakeside resort where he works as a cook – if Fintan were interested. And Fintan was, having already handed in his notice at the DSS the previous week, two days after the police pulled Walt Shea out of the Mississippi, some 200 yards downstream from the Arch, which Fintan had never taken Walt down to eyeball – otherwise he might've blamed himself for being in some way responsible for Walt's wandering along that stretch of water. And so Fintan takes Bobby up on a prospective gig, riding shotgun beside him in a 1963 yellow Bonneville up to Burlington, Wisconsin, one Sunday evening.

\*

The groundskeeper job at the resort had already been filled, but Fintan finds work two days later as a roustabout at a small carnival just across Brown's Lake, which appeared to cater to a different class of clientele from the mostly middle-class Jews at Bobby's resort. Nor is his new boss, Lenny, in any ways the same as his old boss Will. Taciturn and moody, a habitual cigarette lit or unlit in his left hand, his other, withered arm tucked in close at his side. The carnival opened from ten in the morning till midnight, the days both hot and long, though Lenny gave everyone an hour or two off at some point before the evening crowds arrived. The work too came in spurts, the hardest graft by far being the weekly set-up and disassemble, when all hands pitched in to haul everything onto the trucks, before the carnival headed off from one small town to another across the state.

The daily tasks, however, were simple enough: emptying the trash bins into an old Dodge pick-up, which Fintan drove mornings to the nearest dump, or fuelling the gas-powered generators that fired the nightly neon lighting. And once Lenny had sussed his mechanical bent, helping to get any broken-down, midway ride – the Caterpillar or the Renegade, say – up and running again. Most of the stalls along the Gallery of Games were manned by seasoned carney hands along with a few college kids, but Fintan also occasionally filled in behind a counter, collecting nickels, dimes and quarters from little kids, or making change from dollar bills for fathers of families, or the lads of all ages who made a nonchalant show of trying to win a cheap plaster ornament or large teddy bear – which the lucky ones who actually managed to either ring the neck of a floating duck, sink three hoops with an under-inflated basketball, or puncture six balloons with bandy darts, invariably handed over to their girlfriends in a similar, studied, carefree fashion.

Lenny also had him some afternoons on Elvis the Mouse, thinking an Irish brogue shouting out the odds might bring some additional marks to the table. The table itself being more of a gigantic roulette wheel, with forty-eight numbered holes along its sloping, circular edge. The bets placed, Fintan would give the table a spin before releasing Elvis from his little cage at the circle's centre – to race up and down the table until its revolutions slowed sufficiently to allow him to vanish from view down the nearest coloured, numbered hole. The ratcheting gears beneath the revolving table and the shouting punters both struck Fintan as piteous punishment for any Elvis, but the several mice who took turns answering to that name seemed to manage OK, and so he simply tried to have some treats – a bit of cheese or raisins, say – to hand on the afternoons he drew that duty.

Other carnival livestock included three sluggish rattlesnakes in a large glass cage, along with two lizards – an iguana, and another whose species he never got – both of which mostly slept inside another wire cage, and neither of which seemed to eat much at all. That Fintan wasn't really up on his reptiles, per Lenny on one of the few occasions he bothered to string a complete sentence together, was likely down to St Patrick's having driven the snakes out of Ireland. But Fintan knew better, thanks to neighbour Jack Gara. Knew how Ireland never had any snakes to begin with. Had only ever boasted a single indigenous reptile: a small, dark-brown lizard with yellowy spots, one of which Rory and he had managed to trap inside a turf bucket on one of those rare, hot Donegal summer's days, when a lizard might actually sun itself on a whitewashed gable or stonewall, lending an exotic Mediterranean touch to the equally anomalous weather.

And remembering too – as he cleaned out the lizards' cage on another afternoon – a tale Carla had told at the kitchen table back at Lenox Place, of her first year away at college at age eighteen. Of a package that popped up in her mailbox, its brown wrapping with cancelled stamps from somewhere in Africa, but its contents a home-grown, recently run-over, Hudson Valley five-lined skink.

'I'd an idea who'd sent that lizard, so I left it outside her room on the dorm floor.'

'Did she own up?' Monty had inquired.

'She just left it there,' Carla smiled. 'Claimed she knew nothing about it when I asked. So I picked it up and chased her down the hallway with it, herself screaming for the dorm mother!'

\*

The best part of the new job was the nights: the entire carnival awash in neon, Jefferson Airplane and the Stones blasting from loudspeakers above the Carousel, Caterpillar and Scrambler, and the Ferris wheel a perfect circle of white lights. Sometime after midnight Fintan would tumble into bed in one of several backlot trailers, his living quarters, or LQ, as the carney crowd called them. A trailer being what they called a caravan back in Glenbay, though Fintan's was larger than what the Donegal County Council issued to old Mickey Gara up the Glen, after the rotten roof-thatch had slid off his cottage. And Fintan would fall asleep no bother, given the long day's night – apart from the Sunday he lay awake for an hour after hearing the three-note, ethereal call of the whip-poor-will, which Mary Cunnea had first whistled aloud for him and brother Frankie in their Glenbay kitchen.

He shared the trailer with Clem, a Wisconsin lad his own age, just out of college, though like many of his American peers, he seemed years younger. One night three weeks into the gig, he woke to a hand running lightly down his leg, thinking for a befuddled moment might it possibly be Suzanne, aka Madame Mazurka, a bonny red-haired carney colleague who, daily donning a long skirt and low-cut peasant blouse, told two-dollar fortunes inside a small tent beside the cotton-candy stand.

However, his midnight suitor turned out to be Bobby Joe instead, a balding, fifty-year-old sad sack who prepared the carney crew's three daily meals – cornflakes, burnt toast, greasy meat and overdone veg – taken in shifts at two long tables beneath a striped canopy in the backlot. 'Fuck off, Bobby!' Fintan had hissed, so as not to waken Clem. 'Sorry man,' Bobby muttered over his shoulder as he left, 'wrong trailer.'

The job was seven days a week, but you got one morning and another evening off. Not that there were much to do in rural Wisconsin, beyond swimming or fishing in the sandy-bottomed lakes. And even the fishing wasn't up to much, though he managed to land a huge carp one afternoon, having borrowed Clem's rod and reel. Six or so pounds, but no fight to it whatsoever, none of the slash and slither of the far smaller mackerel off Ra Maisha, the heavy drag on the line more like a car tyre than anything alive, as he slowly reeled it in. He'd already heard from Bobby Joe how carp was eaten everywhere bar America, so he slipped the outsized fish back into the lake, where it lay on its side for a few minutes, breathing like a bellows, before slowly swimming off.

One early August night off he made his way to a bar in the tiny town of Green Lake, where they'd pitched camp earlier that week. Had nursed a beer as he watched a Chicago White Sox game on the telly, thinking of 'the young gentleman doctor' whose two small daughters his mother Mary had helped rear in that city. And who, he calculated, would be young women now, maybe somewhere in their early thirties.

This was the same age, it turned out, as Madame Mazurka, whom Fintan now occasionally sought out for a chat after the last punters had departed and the nightly neon wonderland gone dark. Sitting in lawn chairs outside her tiny trailer, where single-mother Suzanne could keep an ear out for four-year-old Tracey in case she woke. No question he fancied her, the gorgeous mop of red curls above the brightly coloured halter-tops she favoured, when not rigged out like a Gypsy Mama, and he wondered, might the attraction be mutual? But the very fact of small, shy, sad-eyed Tracey had him determined not to try to bed her mother, and so they remained just good pals instead, generally chatting for half an hour or so before saying goodnight.

'Blue money's better,' Suzanne told him one Friday night, recounting how she had worked as a carney stripper in her native Vermont two summers back. But once she had custody of Tracey from her daughter's alcoholic father, she turned to fortune-telling, figuring her beloved, dearly departed, French-Canadian grandmother – whose accent she'd adopted for Madame Mazurka – might rest easier with her favourite granddaughter trading as a clairvoyant rather than a striptease artiste. And so she closely questioned Fintan when he spoke of how his great-aunt Cassie had read their cups and cards at the cottage back in Pier – keen to see what, if anything, she might borrow to embellish her act.

*Blue money* was a new one for him, as was *roustabout*, which per their cook Bobby Joe, was Fintan's own job description. Neither had mentioned Bobby's nocturnal wrong turn the morning after, nor did Fintan shun Bobby either, who had a fund of carney stories going back to his first gig as an eight-year-old shill, the lucky little boy who would loudly win at the Floating Ducks or Bucket Bonanza, slowly circling round with his prize teddy bear or Indian chief headdress, before returning them at the back of the stalls. No surprise then, that Bobby Joe knew all the scams: how to best short-change the punters, or how to reset the single bowling pin at the Ball & Chain booth slightly off-centre, so as to give the occasional sucker an actual chance at winning. Or even the safest way to skim the cash-take from the games you ran, though Fintan was happy enough with his wages – even managing to squirrel away a few bob each week – given there was feck-all to spend it on except drink the few hours he wasn't working, and he was determined to keep an eye on that.

Towards the end of August he donned Will's boots for the first time, surprised to find them a perfect fit. Thinking how he hadn't a clue as to how tall Will had been, but pleased to think they'd the same boot size. There were only two weeks left now until the carney season ended, nor would it come too soon either. Even the two surviving Elvises seemed to be running out of steam, needing a gentle poke now out of the box atop their spinning table.

Later that same Saturday afternoon he heard all kinds of screaming coming from the Scrambler, where it happened an elephantine man in an Alice Cooper T-shirt had just blown his lunch – two corn dogs with a side order of fries, funnel cake and a large root beer – spraying the chunky, multicoloured blend all over his fellow riders as the three-seater chair pods, mounted on long, spider-like arms, criss-crossed at high speed within inches of each other. The aftermath looking not unlike one of those medieval paintings he'd seen in Cleveland or St Louis, only painted by a latter-day Bruegel: three or four folk vomiting in turn in the tall grass behind the Scrambler, while Lenny ran around offering free all-day passes to anyone he gauged wouldn't try to hug or clobber him, as Fintan faded back into the crowd of gaping, if not gagging, onlookers, determined not to draw clean-up duty.

The following night they tore down the set before striking off early the next morning like a mechanical, raggle-taggle, itinerant caravan, to motor two hours northeast in a late summer heatwave to their final Wisconsin site on Lake Michigan, south of Port Washington. That same afternoon he tried to picture his mother, Mary Cunnea, a year or so younger than himself, as she too had taken in that same lake for the first time. Its large, placid body of water far more reminiscent of Cleveland's Lake Erie than Glenbay's North Atlantic, but Fintan grateful all the same for both the broader horizon and the promise of what he too now sometimes called *fall*, not *autumn*, already heralding itself in the cooler nights. A few maple trees even flashed a blaze of red or orange, and on the following slow carnival afternoon he drove Suzanne and her Tracey out in the Dodge pick-up to an apple orchard. It was early yet in the season, but they managed to fill half a basket with McIntoshes, which Fintan found, like so much of what you eat in America, to be rather bland.

'You don't have to go?,' Suzanne said later that night, after they had finished off a six-pack of Schlitz, and so Fintan didn't. But only after Suzanne had made it clear there were no strings attached. Nor anything like unfinished business between them – more like a one-night, once-off, farewell tryst. They made love quietly inside the tiny trailer, so as not to waken Tracey at the other end, and being a relatively older woman, thirty-two years to his twenty-three, she had him do something he had not yet done heretofore. Afterwards he lay on quietly, listening as Suzanne described the Licensed Practical Nurse course she would start the following week in Madison, where Tracey was already enrolled in kindergarten.

'Maybe we'll ask that crystal ball of yours?' Fintan laughed, when Suzanne asked about his own plans. Like herself, he was in no way inclined to follow the carney life south for the winter, but beyond that, he hadn't a clue.

Back in his own bed and unable to sleep, he suddenly – for no reason he could figure, lest it might explain why he was lying in a musty caravan on the shores of Lake Michigan – remembered the monkey peering out a caravan window at him and brother Frankie at the wee travelling circus outside Killybegs, to which mother Mary had taken them. And how Frankie and he had talked of little else for days after, like it had been a Barnum & Bailey three-ring circus – not a tiny troupe whose Hong Kong-born acrobats double-jobbed selling admission tickets, their ringmaster busy splicing an electrical cable inside the small tent as they took their seats around a single grassy ring, where the performing ponies repeatedly pulled up short in order to snatch another mouthful. Fact was, Frankie and he had repeatedly spoken of running away to join that troupe, but having already departed Glenbay, Fintan was no longer in need of a carnival life.

# 7

Picture Fintan once again in St Louis – not beneath the Arch this time, but having retraced his steps for the first time Stateside, back to the house on Lenox Place. Planning to collect some stuff stored there, crash for a night or two, before finally heading farther west. Only to find Carla instead, in a turquoise T-shirt, drinking camomile tea at the plank-top kitchen table on the evening he blows in. And not Carla just visiting Shelly either, but residing herself now at No. 127.

Seeing her – with the same bright smile, only framed by even shorter blonde hair – he suddenly wonders, is Carla a reason he might've returned? As if some kind of unfinished business possibly lay between them, and thus not entirely surprised to find her at the scarred, coffee-mug-ring-stained table, offering him the last of her Bit-O-Honey bar.

*

It took a few weeks to suss out some – if not all – of what had gone down in St Louis over the summer. The red-Porsche boyfriend was clearly no longer in the frame, while Carla herself was now sleeping in Shelly's second-storey room with its single queen-sized bed beneath the shelves of grinning dentures. What precisely that signified wasn't entirely clear, however, for Shelly's blue Harley-Davidson boyfriend was by no means history, still roaring up the drive several times a week.

Yet Fintan found himself surprisingly OK with the possibility that Carla and Shelly were also now an item, felt little of the jealousy he could now acknowledge having harboured for red-Porsche man, now that he was no longer in the picture. To be sure, it was not a scenario he would've given much thought to, nor a way of being together that Rory and he had ever puzzled over back in Glenbay, before Fintan found less and less to puzzle over with his pal. Rather he wondered whether Carla's tale of the gift-boxed lizard from her college classmate might've been some kind of unrequited love story, something that hadn't occurred to him when first she told it. 'Did she fancy you?' he would later ask Carla, who just shook her head, 'Naw, just a bit nutty, I think.'

Either way, Fintan tried not to think too much of his two pals in the one bed, whatever about imagining himself therein, as truth be told he had never entirely let go of his initial crush on lanky, leggy Shelly. But what he finally did face up to was a keenness for Carla that had been there from the git-go, though he suspected anything between them was least likely to happen on the red-Porsche rebound, whether or not she'd already rebounded into Shelly's bed. There was also the small matter of sorting a bed for himself, plus hustling for work again if, as it increasingly looked, he was going to linger a while longer on the west bank of the Mississippi.

The bed proved easily enough sorted after a week on an overstuffed sofa in the front sitting room, when Mitch, a skinny, bespectacled engineering grad student at Washington

University, departed early one Thursday morning for parts unknown, owing two months' rent on Fintan's former room under the eaves. And work came almost as quickly, courtesy of Handy Andy, which operated out of a dingy East St Louis storefront, lit by a single, bare bulb hung from the ceiling, the first of several casual-labour outfits in which Fintan would enlist across America in the years to come. The drill was pretty much the same, no matter the city: turn up around 6 a.m. along with the other hoping-to-be-hired hands, some of whom might smell of drink or look like they'd slept rough the night before. But Fintan himself had cut back on the booze, happy just to be back in an urban scene after three months of small-town America, the corn-fed conservatism of the rural Midwest having reminded him of Uncle Condy's disdain for the Irish Midlands farmers back home: 'A muddy Wellington on the accelerator pedal as they drive their Mercs into a field!'

That said, his first gig was anything but handy, rather three weeks shovelling crushed stone out of a dry-bulk cargo barge moored twelve miles downstream on the East St Louis side of the river. Having held neither spade nor shovel since his brief stint on a London building site, his hands blistered up within an hour, his back aching by the time the van returned to take him and three fellow labourers on the half-hour ride back across the Mississippi to South Broadway, where he had locked his bike.

Carla he saw most evenings around the house, where they might talk for a time before one or the other headed out. The fact that she was curious about Ireland, and that she knew little about the place – had none of the shamrock notions of most Americans he met – enabled Fintan to talk some about Donegal. Carla in turn might speak of Indiana, and so it was mostly childhood stuff they shared, managing to find an occasional correspondence, if only how each had enjoyed squinting at a street lamp until it blurred into a horizontal line of light. Though only Fintan had memories of several years before street lamps, and how the initial handful that eventually followed had been confined to the narrow village street in Glenbay with its chapel, shop, petrol station and two pubs.

Carla also told of the old woman who had hemmed her mother's skirts, her front-room lamp hung from the middle of the ceiling, turned on and off by a string instead of a wall-switch like any other house. She knew too of the sour-tasting sorrel that Fintan's mother had occasionally picked to put in a soup, not standard Donegal fare for sure, rather something Mary had read somewhere. But it was wild chives, not sorrel, that Carla and her pal Maggie had picked to eat in her Terre Haute backyard. A backyard, she boasted, 'with the biggest magnolia in the state of Indiana!' Whereas Glenbay had fewer trees of any kind, the odd shelterbelt of pine fronting a cottage, or a stunted oak or sycamore struggling to withstand the salt wind off the Atlantic, nor anything like the magnolia, whose elevated perimeter of branches allowed one to stand within. 'Like being under a giant umbrella of colour,' Carla enthused, describing the saucer-shaped, pink-and-white flowers, which when wilting would brown first along their edges.

Carla also talked about family, sounding at times as if she were trying to explain them to herself as much as to

Fintan. A maternal grandfather she hardly knew, the wealthy owner of a cardboard-box factory, who she felt had lived a hard life. 'He had a lot nice things, but he looked sort of used up?' Another concern was politics, not least her father's reactionary conservatism, which had her at age six thinking Sputnik was an actual dirty word, though neither the Reds nor satellites any longer exercised him.

It happened she too was keen on blackjack, if not entirely best-pleased the evening he had quoted Uncle Condy, how 'You'd've been shot out West for that!' after failing to have him cut the deck before she dealt.

When the fraternal Scientologists, Seth and Simon, departed the house at Halloween, Carla shifted from Shelly's into their vacated room, making Fintan wonder whether she too had simply needed a pillow on which to lay her tousled blonde head. Then, two Saturdays later, they took it up a notch themselves, dropping a tab of mescaline each, which Carla had scored off the cook at the waterfront café where she now waitressed several afternoons a week along with her cleaning jobs. They left the house a half-hour after washing down the pills with a glass of OJ in the kitchen, only to discover an inch of light white powder on the sidewalk, an early snowfall, which looked like it was breathing, pulsing like porridge over a low flame, the trees and houses likewise embellished just for them.

They made their way then towards the aquarium downtown, though Fintan had to stop en route to talk to a long-haired lad hawking the *Riverfront Times* with a picture of Springsteen on the cover. However, it wasn't the Boss who'd stopped him in his tracks, rather the blue eyes of a chap around his own age, who was flogging the alternative weekly on a corner. 'Blue like the sea and sky!' Fintan informed the bloke who – having twigged it wasn't a come-on, given Carla's arm linked in Fintan's – just smiled broadly at them both.

'I don't know where I am, man,' Fintan added.

'S'all right,' the newspaper vendor replied. 'What're you on?'

Fintan looked at Carla, who offered, 'Mesc?'

'It's cut with speed sometimes,' the blue-eyed, handsome man told Fintan. 'So it could be more how fast you're travelling,' he grinned, 'than a question of where you are?'

His easy smile served to settle Fintan, who later wished he'd bought a paper by way of thanks. Reaching the aquarium, they floated amidst mostly parents and kids, marvelling at the colours thrown off by the various fish, flickering neon flashes that swam this way and that. However, a moray eel, which lay slowly breathing in and out, suddenly transported Fintan back into father Packy's small boat in the shadow of Glen Head, whereupon he began to panic until a foul fish and shite smell, wafting suddenly from an enclosure where three small penguins were doing their head-waiter bit for a delighted gaggle of kids, brought him quickly back to Missouri. Peering into the men's room's neon-lit mirror a few minutes later, he marvelled at the greenish pallor of his skin, the enlarged pores across his face, his cheekbones threatening to push through. All of which led Carla, over a coffee shortly after, to speculate that what the short-order cook had sold her was more likely LSD than mescaline.

They held hands some of the way home, where in the kitchen Carla gave him a kiss on each cheek, more like a Parisian than a Hoosier. They segued off then into separate rooms for the rest of the weekend, though not before Carla cautioned him to take it easy over the next few hours, checking in briefly the next day as well to make sure he was all right after their trip. He saw little of her through the following week, himself acting the Handy Andy now on a painting job in a huge warehouse back in East St Louis, before returning home too tired to do other than eat and hit the hay, as Uncle Condy used to call it.

The following Monday they found themselves on their own in the front room after supper, where Carla patted the empty space beside her on the overstuffed sofa as he was heading for the navy-blue easy chair.

'What are you doing for Christmas, Fintan?'

'Jaysus!' he said. 'Trying to ignore it best I can?'

'Would you like to come back with me to Terre Haute? Don't worry,' she added with a smile when he hesitated, 'my parents will be sure to put us into separate rooms.'

'Sure, we've separate rooms here!' Fintan laughed, thinking he might take her hand – only Carla took his first.

'It'd be just a couple of days,' she added, 'which is about all I can manage there anyhow.'

He heard a bit more about her parents that evening. How her father had retired from his father-in-law's box factory, nor got worked up over much else either. 'It's more like he's retired early from life,' Carla said. 'Goes up to this cabin we have on Birch Lake, sits in a rocking chair afternoons on the back porch, a pair of binoculars on his lap.'

'On the lookout for Sputniks?'

'Not even. Just ordinary, everyday planes. "Here comes another one," he'll occasionally announce, lifting the glasses like he really couldn't care.'

Her mother sounded no happier – only more inherently so, like she'd been quietly desperate for years. 'She'd this habit when I was little of laughing over something at the table,' Carla said, 'only she'd lose it then and begin to cackle non-stop, at which point my dad would look over at me and say, "OK, kiddo, it looks like Mom's going to start to cry" – and sure enough she'd start sobbing her heart out.'

Fintan had little experience with this kind of talk – at which Yanks seemed to excel – but Carla's sharing didn't faze either, which seemed enough for her. 'Mom told me once about driving home from her college in New York State one spring during the Depression, all the way back to Indiana. And how she picked up this young guy hitching just outside Poughkeepsie, who showed her these printing plates for counterfeit twenty-dollar bills, which he'd nearly perfected, only for his landlady to throw him out for not paying his rent.'

'She came back to Indiana then?'

'That was her mistake I think,' nodded Carla. 'Like she missed her chance to get out, lacked the nerve of that guy heading west, full of plans for his funny money. Yet she enjoyed telling stories a lot, like she were also saying life in Terre Haute just didn't cut the mustard.'

'What other stories?' asked Fintan, wondering whether he was falling this hard for Carla because she too had a store of them. Unlike those Yanks who talk all the time – about anything or nothing – but don't so often tell stories.

'Anabel,' Carla said after a pause. 'She used to tell me about Anabel, a German cook my grandparents had when she was little, who told her stuff, like how the Kaiser had cut off the hands of all the children in Belgium. Mom said Anabel had her own story too, had been in a reformatory, but she didn't know for what. But Anabel was kind to her, like always leaving the stale cornbread for her to throw to the chickens, which my mother loved doing cuz it made them go absolutely crazy.'

The spuds Mary Cunnea had given him and Frankie to feed their hens weren't so much of a story, never mind his mother's having been in Chicago – like Anabel, a hired hand in another's household. Still, Carla managed to elicit an occasional recollection of his mother, her habit of making a wish upon the first sighting of a new moon, say, or how she never let him or Frankie out of the cottage without first looking for her hairbrush, which Carla, laughing, said explained his perpetually tousled, sandy hair.

They went to bed together that night for the first time, but that was pretty much all they did. Slept together in Carla's bed beneath a large, ersatz landscape the Scientologist brothers had painted on the length of the wall: all Day-Glo oranges and yellows beneath a maroon moon in a black, star-flecked sky. Fintan with an arm over Carla, who had asked only that he hold her, had not asked for anything unsaid, as if whatever was finally in play between them entailed more than just intercourse. It was the same the two or three nights they again slept together coming up to Christmas, by which time Fintan had painted over the bedroom mural with a tin of off-white paint left over from the East St Louis warehouse job.

It proved separate beds in the old, three-storey house in Terre Haute too, just as Carla had promised. Fintan in what had likely once been a maid's room on the ground floor behind the kitchen, while Carla slept upstairs in her old childhood bedroom. Their three-day visit proved as strange as anything he had encountered in America, from the clear plastic over everything you sat on, easy chairs and sofas, to a small mountain of gift-wrapped packages beneath an enormous tree on Christmas morning.

'It's not real?' he said to Carla that afternoon, having rubbed its needles between finger and thumb.

'Nope.' She laughed. 'But there's an artificial pine scent you can spray to make up for that.'

'You're joking?' he said, frowning, only Carla laughed again before pointing at an aerosol can smaller than those he'd already spotted sitting on the cisterns of the toilets both upstairs and down.

The USSR's invasion of Afghanistan on Christmas Eve, together with the ongoing Iranian hostage crisis, loomed large at the Christmas Day table, along with its twenty-pound turkey and enough side dishes to feed an army. Grace, with its few words of peace and thanks, was followed by a heated exchange between Carla's father and her uncle Dave on the efficacy of gunship helicopters in any attack on Kabul. And while Fintan had sampled a fair quotient of jingoism across the bar at O'Connell's back in Cleveland, this rabidness at familial quarters was something new. Not that Carla hadn't warned him on their journey from St Louis the day before, after he'd marvelled out the Greyhound window at a large, hand-lettered front-yard sign: GOD, GUNS & GUTS

MAKE AMERICA GREAT. LET'S KEEP ALL THREE! Only to be baffled some fifteen minutes later by another, smaller, faded square of cardboard – FREE LT. CALLEY – in the fly-speckled window of the small café their bus pulled into for a ten-minute rest stop, until Carla filled him in.

'Wait till you meet Uncle Bert,' she grinned as they were getting back on the bus.

'Who's Uncle Bert?'

'My mother's brother. A right-wing lawyer who plays tuba in the Shriners.'

'And what's a Shriner?'

'Ask Uncle Bert tomorrow,' Carla had said, only Fintan hadn't. Had simply listened as the table talk turned from killing commies to the new Thunderbird Uncle Bert had bought, and from there to cars in general, with which he was far more au fait than geopolitics.

Carla's father at the other end of the table was much as his only daughter had painted him, a young-looking, if somewhat played-out sixty. Her mother, several years younger, with fading strawberry-blonde hair, had kicked things off by knocking a silverware drawer off the dining table in her search for a gravy ladle, its contents spilling in a sparkling, ear-shattering waterfall onto the polished parquet floor, a sideshow that delighted her brothers Bert and Dave no end. And prompting Fintan to keep an eye on her whenever she laughed during the meal, lest she again lose the run of herself and end up sobbing, head in hands.

They all asked Fintan a question or two about Ireland – in between offering him sweet potato draped with melted marshmallow, or a second serving of fruit salad with Jell-O – but once their interest faded he was able to simply sit and listen, not least to Carla's maternal grandmother, who threw out an occasional morbid conversational strand, like an aged black widow spider at a corner of its web, from the far end of the table. Telling of a friend who woke feeling hot along one side, only to discover she was haemorrhaging – fatally, it turned out – from an operation.

'You shouldn't recommend a doctor, lawyer or newspaper,' she later directed at Fintan from down the table, apropos of Lord knows what, as plates of pumpkin pie topped with whipped cream from yet another aerosol can circled round, after which Carla, grabbing the first chance to flee, borrowed her father's car to show Fintan the town with its Christmas-afternoon emptied streets.

'They built the stone steps to keep horses from being ridden into the place,' she remarked as they drove past the county courthouse, reminding him – not that he needed it – as to why he was there, and what it was that, along with her ready smile and cornflower-blue eyes, beguiled him so. An apprehension of times past, along with a sense of place he'd first heard as her voice had quickened at the Lenox Place kitchen table a year ago, while talking about the Cumberland Road – which as she now pointed out – they'd just turned onto. And, yes, her entangled sense of family too – or sense of an entangled family, God love 'em – which no doubt had also helped win his heart.

'They're something else,' she now offered as they drove through a large park, the last of the watery winter sun lighting the Wabash river through the trees. 'Aren't they?'

'They're just family,' Fintan said. 'OK, maybe an as-large-as-life family … But how was it you managed to find your way through all that?'

'Being an only child helps. You have to move quickly, else you won't move at all.'

She nodded then as he held up a plastic baggie, turning her father's Buick Riviera into an empty picnic area by the side of the road.

'Some nights I'd lie with my ear to the hot-air register in my bedroom floor, listening to them bicker in the living room below. It was no mystery they weren't very happy, but I don't think they themselves knew why, apart from the stupid stuff they bitched about.'

They parked and smoked half a joint, after which Carla drove them through her old neighbourhood, pointing out various sites, a kind of guided tour through her schoolgirl past.

'That was my best friend Margaret's house.'

'Where's she now?'

'Right here in town,' Carla said, telling of Margaret's pregnancy in their last year in high school, and of the shower her girlfriends threw for her in an awkward room at the YWCA on the morning of her wedding. 'I'll show you her boyfriend Larry's house now,' she says, making a right turn. 'Larry was out front when I drove home that morning from the Y. Playing with his two dogs on the lawn like he were still a kid, not somebody who was going to get married that afternoon. And I think it was that morning I first realised I had to get out of this town big time.'

'A shower?' asked Fintan, who still encountered daily mysteries about American life.

'A baby shower,' Carla said, 'though they're usually after the wedding. Just a bunch of presents for the baby, plus stupid stuff, like a banana gift-wrapped within a condom – which really wasn't that funny, given Margaret's tummy.'

They managed to spend as much time as possible out of her house over the next two days, took in *The Deerhunter* with Robert De Niro at a downtown cinema, the film like a dark shadow-play to all the flag-wrapped talk back at the house. They lit up again too, this time in Carla's backyard, passing a joint back and forth under the leafless latticework of Indiana's largest magnolia tree, from wherein she pointed out her childhood tyre swing suspended from an adjoining maple, same as he'd seen once in an American film back in Killybegs.

Then, three nights after Christmas, Carla quietly opened his tiny bedroom door not long after they had said goodnight. Standing there in an ankle-length red flannel nightgown, same hue as her sweatshirt on the day they met. Holding a finger to her lips, she beckoned with her other hand for him to follow her upstairs. Pointing with a smile to the hot-air register in her bedroom floor, she then handed him a foil-wrapped condom as easily as she might the last piece of a Bit-O-Honey bar, before dimming the bedside lamp. And so they finally made love for the first time, there in her childhood bedroom, managing to get what seemed to Fintan a never-ending nightgown no higher than her waist as they struggled to make no noise at all, her hand across his mouth as he came.

'No, but I will another time,' she replied when he asked whether she had as well. 'Sex isn't accounting,' she added. 'It doesn't have to balance out every time. Just hold me, Fintan, please,' which he had for an hour or so before stealing back downstairs. "S funny how touch is often enough,' she'd whispered sleepily in his ear before he left, 'and a lot of the time I don't feel like making love.' Yet speaking as if love were very much what they had just made, and love being even less of a balance-sheet affair.

*

Back in St Louis they kept to their own rooms, only sleeping together one night out of every three or four. On the third occasion Carla shed her nightgown altogether, and Fintan saw for the first time beneath his fingers the raised welt which he had only previously felt, running alongside nearly half of her spinal column. 'A horse story I hadn't told you yet,' Carla said in the dark, how Flapper had shied away from a two-foot-long black snake along a river trail the summer she turned thirteen, pitching her down onto a fallen tree. 'Luckily the jogger who came along knew enough not to move me,' Carla explained, telling how she'd spent the rest of that summer in a hospital bed, following an operation to put two screws into her lower back. The scar had felt a livid red to his hands that night, but in the morning's half-light he saw its actual paleness, like a long errant rib having worn its way into view.

At breakfast the next morning Court slagged them both, suggesting they move in together to save on rent, which Shelly told him was pretty rich, coming from a monk. She and Carla were as tight as ever and Fintan, who hadn't asked, figured it was likely just touch between them – Carla's need to be held – not that it truly mattered. 'And I wondered, were you ever going to show your hand?!' Shelly had laughed at Fintan on their first night back from Terre Haute, making him wonder, had it been that obvious?

Yet obvious isn't the same as easy, and three-quarters through a bottle of wine on New Year's Eve, Carla came undone on the sitting-room sofa. Weeping 'There's nothing new, Fintan! Nothing new under the sun!' And then 'No, please, no!' when he tried to hold her. Nor did it feel entirely unlike what had several times happened between him and Noeleen back in Donegal – a kind of dark wave suddenly washing in – though Carla and he had so far managed not to go *seachrán* in either the house or the back garden on Lenox Place.

Nor had they made any big plans either, preferring to just play it as it lay for now. 'It's not you or us,' Carla had said, sniffling. 'It's just old stuff, old, old stuff,' sounding at age twenty-five like she'd a half-century already under her belt. Yet telling him the next morning how she always cried the last night of the year.

A week later Fintan forsook Handy Andy for Vinyl Is Forever, who paid two more bucks an hour. He also bought his first car ever that same week, a yellow 1967 Mustang convertible with over a hundred thousand miles on the clock. 'Yellow's a good colour for getting things done quickly,' Suzanne had told him the previous summer in Wisconsin, something both she and Madame Mazurka apparently believed, although speed didn't matter so much as being able to get to whatever house within metropolitan St Louis his new boss, Mitch, who constituted VIF, had secured for its plastic makeover. Most of their clients owned a single-storey, clapboarded ranch house they'd grown tired of painting, so he and Mitch would scrape off whatever old colour had started to peel before nailing on the sheets of ersatz vinyl clapboard, which came in a selection of half-a-dozen hues, 'Bird-Shit Green', as Mitch called it, being a shade more popular than 'Watery-Piss Yellow'.

'Would you not go back to working with people?' Carla asked. 'See if the Social Services office is hiring?'

'Sure, Mitch is people,' he had replied, fobbing her off as if she and he were folk enough to be working with at the moment. Yet feeling, truth be told, ever further adrift, anchorless in Middle America as January wound slowly down.

'You've a nice way with people is all I'm saying.' But she left it there, as Fintan just shook his head.

He still talked plenty to her of other stuff, though. Showed her the snapshot one night of young Mary Cunnea beside the big Wisconsin summer house with its genuine timber clapboards.

'She's lovely,' Carla said, making him feel it were OK to have taken it out, OK to have shown it to her. She asked about his father too, only he hadn't a photo of Packy. Nor brother Frankie either, who was in Germany, still on the building sites he thought, though it was two or more months since he'd had any word. He wondered too if her being an only child was why it often felt they were siblings, given the easy familiarity in what they shared, the night-time stories of her adolescence that Carla told, as though she were in bed with the sister neither of them had had. Or stories of the gauntlet, say, that she had to run when her thirteenth birthday fell on a gym day, the girls lining up on either side to swat her bottom as she ran past.

'Running as quickly as I could – right down to the lockers, where I discovered my first period had started. That afternoon I looked up menstruation in my mother's copy of *Dr Spock's Baby and Child Care*, who felt I should also be masturbating at age thirteen, only I hadn't a notion what masturbation meant.'

'Your man from *Star Trek* with the funny ears?' Fintan asked, making Carla laugh on and on. But once she stopped, she talked about taking America's favourite family doctor one step better, coaxing her cat Tippy to lie between her legs beneath the sheets at age fifteen.

'I think high school's probably why I'm not that pushed about sex,' she told Fintan another night. 'Or maybe I was only lagging behind, just not ready yet. Certainly not ready for Miss Oliver, the girls' dean, who if she learned somebody was going steady, used to stick her finger in their tummy and ask, 'Putting on any weight, dearie?"

'But I finally got a boyfriend Junior Year. Bobby Allen with an old 1963 Pontiac Cutlass we'd go parking in, out the country with the windows down so you could hear the whip-poor-wills.'

Early February was still too cold for Missouri birds of most feathers, but a day after Fintan told her of his mother's Lake Michigan whip-poor-wills, they headed out in the Mustang, ending up parked somewhere within sight of the Mississippi, engine idling for the heater and Carla reclining against his chest as an occasional riverboat slipped past: all red, green and blue running lights, like the ghost of a Christmas past slowly making its way downstream.

At work Fintan quickly sussed how Vinyl was perhaps not that Final, whatever about the thirty-year guarantee Mitch made a mighty show of presenting to customers when the job was done. He had figured this out not from anything Mitch had said outright so much as what Fintan had pieced together: a comment here, an anecdote there, the fact that Mitch had moved through three states in five years, or how the phone number on the written guarantee was 'out of service' when he tried to ring Mitch one morning when he was running late, having mislaid a second number Mitch had given him when he'd hired him. Or the big bee Mitch had in his bonnet about 'the hit-and-run gypsy outfits who offer to pave your driveway for a song, only for the tarmac to wash away in the first heavy downpour'.

The gypsies however weren't competitors, leaving Fintan to wonder whether Mitch maybe wasn't entirely easy about his own fiddle either. Not sufficiently bent to altogether dismiss the dismay his customers surely felt after a second summer of hot sun produced the first fissures and cracks in the fading vinyl encasing their home. That said, it's not like Fintan had seen a career in Vinyl Is Final, any more than he had in selling Kmart's plastic wares. Yet even a hint of Mitch's potential ambivalence more than fed his own, and he figured he'd do well to stick it out until the spring.

*

In early April Carla travelled back to Terre Haute for a few days, during which time Fintan packed in the vinyl gig, wishing Mitch well. She came back then, along with a massive dose of the blues. A week later Fintan put out how he was heading west, nothing more specific than that single compass point.

'You don't stop, do you? You can't stay anywhere?'

'Well, I'm hardly making you happy here?'

'Love 'em and leave 'em, eh Fintan?' managing a shard of her old smile.

'Come with me?' he asked, knowing she wouldn't.

'Do you think there're people who actually enjoy change?' she then asked in turn.

He hadn't an answer for that – not yet anyhow – so he simply shrugged his shoulders.

'I'll go with you so?' she offered then, managing more like a half-smile this time, his own heart suddenly shunting sideways beneath his shirt. 'At some point you have to stop being somebody's child' – as if to clarify that she was not simply following some lover off into the sunset. 'It gets too confusing otherwise, as to who's the child and who's not.'

He had of course less experience of this, but he guessed she was likely right. And worrying over her mother clearly did her no good, but he didn't offer that either.

Later that evening she told of the first time she had tried to leave home, during Christmas break her sophomore year at college. Having told her parents she was taking the bus to visit a classmate in Louisville, she instead thumbed a lift west on Interstate 70 with a truck driver, bulky, in his fifties, who made her increasingly uncomfortable over the three hours they trundled along, making her wish the big pair of scissors she had thrown into her bag were in her coat pocket instead. Nothing overt, nor suggestive even, just how his right hand sometimes glanced off her knee as he shifted up or down some fifteen gears, or the way he twice lightly touched her leg as he pointed to something with his other hand, a picturesque stand of trees or a snowbound roadside shack, as if the real prospect lay not out the window, but along her thigh instead.

He eventually dropped her at a rest stop near Chesterfield, Missouri, where she'd used the scissors to slash her hair into a ragged, boyish cut under the 24/7 neon glare inside the ladies'. Judging her sheepskin coat, heavy sweater, boots and bag to be sufficiently androgynous, she proceeded to play it all the way by stripping to her waist inside a toilet stall and tightly binding her breasts with a black silk scarf thrown into her bag at the last minute in Terre Haute.

Her makeover had likely only fooled one or two drivers but she guessed only an older trucker and a younger couple – whom she figured had only stopped so that someone could bear witness to the sullen silence between them – had copped straight away she was a girl. Either way, she was making it up as she went along, not sure if she were dropping out of Vassar, nor where she were heading, knowing only that Terre Haute and family were farther behind with every mile.

Then, somewhere off the interstate north of Wichita, she ran out of steam as the traffic too dried up, the odd car blasting past as if she were invisible. Around midnight the gas station where she was stranded turned off its sign, leaving her in a wintry pool of light from the single street lamp overhead. She tried curling up inside a telephone booth, but that proved too cramped and the wind rattling the glass panels far too unnerving, like somebody outside impatient to make a call, or worse.

143

The thought of thumbing again into the dead of night was terrifying, but the prospect of freezing to death, paranoid or not, seemed real enough to send her back out under the street lamp, scissors inside her right mitten, until the steel began to burn with the cold, whereupon she slid them up her left sleeve, just within reach. Minutes later a black Chevy Chevelle braked fifteen yards past her, before reversing in a dead-straight line at speed. The driver, Mitchell, in his forties, told her she was plumb crazy to be taking such chances, as he cranked up the car's heater.

'My brother-in-law is a heart surgeon,' he kindly told her, after she'd shared some of her own story, whose vacation home near the Cheyenne Bottoms was apparently used but two or three times a year, and definitely not at Christmas. 'Put the key back there when you leave,' Mitchell told her, after they pulled in ninety minutes later, having retrieved it from under a cinder block beside the garage door.

She spent two nights on a huge leather sofa in the front room beneath a timbered cathedral ceiling. Slept for hours on end, in between shuffling back and forth across the deep-pile carpet to the kitchen, where she slowly ate her way through the few foodstuffs in the freezer: a half-packet of waffles, fish sticks and a TV chicken dinner like those her mother had served when she hadn't felt up to cooking when Carla was a kid.

'They bang on about American hospitality in Ireland,' Fintan said, smiling, 'but giving you the house was going some?'

'The last night there was the happiest New Year's Eve I ever spent,' she said with a laugh. 'TV unplugged, Bowie on the 8-track surround-sound, and asleep before midnight.' She had the oil-fired furnace turned off before the first sunrise of 1973 then, the key back under the cinder block and her thumb out for Salinas, where she bought a ticket on the next eastbound Continental Trailways bus back to college.

*

Another photograph Fintan will hang on to down the years – *April 14, 1979* scrawled in ink across the back – shows Carla in her red sweatshirt, himself in a blue work shirt, seated side by side on the porch steps at Lenox Place. Photo taken, Shelly had then hugged them both, after which they'd hopped into the yellow Mustang, pointing themselves towards Tulsa, Oklahoma – not entirely unlike a dart thrown at a map – and threaded their way through the city traffic as the morning sun, rebounding off the Arch, shattered itself along the Mississippi.

# 8

Mid-August however finds Fintan once again on his own – stranded this time on the streets of Laredo – as if honouring a promise made to himself the night he had first heard Texarkana singing of same back in Molly's. A cowboy song set to an Irish air, 'The Bard of Armagh', as Uncle Condy would later inform him. Only Fintan is not on said streets this sweltering Saturday afternoon, rather reading a paperback novel in the lobby of the Bender Hotel just off Jarvis Plaza, its lobby marginally cooler than his hot-box single room two flights up a staircase lined with coloured rippled-plastic pictures for sale of Jesus or Our Lady, both of whom wink at him when he passes by, whether he has drink taken or not. *Christ in the Garden* costs about the same as a room for a night, but none of the artwork has shifted in the three weeks since he checked in.

However, Tolstoy – with a map on its inside cover that Carla had quickly sketched of the federal highway system – is heavy going in the heat, and so Fintan lays it down as a bloke a few years older than himself approaches the front desk, the wide mirror behind offering a quick shot of thinning brownish hair, beard and beaked nose. But what catches Fintan's eye is how the stranger, having signed the registration card, leans back then to look at it, as if trying to gauge whether whatever name he's chosen this time will sufficiently pass muster.

*

'What's up?' the mystery man then inquired the next afternoon, sliding onto an adjoining red-cushioned stool in the hotel coffee shop.

"S hot,' said Fintan, not sure he was up for a chat, but this time taking in your man's lined, lived-in face, a silver stud in his left ear, plus the small goatee he'd missed in the lobby mirror.

'Wesley,' Wesley said, offering his hand. 'I knew a crazy Irishman in France,' he offered next, having nailed Fintan's provenance straight off.

'Plenty of them going,' Fintan said, softening slightly, not having met that many Yanks who'd ever gone what they often quaintly called *abroad*. But Wesley had travelled all right – Africa as well as Europe – where he had seemingly met his double, an Egyptian money changer, in the shadows of the Pyramids.

'The Pyramids?' Fintan marvelled.

'Yeah, cooler in the shade,' Wesley allowed, 'but a godawful stench of urine,' shaking his head as if trying to clear his large hooked nose.

In short, the chat proved mighty, spilling out into a bar & grill on the plaza, and lasting till nearly midnight. Most of it was Wesley: a steady stream of biography, anecdote and speculation, offered in a Louisiana drawl upon which you could practically hang your hat. Tales of a Baton Rouge,

Baptist-reared childhood, in which his father had worked the graveyard shift at a petrochemical plant down by the port, prompting Wesley and his brother Darrell to take up chess afternoons at home when their dad was trying to sleep, a board game Wesley would later hustle for money in city parks from Detroit to Baltimore.

Volcanoes were another passion, taking Wesley to Zaire two years previous, where he had trekked for weeks towards Mount Nyiragongo, only to walk out amid its live-lava flow, stepping from one as yet unsubmerged stony outcrop to another. Or how having puzzled over the Grateful Dead's choice of 'Fire on the Mountain' for their encore earlier that spring at a concert in Portland, Oregon, he had then walked out into the ash from Mount St Helens, which having blown its top during the concert, was now falling like a nocturnal snow shower across the city streets.

'Too straight a gig, man,' he likewise informed Fintan about the travelling sales job for an office-equipment crowd, which he'd only packed in the previous week. And pulling out of his leather shoulder bag, after another pint, a pair of the earrings fashioned from peacock feathers, that he'd been hawking at hippy markets – what few were left, from Milwaukee to San Francisco – until sick of being always broke, he'd cut his hair, put on a tie, and begun selling ditto machines, copiers and something called a fax.

A lot of what turned Wesley on struck Fintan as downright daft. His fascination with astrocartography, say – longitudinal and latitudinal lines drawn on a world map in conjunction with your astrological birth chart – that precisely predict where one is destined to find love, be it Boston or

Barcelona, else a heap of money in Buenos Aires or Budapest. Or the medium in Oklahoma his ex-girlfriend Terri Ann used to phone from Minnesota, who after listening to Terri Ann's voice for five minutes, would then describe the various 'entities' who'd seemingly set up housekeeping inside her body. 'He said she had seven of 'em,' Wesley said, shaking his head over their last beer. 'I couldn't sleep easy beside her after that.'

'Bed too crowded?' Fintan grinned.

'Scared they might start messin' with me,' Wesley replied, shaking his head again.

Yet some of it called to mind the medieval-like folk beliefs back in the Glen, be it the poison within a draft from a cracked window, or the peril of sitting on freshly cut hay. And other stuff sounded more plausible: Texan girls being bigger-boned, something Fintan himself had already noted, apparently per Wesley from all the limestone that leeched into the water table. He liked too how one thing with Wesley invariably led to another: his riff on statuesque Texan gals followed by the high rate of tooth decay in New England with its preponderance of granite underground, compared to the richer mineral deposits found throughout the Midwest with its sedimentary soil, lake bottoms and artesian wells. 'All that calcium, phosphates and natural fluoride,' he beamed, 'building blocks for the teeth,' making them sound like old friends he might invite round for supper. Only that very riff had suddenly summoned forth Carla's smile – its quick, white flash and parted lips – making Fintan yet again think how he should've headed back east with her.

A week later he and Wesley cut their overheads by moving into a double room with narrow twin beds on the fourth floor of the Bender, up a further flight of stairs festooned with plastic pictures of the 'Flight into Egypt' and 'The Annunciation'. 'Lenticular', that saw the donkey carrying Mary, briefly keeping pace with them as they ascended. And Wesley proclaiming *'Far out!'* after Fintan described the picture of the Sacred Heart with its small red votive lamp on the wall beside the kitchen door in Glenbay.

*'Bloody kip'* were two words Fintan bequeathed Wesley in turn, upon finding a large chunk of ceiling plaster across the shower floor in the shared bathroom at the end of the corridor. Their roomy, high-ceilinged bedroom was identical to the one Carla and he had shared back in late April, complete with similarly mismatched table and chair, its wooden wardrobe split and cracked from the dry heat. A large fan sat in one of two wide windows, the tiny electric heater stashed in a corner making him wonder at Laredo in the winter. But thankfully there were no sign of the bedbugs Florence had reported of her Laredo night forty years before, in what Fintan figured might've well been the Bender, and he thought once again of sending her a postcard of the town, care of O'Connell's Bar & Grill.

'Army lifers,' Wesley explained, after Fintan mentioned the mostly balding older men – fellow long-term residents – who turned up daily in colourful tropical shirts, sitting on into the evening in rocking chairs along the wooden porch.

'You see them all over the South too. Eking out their pensions in cheap hotels like this 'un.'

The two or three vets who favoured long-sleeved white shirts, ties and suspenders despite the heat were likely officers, Fintan figured, more at ease with metal and ribbon than a large, fading hibiscus across their chest. 'War relics,' he declared a few nights later, having shared a joint with Wesley in a quiet corner of the plaza across from the war memorial, seated side by side like sentries at a long-abandoned outpost. 'Manning the border!' Fintan said with a smile, recalling how the highway had suddenly widened without warning ten miles north of Laredo on the evening Carla and he had arrived. The occasional wooden hoarding they had passed – fading, hand-painted signs proclaiming JESUS IS LIFE – replaced by steel '35' signs. 'Jesus may well be life,' Fintan now preached to his congregation of one, 'but he sure as God didn't give you this fine freeway to traverse it on!'

'Check out the US post office on the plaza,' Wesley said, pinching the roach between forefinger and thumb. 'Big as a frigging fort!' And so it was, Fintan agreed, having posted Carla a letter there the following day. As if any evidence of nationhood needed to be that much more concrete – literally so – this close to the Rio Grande. Nor had Wesley much time for the old-timers on the porch, who simply shook their heads at his leather shoulder bag, or the cornflowers Terri Ann had embroidered on several of his shirts.

'How did you beat the draft?' Fintan asked the following afternoon in a cafeteria off the plaza, where Carla had waitressed during their three months in Laredo.

'Dropped a tab of acid the night before my pre-induction physical.' Wesley laughed. 'Then locked myself in a closet with a tape of Captain Beefheart's *Trout Mask Replica*. Got my 4F-deferment straight away the next day!'

'4F?'

'Yeah, for being totally f-f-f-fucked out of my head,' Wesley replied, grinning over his strawberry milkshake.

Passing the front-porch garrison on his way into the hotel that night, Fintan had suddenly thought of Freddy Rua back in the Glen, haunted by the poisonous snakes that had nearly done for his brother John James in Korea. Freddy being one of the walking wounded who never even went to war, unlike Walt Shea back in St Louis who, unlike Wesley, had neither avoided, nor in the end, survived Southeast Asia.

'US imperialism,' Wesley said, 'name of the game,' offering Fintan a term first heard from Mr O'Connell, his metalwork teacher at the Tech, and applied exclusively to the Brits. Rumour was that O'Connell, who peppered his lessons on the arc-welder with a running commentary on 800 years of British oppression, had been active in the 'armed struggle', but Glenbay was too far from the Ulster border for anything too serious to spill over. And if he now saw an occasional news story on the H-Block hunger strikes, Ireland was a continent and an ocean away, whereas the notion of America as empire suddenly surfacing in Laredo had him now wondering how the cinematic West, on which he'd been partially reared, might have been truly won.

'*Militarism*,' Wesley spat out another night, giving Fintan one more peg on which to hang all that Christmas, Terre Haute, table talk about 'copters, tanks and 50-millimetre machine guns. Yet polemics were but one card in Wesley's deck, who was shortly after onto *ceromancy*: telling of how yet another ex-girlfriend, Hilda, had divined the future by pouring molten wax into water in order to descry the shapes therein.

*

Little doubt Wesley was wired, yet Fintan had needed something of a jump-start in the fortnight since Carla left. He had written to her twice already, bits of a letter on various scraps of paper, as the Bender didn't do hotel stationery. He also rang her once she was back home in Indiana, even though he was no fan of the telephone. Carla had written back too, a proper letter as well as a postcard – of a Mississippi steamboat – which Carlito behind the front desk handed him one afternoon. The following evening he told Wesley of their early April journey from St Louis to Texas, making their way through Missouri and Kansas, fields of green winter wheat pocked here and there by patches of brown earth, putting Fintan in mind of a worn-out pool table.

'You know you're no longer in the germophobic Midwest,' Carla had said with a laugh upon exiting the women's room at their first pit stop in Oklahoma. 'Nobody's afraid to sit on a toilet out here, whereas back home they hover above, and end up peeing all over the seat!'

A few hours later the yellow Mustang threw a piston rod in Pawnee, where Fintan haggled with a garage mechanic, a decent skin, who finally offered him $100 for the car – 'for parts' – agreeing also to send on by bus two boxes of their belongings in the back seat, soon as they had an address. Travelling light, a backpack each, they stuck out their thumbs and got their first lift high in the cab of a semi-truck, the dual oval orbs of the driver's aviator-style shades like tiny TV monitors, wherein Fintan saw Carla, himself, the road and its rig unreel. And if Pawnee had not been sufficient, they bypassed highway signs for Lone Chimney, Stillwater, Shawnee as well – and best of all Fintan thought, Tecumseh – where they crashed that night on the couch of a couple who, heading home from a church-revival meeting, confessed they had thought Ireland was actually attached to England, like Scotland or Wales. 'Refuse nothing, only the blows!' he'd quoted Uncle Condy to Carla, who had hesitated at accepting an overnight invitation, only to find herself up at dawn, helping their hostess Shirlee whip up a batch of breakfast biscuits.

They got away early, got one long lift after another, and, having ring-roaded both Dallas and Austin, found themselves by mid-afternoon somewhere south of San Antonio on the I-35, where the still verdant landscape levelled out in earnest, no sound but the wind and locusts, and more sky overhead than Fintan would've thought possible. Nothing to break the horizon in any direction but the occasional mesquite tree like a tiny distant twig. Richard, a Native American lad in the employ of Southwest Bell, then gave them a lift in a VW bug a further fifty miles south, his improbably Anglo name offset by high cheekbones, glossy black hair and a handcrafted leather bracelet round his right wrist, which rested in turn upon a steering wheel wrapped in rawhide. From the passenger seat, Fintan watched what looked like distant pieces of chaff suddenly blow up life-size, inscribing themselves in chromatic smears across the windscreen.

'Locusts,' said Richard, who shortly after exchanged a few words of English – in a cadence unlike anything Fintan had yet heard – with the lad at the petrol pump where they'd stopped for gas, who looked like he could've been a brother.

It remained flat and green on all sides to the horizon where Richard dropped them off, some sixty miles north of Laredo, beneath a sinking sun and several towering cumuli flattened out overhead: more like the painted backdrop out a car window in an old black-and-white movie, or so Carla said, than anything real.

Standing once more beside the highway, Fintan espied a string imbedded along its macadam edge and the loose gravel of the soft shoulder, no doubt the handiwork of a departed highway-paving crew. A string which tautened like a fishing line as he lifted it, freeing itself before him as if he were unravelling the entire road, a fine seam running southwards across the border into Mexico, where slowly unstitching itself past countless cacti, it would eventually vanish from even his own inner eye.

Nor were they waiting long before a Ford pick-up pulled over, its red paint still bright beneath its dust. 'We go twenty miles,' offered the older of the two Chicanos in the cab, leaning across the driver, who sported a sleepy eye and straggling moustache.

'Thanks, but we'll hold on for Laredo,' Fintan said.

'OK, man. We go to Laredo,' the older bloke replied, matching Fintan's demurral with equal insistence. 'We eat breakfast tonight in Nuevo Laredo,' he said, looking at the driver, who shrugged and nodded simultaneously.

And so Carla and he climbed into the cargo bed to sit with their backs against the cab. The wind whipping by on either side made talk difficult, so having smiled their luck at one another, they simply watched the white lane-lines behind them disappearing northwards until ten or so minutes later, when the truck gradually began to slow.

They saw nothing as they peered around both sides of the cab, the truck apparently pulling over in the middle of nowhere. And Fintan thought he knew why too – confusion sliding into fear, giving way like soft sand underfoot – as if this moment had been awaiting dead ahead, a speck on the horizon, awaiting them ever since they'd waved goodbye to Shelly three days ago. His heart now accelerating in a strange counterpoint to the slowing vehicle which, as in any melodrama, was taking an eternity to stop, fear now a tangible ripple in his blood, a stream of tiny bubbles bursting in rapid succession beneath the skin along his upper arms, as the truck finally eased to a dead halt.

When both driver and passenger doors opened, Fintan knew they were truly fucked. Rising from a half-crouch, he turned to face both men as they came round either side of the cab. And once again it was the older one who spoke, with a genuine smile.

'Hey man, why sit in the wind – plenty room inside?'

Fintan could feel a nerve still jumping in Carla's knee, pressed against his own, after they had squeezed into the cab. The truck then stopping once more some five miles on, this time at a small yellow-adobe roadside café, its single, old-fashioned, bubble-headed petrol pump slouched beside the screen door, like someone loitering in the gathering dusk. Inside, an oversized fan, suspended from a deceptively high ceiling, spun slowly like a giant propeller in the yellow light. Their driver lifted six bottles of beer from an ancient Coca-Cola cooler sweating in a corner, as his companion chatted to three old-timers sitting at a table festooned with more beer bottles.

'*No, gracias,*' Fintan said, using two of his ten words of Spanish as the driver waved a beer at him, pointing himself at the two bottles of Fanta orange that Carla had fetched from the same cooler. Sodas paid for, they exited the café ahead of their companions – only to hear a telephone ringing somewhere off to their right. Turning, Fintan saw a phone booth, unlit and incongruous at the edge of the building, like it had somehow sprung up, mushroom-like, overnight.

He started towards it, only to stop as Carla said, 'Don't!' and then 'Don't!' again – as if asking they not tempt fate twice in the one night.

'Right so,' he agreed, taking her hand as they turned towards the truck. 'But we're sorted now, these lads are sound.'

Night had nearly fallen, bar a pale yellow band of luminescence along the western horizon. Once underway, the elder hombre launched into what sounded like a sermon, half in Spanish, half English, lacing his religious exhortations with an occasional profanity, while urging greater speed. Their driver, however, simply downed his beer, tossing each empty bottle out his window, its tiny *pop* on the hardtop barely audible behind, like a distant gunshot muffled by wind and engine.

Carla and Fintan hopped out then at a large, palm-lined plaza in Laredo. Waving their benefactors off in the direction of the International Bridge and breakfast, before pausing to read the names, lit by the flame, of a war memorial on the square, many of them Latino, reminding Fintan yet again how it was not as a rule the poor you need fear.

After downing a bowl of chilli in a cafeteria across the street, they found their way two blocks west to the Bender Hotel, an ancient, wooden, three-storey affair with a pale-green lobby, above which three overhead fans hung motionless, their blades like giant petals. Behind the front desk a night clerk in his sixties wearing a sharply creased short-sleeved shirt and sporting a neatly trimmed grey moustache took cash up front before handing over the keys to their double room, where another overhead fan was shredding the street-lamp light through the window blinds into a shadow dance up and down one wall.

Minutes later they fell into bed, where Fintan lay listening, his eyes shut, to Carla already asleep. Only to see, out of nowhere, the dark interior of the byre in Glenbay, looking like an overgrown shed compared to the barns he'd seen in America, the same byre to which Frankie and he would race one another in the morning to see what eggs the hens had laid for Mary. As if once upon a time it had needed far less to take him out of himself: spaces far smaller than the unrelenting sweep of sky that would hover overhead all that day, until somewhere south of San Antonio he swore he could feel its gentle tug, like a fish's first, tentative dart at a baited hook. Wrapped now in white linen and slipping into sleep, the last thing he saw were tiny brown shards of broken bottle glass, shaping themselves into petal and thorn patterns over the highway, like some unknown desert flower blooming in the night.

*

Two days later Carla and he sublet a small wooden bungalow on the western edge of town, three rooms and a bath, plus a strand of purple bougainvillea at the front door, which Fintan thought his mother Mary would've loved, given the care she'd lavished on the potted geraniums outside their cottage door. They both successfully hustled work before the week was out – Carla double-shifting as a motel chambermaid in the morning, then waitressing in the afternoon in the same cafeteria on Jarvis Plaza where they'd downed the chilli that first night – while Fintan was hired on as a flatbed-truck driver for a local lumber-yard, delivering timber throughout the town, or fencing posts to outlying ranches. And once he had the rhythm of it, managing most afternoons to call into Carla's café, ordering a takeaway coffee at the counter, where they might manage to exchange a few words. And if he no longer stared at the Stetson and cowboy-booted customers who walked in and out, Laredo – with its outlying ranch cattle pens and dusty pick-up trucks with gun-racks cradling .22s – truly felt like the West at last.

That said, he hadn't yet bought a big hat himself, and still wore the steel-toed work boots he'd bought to shovel gravel out of the Mississippi barges. Still he let Carla pick out a Western shirt for him, a belated twenty-fourth-birthday gift, having sung dumb about it back in February. Not any rhinestoned, nylon-fringed affair, however, rather a blue-and-grey-checked cotton number with pearl snaps on the pockets and cuffs, which he wasn't at first sure he could wear out onto the streets of Laredo, however much he might've killed for such a shirt as a kid.

He donned it however the night he borrowed a workmate's old Pinto to take Carla to a drive-in movie north of the town – as if his childhood love affair with American cars and film had been all along leading to that Friday night. The double bill was dire – John Travolta in his own cowboy shirt astride a bar-room mechanical bull, followed by an equally cheesy sci-fi flick – but Fintan was happy simply to take it in, an actual movie theatre fashioned out of a large dusty parking lot, ringed with rows of cobbled ridges that tilted each car up at the giant screen, beneath which sat a few swings and a small roundabout where a handful of kids, half already in pyjamas, played in the waning light before the first feature began. Some of the audience had brought beer along, but Fintan was happy sharing the Coke, popcorn and ice cream ferried back from the concession stand for Carla, though he told her – after she sent him back for a chilli dog – how she'd have been drummed out of the St Louis Food Co-op for even looking at such garbage.

'All that emphasis on a healthy diet is basically unhealthy,' Carla said, grinning at him between mouthfuls. 'Too Californian for my liking.'

'Sure, more have died for the want of it,' Fintan replied, echoing old Jack Gara who – come to think of it – had sounded like an early card-carrying member of the wholefood crowd himself. Jack, who had stopped eating store-bought eggs after they started feeding fishmeal to hens, informing Fintan, 'It's not natural unless it grows in the earth with just the heat of the sun.'

They grabbed a day off work then either side of the July 4th weekend in order to head south of the border, walking across El Puente to board a train in Nuevo Laredo for Monterrey. The moon rose shortly after from behind a ridge, its top slightly frayed, and its light bathing giant cacti everywhere. A blind boy with an accordion boarded at a stop farther south to make music down the aisle, shadowed by an even younger lad, possibly his brother, hat in hand.

Once in Monterrey, they hopped off and straight away back onto a bus east, reaching Tampico on the Gulf at first light, where they dozed for an hour on the orange-peel and cigarette-butt-flecked beach, until church bells awakened them, followed shortly by a bloke shouting at his donkey as it pulled a large sheet of plywood with its painted, mock-up of a pirate boat – *El 7 Mares* – along the sand, two circles cut out of its dual, painted deckhands for tourists to stick their heads through and pose for his camera.

After breakfast in a nearby café, they found a one-room, two-dollar-a-day beach cabaña, with four whitewashed walls and a blue ceiling from which another airplane-propeller-sized fan stirred up the mouldy, tropical scent within, plus a tiny outdoor toilet at the back. A small kerosene hotplate sat on a corner table, though they chose to lunch on the veranda of a restaurant above the beach, downing a cheese-and-chilli soup, followed by crêpes soaked in a sweet goat's-milk sauce.

Afterwards they swam throughout the afternoon, the waves about their heads at sunset tinged a pinkish hue, matching the stains on the cabaña towel onto which they'd peeled pomegranates bought for a peso each, yet another first for Fintan, its flavour sweet and piquant both.

They tried making love too in the water late on their second night, only Carla proved too skittish each time they came close. 'I keep thinking it's an eel or something!' she laughed, spitting a mouthful of salt water at Fintan before pushing him away.

On the morning they were to head back, Carla awoke from a dream in which someone had painted, in large, red letters along a wall, GOD IS ALIVE IN TERRE HAUTE AND $5 WILL PAY FOR ANY SIN.

'Sure, indulgences went out of style back in the Middle Ages,' Fintan quipped, only for Carla to turn away on her side of the small double bed.

'You want to borrow five bucks so?' he tried again.

'I'm thinking of going back to St Louis for a while,' she eventually offered to the whitewashed wall.

'What are you saying, Carla?'

'For a while.'

'I thought we were doing OK?'

'We are,' she said, turning to lay a hand on his collarbone. 'It's better than OK with you, Fintan, but this kind of drifting doesn't allow for a lot of purchase on things.'

'Sure, you can save up to purchase anything you want,' he tried one last time – as if there were any chance of humouring her away from where she was headed.

'Nor is Laredo really that different from St Louis – just another gateway town to nowhere,' she spoke to the wall once more.

'And Terre Haute is somewhere?'

'I don't mean going back home,' turning towards him again. 'But maybe back to school? So I can teach? Get a job in a little school house on the prairie,' she said, smiling faintly, having told him months before of loving Melissa Wiley's books as a child.

'I don't dream of Donegal at all,' Fintan offered after a time, as if Carla had been speaking solely of her dream. They lay on for a while so, hands on each other as if touch alone might yet again prove enough. Tracing the long white scar along her spine with his thumb, he recounted how Will Woodward had once challenged a doctor on a house call to examine his sore shoulder. 'You haven't touched me once,' he informed the medico, peering up at him from his wheelchair, 'like you would with another patient?'

And remembering as Carla's hand then brushed his neck, how his mother used to steady his head with a hand as she brushed his sandy hair. Unlike Packy, who'd rarely touched him, lest it were to give him a clatter when he was small. Or handling him like an animal – had he needed tending – removing a splinter from his leg, say, in much the same manner he might squeeze the suppurating pustule on a cow's back in order to extract the egg deposited under its skin by a warble fly.

On the crowded, smelly bus back to Monterrey, Carla told how it had taken her several years to place its same acrid scent on her school bus as urine. 'Off the poorer kids who probably slept three to a bed, where all it needed was for the youngest to wet himself.'

'My brother did that for a bit,' Fintan said, 'but we had each our own bed.'

They dozed off then, once aboard the train, waking an hour later to the same blind accordion player working the aisle, only this time followed by what might've been his sister, a dirty Styrofoam cup outstretched in either hand, into which they deposited what coins they had. Out their window distant mountains rimmed the horizon, a smaller moon overhead with scattered stars, cacti and sagebrush rampant alongside the tracks. Waking once more, Fintan saw how the mountains had closed in, the rail-line now running beneath rocky walls either side.

*

Carla left for Indiana three weeks later, the last week in July, boarding a Greyhound bus early one Monday morning. Their time together since Mexico had been rocky enough, Fintan doing his best to persuade her to stay on through the fall, before offering to accompany her back east for a spell, little as he wanted to see the Corn Belt again, having at last found his way out west.

'Can I get anything for you?' he'd asked Carla the previous Friday evening after yet another strained exchange.

'Lost,' she'd replied, which saw Fintan slam the door behind him, only to turn back halfway to Chuck's chilli place. Sitting together on the front step they talked it through once more, finally reaching some manner of accord.

'It's just a nine-month course,' Carla said as they undressed for bed. 'And I'll find a teaching job then this side of the Mississippi.'

The night before she left, Fintan again borrowed his workmate's Pinto and drove them out to the drive-in. Only they got nowhere near the concession stand this time, had each other fairly unzipped and unbuttoned before the first feature ended – a decent thriller – but not half as riveting as they found each other. 'We're worse than teenagers,' Carla laughed as she tried to hold him off, hands against his chest and endeavouring to keep the gear stick between them. Nor had they bothered staying for the second film, as if touch for once were simply not enough – whatever about an impending sense of certain loss, come tomorrow.

'Hurry back,' Carla whispered as he dropped her at the house, before leaving the Pinto back a half-mile out of town. They made love then after he'd hoofed it back, Carla having left a trail of lit candles from the front step through the small sitting room to their even tinier back bedroom. A few hours before dawn they came together again, Fintan gently holding her shoulder as his erection traced the scar along her back – not unlike a carnal dowsing stick – as if trying to divine whatever lay between them.

'Do you think leave-taking comes from leaves falling?' she asked at breakfast. 'The way saying goodbye can feel like autumn inside?'

'There's some poet who talks about interior seasons,' Fintan managed. 'But he obviously never lived in Texas without a window fan.'

'Always the joke, Fintan,' Carla said with a shake of her head before going upstairs to finish packing.

Fintan juggled his afternoon deliveries in order to drop her to the bus station not far from Jarvis Plaza. Unable to park the lumber-yard rig, he had to settle for a quick kiss on the sidewalk and a final wave as Carla disappeared with her bags inside the depot. That night he packed his own duds into the army-surplus duffle bag he'd brought from

St Louis, gave the kitchen and bathroom a quick lick, then checked into the Bender the following evening after work. It happened the rent wasn't due for another fortnight, but no way did he want to be within those three rooms and a bath without her.

*

'It's cuz you're an Aquarian,' Wesley informed Fintan after he'd chanced talking a bit more about Carla a few weeks later. 'Too singular to commit!'

'Astrology's bullshit.'

'Too private for your own good too,' Wesley added with a laugh. 'Typical Aquarian.'

'It's bullshit. My brother Frankie's birthday's two days after mine, and he's not a bit like me.'

'Yeah, like I said, too particular to think anybody else might be anyways like yourself.'

'Least of all my brother.'

'Brothers are usually the least alike,' Wesley conceded with another laugh, before telling how his own had re-upped in the army. 'Hard to believe we were two pups from the one litter.'

'Where's he stationed?'

'Korea, last I heard, working in military intelligence. Though that's an oxymoron, I told him.'

'And what's an oxymoron when it's at home?' Fintan asked. 'A retarded cow?' And then, 'Do yous get on?'

'Ah, Darrell's all right. Better at chess too, which he gets to play now against Kim Il-Sung.'

In mid-September Wesley announced he was heading up to Dallas, where his ex, Terri Ann, had found work as a barmaid and, cleansed of her seven entities, was once more sleeping on her own. Yet the night before Wes split, Fintan awoke to find the wastepaper basket in flames from a smouldering roach of the farewell joint they'd smoked before they'd called it a night.

Hollering at Wesley to wake up, he hightailed it down the hall to the bathroom sink with a Coke bottle, only to find Wesley pissing into the wastepaper basket when he got back.

"You've got flame in that basket is what you're meant to say,' Wesley then informed him, citing an elderly head waiter who had given him his first summer job as a busboy at a country club outside of Baton Rouge. 'And you don't shout it either,' he chided Fintan, sitting in his boxer shorts at the edge of his bed and rolling another joint.

'For fuck's sake, Wesley.'

'It's cuz I'm an Aries.'

'Jaysus, don't start!'

'It's true, man. This must be the third or fourth fire just before I leave somewhere.'

'Watch where you throw your roaches, so?'

'Uh-uh, man. One time somebody firebombed this community house in Denver the night before I moved out.'

'Community house?' Fintan asked, despite himself.

'A commune really,' Wesley grinned, 'with most of the heads there into grassroots-organising. You know, getting people to not pay their pricey rent and shit like that – nor did they want folks thinking we were just hippies.'

'Why Aries?' Fintan asked, once more despite himself.

'It's a fire sign, Fintan,' Wesley said, sounding like a weary teacher addressing an especially slow pupil.

'So all you Aries folk nearly get toasted alive?'

'Nothing happens to any class of everybody, Fintan,' Wesley said, even more patiently. 'The world don't work that way.'

'Good job Texas hasn't volcanoes anyhow.'

'You got that right!' Wesley grinned. 'You wanna toke?'

*

Fintan headed north three weeks later. The sawmill gig had already begun to sour back in August, the new foreman, Duane, a skinny runt with a bad leg, making life miserable for everybody, and so Fintan gave only a week's notice. Yet when that week ended, Duane announced how he'd get nothing till payday the following Friday. So Fintan had stopped at a liquor store on his next delivery run, before driving back at lunchtime to the lumber-yard, where he stretched out with a bottle of Flame Tokay on the conveyor belt fed by a huge circular saw.

'You going back to work?' Duane asked when the whistle blew.

'Sure am,' Fintan said, cocking the bottle at Duane, 'once I finish my wine.'

'Well, finish it elsewhere, Irish, cuz I just fired your sorry ass.'

'Suits me,' Fintan said, 'so long as you pay my sorry ass now!' Following which he duly informed Duane of the Texas Workman's Compensation Act, which, per Wesley, provided for immediate pay upon a summary dismissal. It took Duane another half-hour and three confirmatory phone calls to both calm down and pony up, during which Fintan took it handy with the Flame Tokay, not wanting to end up half-hammered under a blazing Texas sun.

That night he rang Carla, who sounded buoyant, her teacher's training course already underway back in St Louis. The following morning he checked out of the Bender, snapping a salute to three ex-army early birds already nesting on the porch, before walking the several blocks to Route 35 north. It took him ten or so lifts to cover the 430 miles to Dallas, the first car that stopped being a Chevy Nova with two Chicanos and a stove-in front door. The driver, long black hair and crimson shirt, repeatedly turned round to Fintan in the back to complain about the bribe he'd had to pay a Mexican cop earlier that morning, south of the border, who had stopped him for speeding, and then the small white hairs all over the black upholstery from a sniffer dog, which US Customs officers had put into the car an hour later.

Yet either the bribe or the border crossing had seemingly wiped any speeding-violation slate clean, as the Nova was easily clocking ninety, only to suddenly brake five or so miles further on for three more hitchhikers – two French guys and a gal, all of whom somehow managed to squeeze into the back beside Fintan. Both the driver and his shotgun-riding pal were now drinking something from a jam jar, maguey or tequila maybe, while bullshitting the anxious French trio how it was only nitroglycerine for a bad heart, making out how they had to hold it in front of the air-conditioning vent, lest it get too hot and blow them all to hell.

Fintan figured they'd need to stop for a leak soon, at which point he would excuse himself, but it happened the heavy load, heat and high speed shortly put paid to the right rear tyre, throwing off a large patch of tread that gave the undercarriage an almighty bang, rocketing Fintan and the French lass into a tight embrace as the driver, suddenly needing both hands on the wheel, dropped the jam jar as he struggled to control the skidding Nova, before finally bringing it to a halt along the hard shoulder.

The Chicanos were hell-bent for driving on – 'We not go so fast!' – but both Fintan and the French begged off. Though not before Fintan had changed the tyre, figuring that was better than overtaking them – overturned and dead in a ditch – somewhere up ahead. Tossing the tyre iron back into the boot, he said *Adios* to the Nova pair and *Adieu* to the three French on the roadside, knowing there was little chance anyone would lift four of them ensemble. But he had only walked a half-mile on ahead before a Chevy pick-up pulled over, *les trois François* waving at him from its open cargo bed, and its driver in turn beckoning him into the cab, only to show Fintan a few miles on the .38 revolver tucked into his belt, should the .22 Winchester with scope on the gun rack behind his head prove insufficient firepower.

San Antonio was as far as the pick-up – and as it happened the French – were going, so Fintan bade them farewell again, only to snag a lift five minutes later with Clyde, an ex-US Marine a few years older than himself, who was bringing a few gallons of milk and a bag of second-hand clothing to a Children of Jesus settlement house. 'Crackier than the Children of God' – another Christian outfit, Fintan gathered – 'never mind too lazy to work,' Clyde added, 'but I don't mind helping out.' And offering another wide-toothed smile as he dropped Fintan off a few miles south of San Marcos: 'If we lack, it's because we haven't asked, so just pray for a ride, y'hear?'

Clyde must've offered a prayer too for Fintan's luck held, his next lift being with a German bloke, his Mexican-American girlfriend and a tiny terrier in a blue T-Bird. Originally from Cologne, Hans had visited Ireland and seen Kerry and Clare but not Donegal. By late afternoon one lift had begun to blur into the next, though he managed to describe for Wesley the following day the skinny, taciturn guy with a cleft lip and old mattress in the back of an ancient Plymouth station wagon, who got him as far as Waco, plus Gilberto, an enormous Chicano, tiny goatee, huge belly and slight stammer, a soundman for Sunny and the Sunliners, who also doubled as driver of their two-ton van full of amps, saxes, guitars, speakers, both sides of the truck emblazoned with the band's name in flowing Day-Glo script.

Gilberto dropped him in downtown Dallas around ten that night, too late to find his way to Wesley's, so he booked himself into an old hotel with its own motley crew of residents – long-haired dudes and what looked like yet another squad of balding, ex-military pensioners. Having paid, he took the pokey lift up to his $12.60 single room on the ninth floor, where the view from his window showed several large half-lit office blocks, floating like huge crystals in the near distance. The following morning he spotted just below him, plain as day, that infamous grassy knoll, recognising it from black-and-white film footage he'd seen in some TV documentary. And, sure enough, there two blocks to the west was the School Book Depository itself.

Sitting with a coffee in a nearby cafeteria, Fintan waited until the busboy chalking up the Fried Catfish Luncheon Special on a board at the door had finished, before showing him the scrap of paper with Wesley's address. Fifteen minutes later, at a bus stop just past the School Book Depository, an elderly Black woman turned to inquire of him, 'Are you a Christian?' Only to promptly move away after he'd politely informed her, 'Where I come from, missus, a Christian is somebody who kills other Christians.'

It took him another hour to find the house, a squat, one-storey bungalow with a front porch and small backyard. He and Wesley hugged one another like long-lost brothers, then another brotherly hug from Terri Ann, a compact, cropped-haired, brown-eyed gal, who arrived home from her bar shift at suppertime. 'You make us all an omelette,' she ordered Wesley, before directing Fintan to sit on a large broken-back sofa and tell her all about himself.

All about himself was hardly his strong suit, but Fintan managed for a few minutes until Wesley, unable to find the jar of jalapeños, opted to go out for a six-pack of Lone Star beer instead, while Terri Ann disappeared into the kitchen. He stayed with them four days altogether, reading on the sofa mornings until Wesley stumbled out of bed, after which they headed into downtown Dallas for a few hours, before coming back to get the supper on.

'Don't you miss home?' Terri Ann asked Fintan one evening, which he allowed as how he did sometimes, before quickly asking, 'How about yourself?'

'What's to miss?' said Terri Ann, whose home was Montana – not Uncle Condy's Butte, which was all Fintan knew about the state, but Bozeman, sixty miles east, which she'd left at nineteen, hadn't seen in the four years since, and hoped never to see again. Later that night, lying on the sofa and trying to tune out the sounds of Wesley and Terri Ann in their entity-free bed, he found himself thinking of the Glen for the first time in several weeks. Thinking of the stories Uncle Condy had told him of Montana, and of Cornelius, Fintan's miner granda, whom Fintan had never known.

'Butte,' he announced then at breakfast the next morning, a Saturday, which saw them once again round the tiny table in the kitchen.

'Why in God's name would you want to see Butte?' Terri Ann asked, waving her empty coffee cup at Wesley, who was looking in the kitchen closet for an old sleeping bag he'd promised Fintan.

'It's on the way.'

'On the way to where?'

'Everywhere, nowhere?' Fintan smiled, hearing Condy once again advising him: 'If you don't know where you're headed, any road'll take you there!'

*

However, a straight line was something he had yet to master, and after getting as far north as Oklahoma City, he swung left with Paul, a Heinz Beans advertising salesman, who drove through the night on Interstate 40, Fintan thinking it the same roadway Carla had grown up on, only for Paul at the wheel to explain the difference between highways and interstates. Dozing off as they dipped back into Texas and across to New Mexico, he awoke to see an exit sign for SANTA FE, 54 MILES, and waking again in Arizona, where Paul had finally pulled over somewhere west of Flagstaff, flipping Fintan the keys before crawling into the back seat to sleep.

Taking the wheel, Fintan thought again of the family man who'd handed Uncle Condy the keys to that black-white Buick over thirty years ago, only to laugh aloud some 180 miles later as they too blew through Needles, having crossed the state line into California. Paul, LA-bound for a sales conference, then took the wheel again, dropping Fintan off at Barstow two hours later, after handing him a Bounty candy bar from the glove compartment.

Fintan would not get to Los Angeles on this run, nor see the Pacific, but he did get clear to the top of Mt Whitney, after a trucker informed him it was the highest peak in the Continental US, before dropping him off at Lone Pine, 150 miles north of where Fintan had waved Paul off. Dark was falling as his lift in yet another pick-up took him through the surreal rock formations of the Alabama Hills, its driver, an older man in a battered cowboy hat, warning him to watch out for rattlesnakes that lay on the still sun-warm rocks 'long after the lights go out'.

Having slowly picked his way over a cluster of large flagstones sloping below the road, he unrolled his sleeping bag on a level sandy patch and fell asleep straight off. Waking at 4 a.m. from a dream in which Mary had been telling both him and Frankie 'It's time to rise and shine!', he rolled onto his back to see a belt of cold, crystalline stars so low as to seem nearly within reach. Rising two hours later, he got a lift straight away with a truck laying hot oil on the dirt road to settle the dust, then walked another mile until he reached the trail portal up to Mt Whitney.

The 14,505 feet took him just under eight hours, allowing for a quick stop above Consultation Lake, where he wolfed down a tin of tuna after slicing his thumb opening it, then wiped the blood onto a rock where it quickly drew two wasps – or *yellow jackets*, as he now knew to call them. The final two miles were the hardest, the air thinner than any he'd ever known, but the view from the peak was well worth the climb, a further blue-green lake to the west, its mirror-like surface throwing back the yellow peaks. After scribbling Fintan Doherty, Glenbay, Co. Donegal in the visitors' logbook, he hightailed it down three miles in the fading light, not wanting to spend the night anywhere near the exposed summit. Only to find himself still awake, half-frozen inside Wesley's sleeping bag under the stand of pines where he'd finally stopped, and so he breakfasted on the tin of Heinz spaghetti that Paul had given him for a laugh, warming it up over the small butane-canister hotplate that Wesley had gifted him.

The hike down was far quicker than ascending, if sorer on his shins and knees, legging it over logs thrown across chilly melted-snow streams. It was early afternoon when he reached Lone Pine, high time to angle back towards Butte before the weather got any colder. He caught a lift straight off in the back of another pick-up, no gun rack this time, just a seventy-five-minute straight run north, the truck climbing bumpily up from the empty, semi-arid landscape and over a high pass – all dust, wind, mountains, sun and clouds – then down again until your man announced, 'That's as far as I'm going, bud.'

A half-hour passed before he got another lift, nor did it get him very far, his chauffeur a grizzled, laconic ex-army man in an ancient Chrysler Valiant. 'Have a slug?' he offered, pointing to a half-gallon jug of the red wine Fintan had already smelt on him, the bottle halfway beneath the seat. Growling 'Down boy!' at the few cars that overtook them, or intoning 'Highway 395' at the occasional, eponymous, steel road sign, 'An old Indian trading-route, once upon a time.'

Then 'Poor fucking Japs' a few miles later, shaking his head as he gestured over his shoulder at the former site of one of ten relocation camps wherein the US government had interned some of its 120,000 Japanese American citizens after the bombing of Pearl Harbor. And finally: 'I'm going to see an old buddy here,' pulling up at a side road with its small, white sign reading SANITARIUM.

Thumb out once again, Fintan continued walking north, calculating his chances as an occasional car rocketed past, most of them easily doing eighty. But any anxiety gradually gave way to awe as he took in his surrounds, the White Mountains at his back, and across the road the eastern slopes of the Sierra Nevada, only fronted now by a vast expanse of sun-soaked desert behind the three-strand barbed-wire fence, room aplenty to unroll his sleeping bag if he got stranded.

And if all were unknown, nearly anything felt possible. Not only the prospect of a night unlike any other, but a buoyant feeling of unbounded potential – of freedom if you like – made palpable by a late-afternoon golden light that bathed the sweeping vista on all sides. As if here was what America truly offered, boundless space as opposed to implacable time, the latter with its overriding sense of a buried past drilled deep into the clay and bog back home in Ireland, only *home* no longer seemed to fit.

Bathed by what the old-timer in the Valiant had described as 'a last burst of Indian summer', he felt as if the sun on his face might go on forever, same as the mountains, sky and the golden light, same as himself. Nor was there anything of a 12-inch black-and-white TV screen about this West, nothing remotely resembling Father Boyle's long-ago Donegal kitchen in the amber light now washing across the rusted rock and ochre terrain, a trio of yellowish dust devils chasing one another as he looked on, leaving Fintan suddenly and utterly at Home On the Range – as if Texarkana had been singing that song for him alone, way back when in Molly's.

*

A Lincoln Continental with a couple and their twelve-year-old twin daughters eventually picked him up, your man in the music business and his wife a serious reader, asking Fintan what he thought of *Armies of the Night*, which she had spotted sticking out of his duffle bag, a paperback handed on by former US Army PFC Walt Shea back in St Louis, before he fell, or more likely jumped, into the Mississippi. 'Try Henry Miller next,' she suggested, telling how she'd known the author back in the mid-1960s, 'a little old man who had to go the john at parties every half-hour.'

They dropped Fintan just below Mono City, at a small roadside café where he hoped to buy a postcard on which to scribble Carla something of what he'd felt back down the road – all that stuff about space and time, light and colour, mountain and high desert – all of it somehow having felt of a piece with her blonde-haired, blue-eyed self.

Only the café didn't see enough tourist trade to bother with postcards, so he dispatched a page of his already tattered road map, confident he could talk the next *gas* (not *petrol*) station attendant into giving him another, and having scribbled a few lines below the very terrain just traversed, he asked might there be an envelope going of the tired-looking, older waitress – *Mary* per her nameplate – who produced one, 'Free of charge, honey', along with a 15¢ stamp from her bag. Pushing back the dollar bill he'd left for a 40¢ cup of coffee, she also promised to post the letter on her way home that evening.

# 9

Butte looks unlike anywhere Fintan has yet seen: both the town, pitched on a hill within its mile-high valley, and the golden mountains that ring it round. The vista also remains sky-blue the entire week he's there, the mid-October air already sharp with its promise of winter, with a light frost each morning, then a half-inch of snow early the morning he departs, dusting the grass and distant peaks.

Although it looks unlike anywhere else, it feels oddly familiar – as if he already knew this place, singular as it is. He had of course heard an occasional story of Butte growing up, along with those Uncle Condy later shared of his own father, Cornelius, who'd worked the mines here, but it seems somehow more than that, if nothing he can begin to express: how, for the first time in three years overseas, he feels something of a fit.

The journey here was pretty much a straight run northeast from California, just under a thousand miles, cutting across Nevada and up through Idaho into Montana, its rolling hills dappled by cloud shadows that doubled their contours – nothing but rolling, empty western land – an occasional speed sign advising REASONABLE AND PRUDENT, while others warned of LIVESTOCK AT LARGE, with a mock cattle-guard painted here and there across the blacktop.

When he asks his lift, Jim, a car dealer of some sort, about the speed limit, Jim just points to the speedometer needle on his Custom Chevrolet pick-up truck – which had been pretty much at 105 mph for a good twenty minutes. 'I'd no idea we were doing that,' Fintan marvels. 'Good shocks and a great suspension,' Jim says with a grin, before dropping him off in Dillon, where Fintan takes a quick look around the Log Cabin Museum – with its combed beaver pelt and stuffed seven-foot rattle snake – before walking to the edge of town to stick out his thumb again.

The jaunt north had taken some twenty-four hours, so Fintan is all but running on empty when a rancher in a beat-up Datsun, bringing his ailing four-year old boy to the doctor in Butte, drops him on East Mercury Street with the sun going down in a reddish-orange blaze behind him. Standing on the sidewalk, he sees what looks like his own name in the large white script above a nine-storey building a block away, just a few letters out – HOTEL FINLEN – which answers any question of where he might spend the night. A fire escape cuts a black diagonal across the window of his spacious, simply furnished fifth-floor room, along with a threadbare bathroom towel, but the sheets looks clean. Moments later he's asleep, staying so till the morning sun breaks through the window nearly twelve hours later.

\*

He spent the next two days walking the town, most of it built on a southward-sloping hill. For all the draw of the distant mountains, the cityscape was what held his eye, the large red-and-yellow brick or granite buildings *uptown*, as the locals called it, seeing how the commercial district sat on the higher end of the hill. Though lack-of-commercial-district might've been closer to it, given its general dinginess, shop windows either half or haphazardly filled.

A hint of home had likewise suggested itself – a Shamrock Travel Agency or the towering Hennessy Building – even before Mike McGann, a miner he met at the bar in the M&M Cigar Store, told him to check out the phonebook, which McGann claimed was over 90 per cent Irish. Paddy's Day was seemingly a mad blow-out too, far more so than in Donegal, where Mary had simply sent him and Frankie off to Mass with a small spring of shamrock pinned to their shirts, while those like Packy, having given up the drink for Lent, granted themselves a one-day dispensation, heading early for the pub where they then stayed till closing time.

The town itself was not large, and he soon had a sense of its layout: from the huge open mining pit beyond his hotel on the upper east end to the winding residential streets on the western side, small wooden houses and grass lawns all ajumble, criss-crossed by telephone wires overhead, plus weed-choked lanes with the odd derelict car. Yet the mining industry that had built Butte was still in evidence too: the huge, iron-latticed head frames with massive gears and cables that had once lowered his grandfather Cornelius in cages into the mines, looming now like gargantuan mechanical scarecrows over a row of houses.

Easy to see too, even before McGann filled his ear, how the economic boom that built Butte had passed over like a lightning storm some years before. Most of the underground mining had finished by the early 1970s, outstripped by the massive Berkeley Pit mine that had opened in 1955 and proceeded to eat up a large hill to the east of the town, creating in its stead an enormous terraced hole, ringed by waste rock and tailings. But word now was, both in the pit and on the street, that what had once been dubbed the 'Richest Hill on Earth' was itself destined for closure.

Few of the buildings Fintan saw uptown were purpose-built, nor housed anything for which they had originally been designed. Instead, shabby storefronts offering RADIOS AND BICYCLES or QUALITY WELDING occupied the ground floor of former hotels, while an empty machine-shop gathered dust in what had once been, per the painted legend high on a gable, the SHEEPSHEARERS' UNION BUILDING. Fact is, you could read Butte's past from the faded lettering on building after building – a carpenter's union hall, a Chinese noodle factory, another union headquarters now a dingy bar – together with painted ads for long-vanished beer and cigar brands, or furnished rooms no longer furnished. It wasn't hard either to spot the old-timers who had spent forty or more years in the mines, now shuffling slowly, stoop-shouldered, along the sidewalks.

Cigars, once in huge demand, were still on offer in the M&M, as Fintan discovered on his second night in town, a spacious bar with a short-order lunch counter, together with a gambling room behind a curtain grey with cigarette smoke, which he learned two nights later from Mike McGann was an illegal establishment.

'Illegal?'

'Hell, yes!' McGann said, laughing. 'With half the town cops in there half the time, buying drinks for the mayor and his cronies.'

'You been down to the Dumas brothel yet?' McGann grinned as Fintan slowly shook his head. 'A hundred yards or so from the police station over on East Mercury.'

'Illegal, surely?'

'You got it!' McGann said, ordering them another beer.

It so happened Fintan had passed by its small, two-storey, red-brick Victorian facade the afternoon he arrived, though he turned down McGann's offer to accompany him there later that evening. He did, however, give the casino a go the following night – losing $10 on the red 23 – before figuring Wesley's magic number were not his own.

McGann, a small, wiry fifty-year-old with work-thickened hands, reminded Fintan in a way of Packy back at home, an air of disappointment that might flash into bitterness, but like his da, no blow-hard either. Like most in Butte, McGann was a lifetime union man, though the unions could currently do little, if anything, to slow the wave of closures and lay-offs.

'I knew the gig was up the minute I heard an oil company had bought out Anaconda Copper,' he told Fintan that first night in the bar, along with a potted history of the copper mining that had seen three times as many folk in Butte in the early 1900s – over 100,000 – than lived there now.

'But the problem's not just management,' he informed Fintan the following night. 'There're also fuckers like that fellah there,' pointing to a bald man around his own age in a checked cowboy shirt six stools down the bar. 'A garage full of fifty-thousand bucks' worth of tools he pocketed out of the mine, a socket at a time.'

The following morning Fintan walked from the hotel up to the Berkeley open pit for a closer look. Walked past small, jumbled single-storey houses, some just a step or two ahead of shacks, others brightly coloured – cherry-red, yellow or lime green, along with an occasional sky-blue roof, as if the seemingly perpetual azure sky overhead were not enough, plus plentiful lawns right up to the kerb, some tended and some not. He then passed a long stretch of plywood fencing before the massive chasm appeared below him, like a gigantic wound torn out of the earth, the block-like ledges carved out of the far wall descending like steps, and its gigantic earth-moving trucks on the bottom looking only inches high.

He stared down into the pit for a time, keen to describe it in detail to Condy when he was back home again – as if payment in kind for the tales his uncle had told him of the place – given how the huge hole below was but another hill above the town in 1944, when Condy himself had passed through Butte.

Then, walking back down to the town, he recalled a story Condy had heard from his own father, Cornelius. Of a deep Butte mine calamity that had killed a fellow Irishman, an acquaintance of Cornelius's, whom the foreman asked to accompany him as they went to inform the wife that she were now a widow.

'Your husband's met with an accident,' the ganger began as Cornelius stood beside him.

'An accident?'

'He's dead,' the ganger responded, as what else was there left to say?

'A dead man's no use to me,' the woman replied, turning back into their one-room cabin and shutting the door behind.

And had she spoken in Irish? Fintan wondered now, thinking suddenly of Da Packy's *'Fuair sí bás orm*, she died on me' at the kitchen table on that April morning thirteen years ago. And then how much he had been thinking of Donegal since hitting Butte – of his father, whom he'd not heard from in six months, and brother Frankie who'd finally written from Glenmore, home from the London building sites after their da had been hospitalised in Letterkenny for a fortnight with pneumonia.

He took a Chinese takeaway out his window onto the hotel fire escape that evening to watch another technicolour sunset, all crimson and yellows. Bundled up in a fleece-lined Levi jacket from a Salvation Army shop, he saw over his shoulder a gigantic letter M that lit up high on the hill as night fell. 'M for money, mother, or McGann?' he'd ask of Mike in the M&M the following night. Or maybe M for mineral? after McGann told him it belonged to the Montana School of Mining.

He set out the following morning in the letter's direction, passing any number of older, grander houses en route, a hodgepodge of architectural styles from when copper had been king, funky with turrets and cupolas, large second-storey balconies or huge porches flanked by Ponderosa pines.

Stopping some fifty yards short of the massive letter, he sat for a time on an outcrop of granite surrounded by golden dirt in which nothing grew – a mixture of processed residue and chemical-laced soil, McGann had informed him, that had been fed into a crusher to extract its copper. Clearly no need here for a museum with sepia-tinged photographs or desiccated rattlesnakes, seeing how Butte's past was right there underfoot, there in the dusty smell of time itself that clung to the old buildings and scarred landscape that cradled the town in its large bowl below.

Hungry from hiking, he chanced going into the Chinese takeaway again upon his return, where the white-haired proprietor clocked his accent straight away. 'You Irish?' he asked. 'Real Irish?' After shouting Fintan's order – No. 17 with fried noodles – through the small hatch behind the counter, he filled Fintan in on some of what McGann had overlooked, how Chinese miners had been the first to arrive after traces of gold were discovered in Silver Bow Creek in 1864. 'Chinese here long before any Irish!'

Sitting once more outside on his fire escape, he wondered, was it that palpable sense of its past that had seemed so familiar about the town? Certainly more like Ireland, that – along with how you'd once needed to literally scrape and dig for a living here – something else you took for granted in Ireland, but which he'd not heretofore encountered in an America that seemed now hell-bent upon the pursuit of an easy life. Whereas Butte was far more of a hard-scrabble, blue-collar town, devoid of yuppies and its quotient of long-haired hippies looking more like extras for a Western – Altman's *McCabe & Mrs Miller*, say – which Fintan had thumbed back into Killybegs to see for a second time.

Later that night back in the M&M he tried some of that out on McGann – who laughed, nay snorted, then said how Butte was fecked by its past and present both, with feck-all of a future. 'We dug up an entire mountain,' pointing a thumb over his shoulder in the direction of the Berkeley Pit, 'and now what?' But he mellowed some after another beer, rounding back to Fintan's theme. 'You left out what's still underground. The tunnels.'

'Tunnels?'

'Two thousand miles of tunnels – everywhere under the town. There's a damn tunnel underneath this bar!' McGann said, leaning back on his stool to point both forefingers down at the floor. 'Sinkholes forming every time the ground shifts, a new pothole every week you drive down a road. We'll all wake up underground some morning – yet be better off, who knows?'

Still Fintan woke up five floors above ground the following morning, head sore and mouth dry. McGann had offered again to take him down to the Dumas – insisting he couldn't leave Butte without visiting the brothel – only to end up talking about his divorce a few years back after Fintan had once again declined. 'The Night Owl at nine tomorrow night,' he reminded Fintan when they parted, having sketched directions on a napkin to a live-music bar down in the Flats.

However, the desk clerk in the lobby waved a postcard at him as he headed out for a morning coffee, an aerial shot of the Mississippi with its arch like a bent silver teaspoon, and on the other side four lines from Carla, saying how much she missed him. And so by half-nine that night, when McGann finally stumbled into the Night Owl, Fintan was nearly in Nebraska, listening to a trucker named Tommy explain how the slipstream of the rig ahead was saving him a few cents on the gallon as they barrelled east along Interstate 80.

\*

The next two months till Christmas were as good as Carla and he had known together, albeit not literally together, as overnight male guests of prospective primary-school teachers were in no ways welcome at Carla's St Louis University dorm. Fintan had hoped to temporarily move back into Lenox Place, but Court and Shelly had both shifted on: Court across the river to a live-in studio on a warehouse floor in East St Louis – 'At half of what it would've cost me on the Left Bank!' – while Shelly had finally moved in with her motorcycle man. So Fintan ended up renting a room from Manny, married that past summer and expecting a child early in the New Year. 'They still look weightless,' he told Fintan the evening he called in, pointing at Will's boots after they'd hugged, 'even on you.'

He had thought of going back to work at the Food Co-op until January, only to find it had closed its doors four months before, suggesting that whatever the 1960s had offered the 1970s was no longer of much interest to the 1980s. Less interested himself, as winter loomed, in whatever outdoors work Handy Andy might throw his way, he hired on instead at a Xerox copy-shop, waiting on customers and, once sussed, taking on the maintenance of the photocopiers too.

As Carla was flat out with her course, they saw each other mostly weekends, going for long walks in Forest Park, an occasional movie or out for a couple of beers. She also stayed with Fintan some Saturday nights, returning to the campus early on Sunday to prepare the lesson plans for her upcoming student-teacher placement.

Then early one December Sunday, she borrowed a classmate's car and took Fintan horseback riding ninety miles south on the edge of the Ozarks. His mount was a roan, more spirited than the stables lad had promised, but after clinging on for two hours as they looped along woody trails, he managed a final canter down a long colonnade of leafless sycamore trees.

'Just be thankful it's not summertime,' Carla said with a laugh when she saw his face, telling how the sunlight flickering through leaves overhead had created some kind of disorienting, manic effect that made her Flapper madly race. 'You'd've liked the big white mule on the farm across from my grandparents on which I learned to ride as a kid, so big it was like sitting on a sofa. With a length of chain in his mouth for a bit, but I still couldn't turn him.' He loved it when she talked storybook stuff like that, loved watching her flick her cropped blonde hair in the rear-view mirror as they reversed out from the stables onto the road, a robin-egg-blue sweatshirt above her jeans, his all-American lover.

Driving them back up north in the last of the light, she told Fintan another story: of Walter Cuzak, who sat next to her in Algebra her first year in high school, where he more often than not borrowed her homework to copy. 'He was sweet on me, I think, but not so keen on school. Then two years later, just before our class graduation, a horse that had bolted from a barn beside Highway 20 went clear through the windshield of Walter's car, decapitating him. The guy who owned the horse moved out shortly after, and the house just stands there now, windows broken and the barn burnt out.'

This last tale was admittedly less storybook stuff, and they drove on silently for a time, Fintan thinking how cars rather than horses had come to mean America, once he and Rory had outgrown their six-gun stage. Nor had he anything similar to share from Donegal, where Rory's father only suffered a dislocated shoulder after his Ferguson tractor mounted a grassy ditch to overturn just short of their meadow gate.

'*French fries*, Fintan,' Carla teased when they stopped for a burger and chips a few miles shy of St Louis, though chips, like autumn or anorak, were some of what he still spoke four years on. 'I suppose they're not good for you, no matter what you call them?' Carla conceded, after swiping the last few from his plate.

'You enjoyed the riding?' she asked as they pulled up at Manny's house.

'Always do,' he said as Carla, laughing, shoved him out.

*

It stayed that easy between them up right through the Christmas, which they spent back down in the Ozarks, after a fisherman pal of Manny's offered Fintan his tiny lakeside cabin, lending him a beat-up Renault to get themselves there as well. 'Christmas doesn't have "the" in front of it,' Carla informed him on the drive down, but Fintan assured her it did where he came from. Better yet, he finally told her on Christmas Eve, seated in front of the cabin's pot-bellied stove, of the trip he was taking back there early in the new year. Showed her the ticket from Chicago's O'Hare Airport – 'Not to worry, round trip, for ten days only' – purchased at the Shamrock Travel Agency two days before he'd left Butte.

'How come you're only telling me now?'

'I don't know,' he confessed, not even sure now why he'd bought the ticket, apart from how much a Montana town had put him in mind of home. 'Afraid maybe you'd think I could never stay put?'

'Going back home isn't the same as flitting here, there and everywhere.'

'I amn't a bird and I don't flit,' he said, wondering whether they might have a row now after all.

'OK, you don't flit, Fintan,' Carla said, smiling. 'But you're one strange bird. Though there's nothing strange about visiting your family,' she continued, laying her hand on his arm.

He blew a little air through his lips at that – as if the da, brother and uncle back in the Glen fell somewhat short of *family* in the way Carla spoke of hers. Telling him two weeks earlier how she felt so enmeshed by her own kin that yes, she'd spend Christmas with him in a cabin in the woods, rather than drag them back to Terre Haute two years running. 'My mother'll have a fit,' she told Fintan, before heading home the following weekend to reassure Betty of her love.

'I know too much of a mother's not the same as too little, Fintan,' she also offered. 'And of course you should go home to see your dad.' Only Fintan felt there were no *of course* about it – *of course* feeling too much like yet another way in which family works to entangle you, as if family were more of a force field than a narrative. Besides, it was Mary who had managed to create something larger than the sum of their individual selves, and Mary who then took that with her when she died. And so his mother was as much the reason –

as much as father, brother or uncle – that he was going back. To visit her grave, surely, but also to see where else he might find a trace of her. A memory embedded in their cottage kitchen say, or something he had possibly forgotten of her where the village street turned at the post office, or down along the Big Strand – lest she fade further away and all but vanish for a second time.

*

Still, neither of them slipped into old stuff that Christmas Eve, apart from Fintan foraging to find half a candle to place in the window that overlooked the by now moon-painted lake. That done, he threw three more birch logs into the stove and opened a bottle of wine as Carla dished out a simple bean and cheese casserole she'd prepared back at her dorm. They finished the wine on the couch then, promising each other to always head off somewhere at this time of year, if not as far as Wesley had got on his own Christmas Eve soirée along the Seine, seated on an embankment wall beside a lit-up Eiffel Tower with a French lass he'd met on the train from Toulouse.

'Somewhere out West,' Carla said when he'd asked where she wanted to teach. 'Oregon or California maybe. You'll come back from Ireland?' she then asked in turn.

'For sure.'

'And out West again would be OK?'

'Out West's where it's at!' – which made her smile. 'We'll have a car,' she said a while later. 'My mother's getting a new one and giving me her Ford.'

'Refuse nothing,' he again quoted Condy at her. 'Only the blows.'

'Refuse this?' she countered, unbuttoning her cardigan and paisley shirt, before drawing him down onto the musty, mustard-coloured couch.

Bundled up again, they walked down to the lake waters in the silent dark, broken only by a bird crying in the woods behind.

'There could be loons here this time of year,' she told him.

'Sure, we've two right here now,' he said, putting his arm around her.

'Are there loons in Donegal?'

'A village full.'

'Seriously.'

'No loons. But you might hear a curlew if you're out at night.'

'What's a curlew sound like?'

'I amn't a bird,' he said with a laugh, 'and I don't sing. But neither does it, really. More a cry – like it's saying its name, only elongated.' And seeing a stretch of the bog on the way home from Rory's house as he spoke.

'Will you take me there sometime?'

'I might.' He smiled, thinking how having Carla there might change the place itself, the way a camera filter can alter a landscape.

'Merry Christmas,' she said, turning them away from the lake.

'Happy Christmas.'

'Christmas is not happy,' she said. 'Christmas is merry.'

'This one's as good as it gets.'

They made love again back at the cottage, in the single bedroom behind the front room-cum-kitchen. More slowly this time, tending to each other until they lay utterly spent, arms still entwined.

'Thanks for hanging in there with me, Fintan,' Carla whispered just before she fell asleep.

'And you with me, babe' – thinking this must be what it felt like to be blessed.

# 10

Daft as it is, he suddenly fears FINTAN DOHERTY will be among the signs held up for JACK KELLY or MRS THORPE behind the red-braided rope as he walks out the Arrivals door at Shannon Airport ten days later. Heading over to the yellow Hertz sign, where he counts out a cash deposit in $10 bills, then signs for an Opel Kadett. Having hardly slept on the eight-hour flight from O'Hare, he pulls off the road under a shelter belt of pines just past Ballyhaunis, Co. Mayo, where he dozes fitfully for an hour before resuming his journey north. He's struck again by how verdant in early January the place is. The green fields that had flashed beneath the plane as it banked into its descent earlier that morning, and the green swathes of rushy meadow behind stone walls either side of the road now, as he rolls down a window to keep himself awake.

It's teatime when he finally reaches Glenbay, the last of the daylight slowly leaching away as he pulls the Opel into the lee of the byre, with no sign of Shep waiting, Argos-like, for his return. Not that he remembers Odysseus' dog from the tattered yellow paperback Mary had sourced a year before she in turn had departed. Lifting the latch, he finds Packy at the kitchen table, feasting on a blackened herring roasted on a pair of tongs on the range, a pile of skins from a feed of spuds beside a page of the *Donegal Democrat* that serves as a plate.

'Jaysus, I nearly choked,' his father says, rising awkwardly to greet his elder son.

'How's the chest?' Fintan asks, thinking his da looks far more than five years older.

'I'm off the fags anyhow.'

'Lent must be wild early this year so?'

'Hateful old place, the hospital.' Packy shakes his head. 'You'll have a cup of tea,' he declares, turning toward the sink.

'Frankie?'

'He goes for a pint after work.'

'He's working?'

'A few afternoons a week with the county council. Cutting rushes and clearing the drains on the road to Carrig.'

'Shep?'

'Ach, Shep's dead these three years,' his father says, spitting into the range before throwing in a half-shovel of coal. 'Did I not write?' He hadn't written, but tells of having looked down at Shep the day Callahan, the new village Guard, had darkened the door, declaring, 'Die dog, or shit the licence.'

'I bought a licence off Andy Beag at the post office the next afternoon, only for the fecker to die on me three days later!'

'At least you've the free coal now,' Fintan says, turning so his father won't see him smile at Shep having finally got some of his own back. And thinking too how little has changed inside the cottage, a layer of coal dust adding to the general clutter, yet the coolness of the rooms oddly reassuring, more elemental after central-heated America. Knackered, he makes up his old bed in the upper room, where he fails to hear Frankie stumble in after midnight.

\*

The cottage was like an icebox the next morning, Frankie still snoring it off and Packy yet to surface either, so after balling up the greasy newspaper place mat from the kitchen table, Fintan threw it, along with a few bits of dried fuchsia, onto the embers, bringing the range back to life so as to manage a couple of sods of turf. Ferreting out an old pair of wellies in the byre, he headed out to the sodden fields down to the Wee Strand tucked into the claddagh on the north side of the bay. Only to find when he reached the rocks that spilled down to the strand that the tiny beach itself had vanished, no sand whatsoever, only the sea, which, having reconfigured the shore, now rose to the very rocks.

'The old buck says it disappeared last winter,' Frankie told him that evening in Molly's, where the brothers bought each other a pint before heading back to the cottage in the rain. A small thing, to be sure, but it played round in Fintan's head for the time he was home. How the changes he noted – an extension on the national school, a handful of new houses sprung up, or the way Frankie's upper body had filled out from the hard graft of London building sites, along with the odd complaint about the 'Pakis' over there – were not the only changes that years bring. Even if Molly's itself seemed little changed, the same dimly lit space, the three or four drinkers, auld fellows in dark clothing murmuring to one another, while Jackie Villy from up the Glen downed the rusty mackerel Molly threw on a plate for him at the end of the bar.

The rain had lifted by the time they climbed the north side, so they stood for a minute outside the cottage, stars bright above, and moonlit clouds slowly moving in over Glen Head. Early the next morning a gale began to blow, showers of hail and sleet rattling the bedroom window, and the bay below aboil with waves when Fintan finally rose. After a bowl of porridge he made his way over to Jack Gara's, knocking before letting himself in, as they do in Donegal. Greeted by the soapy film of Jack's Condor pipe tobacco in the warm interior, he found Jack propped up in a bed across from the range.

'Who is it that you are?' the old neighbour said with a smile at Fintan, who felt for the first time as if he were maybe truly home at last.

'Like Siberia out there,' he smiled back.

'No different,' Jack agreed. 'Only their bread is black.'

They talked for an hour or more, Jack keen to hear anything, everything, about America. He rose then as Fintan put on a kettle, and having pulled a pair of trousers over his long johns, set out a small mirror, cup of hot water, soap dish and brush on the kitchen table, then sat to shave himself.

The following day Fintan tried to place a phone call to Carla from the kiosk across from Molly's, only the operator in Donegal Town was unable to get an international line. Back at the cottage he made Packy a dinner of boiled bacon and cabbage, leaving Frankie his share in the pot for later. Packy was still weaving – no longer tweed but small, striped hearth rugs that Leno in the shop sold to tourists in the summer. His father asked the odd question about the States, the price of a pint of milk, say, or what the weather was like in January, but there wasn't a whole lot more chat between them than there'd ever been. Dinner done, Fintan took off over the hill to Pier, knowing Uncle Condy would call into them once he had word, and wanting to spare his uncle the awkwardness of a visit.

A line of snow clung like a salt rim along the brown basin of a cut bog en route, a thin skin of ice underfoot over muddy tractor tracks. He could hear the wind playing faintly in the radio mast at the height of the hill, then smiled at the ornate paving on its small transformer shed, as if anybody other than sheep would admire it, and thinking to ask Frankie whether it was more of the county council's work.

And smiling yet again at the dented blue lorry door and a swathe of fish net, improvised sheep guards both, on either end of the small bridge over the stream at Pier itself, sure signs Condy was still drawing down the yearly headage bounty for his flock.

'Tis yourself,' Condy said, after Fintan knocked and lifted the latch, 'and you're welcome home,' rising from his chair to shake hands with his nephew.

'You look well, Condy,' he said, and he meant it, his uncle seeming much the same, never mind altogether fit for a man of sixty-four. The cottage looked little different too, the same bachelor clutter everywhere, his battered steamer trunk having emigrated from under his bed in the lower room to a corner of the kitchen. Yet apart from its faded shipping labels, there was nothing about man nor room to suggest he had ever departed Donegal.

'I owe you a few letters.' Condy smiled.

'A cup of tea will make us quits,' Fintan said with a laugh.

'So tell us,' Condy said, after pouring them each a chipped cup's worth.

*

Yet it was a story of Condy's that knocked around in Fintan's head on his way home over the hill, much as they always had. 'Sure, one of his paintings used to hang right there,' Condy had said, pointing at the wall beside the kitchen dresser, after Fintan mentioned having seen a woodcut of Randall Hart's – what looked like a Donegal landscape – in the Cleveland Museum of Art.

'A painting here?'

'A painting of your mother. A smaller version of that the Yank who visited years ago was talking about.'

'The one where she's lying on the hill?' Fintan said, pointing in its direction over Condy's shoulder.

'Aye.'

'You never mentioned that before?'

'Sure, why would I?' Condy shrugged. 'Didn't Mary break it up and feed it into the fire?'

'You're joking?'

'Said she was sick of looking at it.'

'What'd it look like?' Fintan asked, not quite believing his ears.

'Covered in blue mould after falling down behind the dresser?'

'No. The picture itself.'

'A painting, just. Herself lying there, looking out to sea.'

The wet stones on the path underfoot gleamed in the last of the evening light as he made his way back over the hill, a filigree of dead bracken on all sides glowing with a near drug-induced vividness. The notable impact of such small detail had struck him upon his return – the wind teasing the broken gutter above his bedroom window upon awakening, a black cat crossing a green field below the cottage, or the one or two grey woodlice most mornings in the bathroom sink – the way Donegal draws you in, not like the wide-open sweep of America, more like small print surrounding you on all sides.

*

He drove into Killybegs the next morning, called into its chemist with a script for more of Packy's tablets. Recalling what a Limerick lad had told him on a building site his first week in London, he then asked your man in his white coat behind the counter for a bottle of Dr Jones Cough Elixir. 'It's no longer sold,' the man said. 'It was being used for drugs,' fixing Fintan with a stare.

'Unlike all those pills behind you?' Fintan quipped, only your man failed to smile back. And so it had been used, per his Limerick workmate, who claimed pouring the contents into a skillet to simmer slowly left you with a sticky residue of opium.

The sun meanwhile was out for a change, and so Fintan wandered down to the pier, passing a fuel tanker whose rear tires were sunk in a muddy track. Two super-trawlers, big as buildings, were unloading massive catches of mackerel, their cranes dangling immense, purse-like nets dripping a bloody shower as they dumped the fish into enormous bins below. Small red-and-yellow fish boxes, strewn nets and pink bits of flesh littered the ground, as forklifts driven by cowboys in orange oilskins cut back and forth at speed, the stench of fish, salt water and diesel nothing but the smell of money, as sunlight glinted on three or four more lorryloads of fish farther down the pier.

He bought a plate of fish and chips at Melly's for old times' sake, no sign this time of the New York docker in his peacoat and blue watch cap – himself the returned Yank now if it came to that, not that it ever it would. Last call was the butcher's to buy Packy and Frankie a chop for their tea, plus a couple of pounds of rashers, some steak and a roast for Sunday, patently acting the returned Yank now as he counted out pound notes at the till.

Back in the Glen by two o'clock, he handed Packy his tablets, stashed the meat in the small fridge beside the sink, then set out again, taking the back road towards Carrig this time, where Condy said the Walsh brothers now lived in a county-council house beside the fish factory, the hour-long trek out and back to Glenbay having finally proved too much. 'You wonder they didn't grow wool themselves,' Condy had scoffed, 'out after sheep all of their lives', as if he'd been out on the hills any less, bar his nine years Stateside.

The creased lane up to their house with its ridge of crushed rock felt like a spine of stone underfoot, while a cock on the dungheap at the lower gable eyed him askance. The younger brother – Micheál, small, stooped, with a thatch of white hair – answered his knock, as Fintan simply would not lift a latch this far from home. His elder brother

Paddy was abed with the flu, Micheál said, waving him into the large kitchen with its fierce smell of tomcat. A battered table, chairs and ancient dresser were all pushed back against the walls, as if to better display the mud-streaked, green linoleum, along with a small black-and-white telly, its screen flickering with a printed message apologising for the loss of programme.

Fintan didn't stay long, nor did he learn a lot more about Randall Hart, to whom the Walsh brothers had let the small outbuilding that the painter had inhabited in Glenelg. 'A baldy man,' according to Micheál, whose slurred speech Fintan had trouble following, as if the gears in his voice box had been stripped by old age. 'Oh, he was wild handy,' he added, describing a wooden floor the Yank had fashioned in his one-room dwelling from an armful of six-by-twelve-inch beams that had washed up onto the claddagh.

Fintan said nothing back at the cottage about the Walshes to Packy, who had seldom if ever spoken about Hart himself, apart from that afternoon the art professor Yank, who'd come to Ireland on the painter's trail, called by. Nor did Fintan say where he was headed the following day, this time driving the long way round to Pier, where he called briefly into Condy before heading on foot north over Pier Hill toward Glenelg. It proved, as so often, one of those deceptive climbs, the way a hill can repeatedly seem to crest, only to reveal a further incline the higher you mount. He followed the cliff-line to his left once he reached the plateau, same as he had the first time he'd made this trek, the summer before he left for London. Not dull like today, but a bright, breezy afternoon, the lobster buoys on the sun-splashed sea like tiny coloured floats on a fishing line, and a seal, which he first mistook for a large pollock below, swimming slowly northwards.

A heavy grey mist had begun to drift in from the east, not as far as the cliff edge yet, but filtering out swathes of the level terrain to his right, the odd, grassy tuft of bog stranded here and there in the middle of a cutaway bank like a tiny island. Not wanting to go astray, he continued to track along the seaside cliffs until he saw Glenelg far below him, the Walshes' old cottage tucked into the butt of massive Slieve Looey, and high away to the east the bog lake that had given the small glen its name, like a brooding body of black water tucked into the flank of the eponymous mountain.

A weak, watery sun broke through as he began the long descent, noting how the well-tended homestead he'd seen earlier that summer had largely vanished. No tidy haycocks, nor long green fields marked by cleared drains, nor indeterminate black shapes of what had proved to be a cow and calf. No dog tied to the byre either, barking faintly up at him before he'd turned back on that occasion, too unsure about calling on the Walsh brothers, whom he only knew by sight from Mass.

He carried on then to the bottom of the Glen, crossing the rushes-choked meadow, and fording the narrow stream via three or four large rocks, before threading his way through a waist-high stand of nettles up to the padlocked front door of the cottage. It would've been easy enough to force a window, but that was not the done thing he felt, despite large clouts of the roof-thatch having fallen in, and the wooden door beginning to rot. The thatch on the two outbuildings he'd first glimpsed from on high that summer had fallen in, and after stepping into the larger, he kicked aside more nettles and several inches of dirt, straw and turf mould only to find the rotting driftwood beams that had constituted the American painter's studio floor. He exited the open doorway then, wondering if this were what Hart too might've seen of a winter's day some thirty years before, a small V-shaped crotch of blue sea, framed by the ascending sides of the narrow glen with a leaden sky overhead.

Darker clouds had again blotted out the sun when he turned toward Pier, climbing steadily, as he didn't want to be caught on the hill by any class of wintery showers. His luck held too, for he was nearly back to his rental car at Condy's gable when the first sheets of sleet descended, the wind sharp behind them. And it was still coming down when he reached Glenbay, pulling over to lift Frankie as he exited Molly's.

'We'll nip back in for one?' his brother offered.

'We won't. I'm trying to stay out of the pub.'

'One'll do you no harm.'

'One's too many, and twenty-two's not enough,' quoting Jack Gara, who'd eventually given up the drink. 'You want to see you don't take up residence in there yourself.'

'Feck-all else to do here,' Frankie said, shaking his head. 'And my county-council gig finishes up next week.'

'What about getting a berth on a boat in Killybegs?'

'I'd sooner slit my wrists.'

'So go back to London?'

'What about himself?'

'Himself's nearly back to himself,' Fintan said. 'And he's the sister here now to look in on him.' The sister, Myra, an unmarried aunt they had scarcely known existed, home now from Cincinnati where she'd nursed for years, and living on her own in a wee house just down from the chapel.

'"Sidewalk woman" the old buck calls her!' Frankie laughed, telling how she would walk her dog on a lead up to the shop. 'He'd probably hunt her if she did call in.'

'Just don't get stuck here yourself,' Fintan cautioned his brother as they pulled up at the home place in the last of the January light.

In bed that night, he thought of a story Jack Gara had told him as a child, of an old tramp who turned up in the parish years before, stopping in a few houses where he played a handful of local tunes on a fiddle well enough that Jack's granda wondered might he not be Francie Joe McGinley, who had departed the Glen some fifty years before? Determined to query him the following morning, his host rose to find the visitor already departed, a half-plug of Crowbar tobacco on the kitchen table in exchange for his keep. Whereas Fintan himself had returned as a younger man – and under his own flag too – yet like your man, already keen to depart again. And keenest of all to see Carla, whom he had failed once more to raise by phone.

*

Fintan had visited Mary's grave shortly after landing home, but three days before his flight back to America he chose to walk up to Colmcille's Holy Well, hoping he might get some fleeting sense of her, some hint that the lichen-covered headstone at the back of the crowded graveyard had utterly failed to transmit. Much as he had looked out the Greyhound-bus window at the Chicago streets the night before his flight from O'Hare, wondering had his mother walked along any of them, a small daughter of the young American doctor and his wife in either hand. And wondering too what – if any – memories they might have of his mother, not much more than a girl herself. Never mind how strange to think someone you would never meet might have memories of someone you will never again see? And how – as the bus turned down another avenue – he might try to locate the daughters, had he anything more than their surname, Sweeney, which neither might any longer have themselves.

There were no flowers in January for the tiny shrine, but he had brought along a small, egg-shaped white stone lifted from the shingle at Pier to add to the cairn, whose rounded mound now rose, like a whale slowly breaching, above the tiny well. The previous jam jar and chipped mug were long gone, but someone had brought up a wee statue of the Virgin Mary – headless now – with a few coins scattered at her feet on the stone shelf above the well. Taking out a dollar bill happened upon in his Levis the night before, he rolled it into a tiny tube and anchored it under two 50p pieces. Turning, he saw it then – a small gout of bright blue – filling a wee, wind-torn aperture in the dark cloudbank above Glen Bay.

\*

His final outing in the parish was with Frankie the following night. Leaving the Opel at the cottage, they walked some three miles up the Glen in that soft, west of Ireland rain – more like a mist, really – that you scarcely note falling till you find yourself well wet five minutes on. Their destination was an old one-room national school in the townland of Moneen that had closed after an extension was built on to the village school beside the chapel. A small kitchen corner – sink, counter and oven – had converted it more or less into a home for a succession of blow-ins, the latest a South African bloke, Jonathan, and his partner Nicole, who Frankie had fallen in with upon his return from London.

After a cup of tea, his brother doled out four tabs of acid scored in Killybegs off a former schoolmate, now working in the fish-processing plant. As they waited to get off, Fintan took in their hosts – thin Jonathan with a bent back and exceedingly long fingers, and slight Nicole with a head of light-brown curls – who were taking turns telling stories of a club they had frequented in England, 'where you took twenty blues and danced all night with the Blacks'.

The acid, when it kicked in, seemed more of a body thing than his and Carla's trip, a warm sense of well-being deep in his femurs and down along his throat. Later on, trying to explain something to Nicole, he found himself suddenly disinclined towards language, heard himself letting go of words in mid-sentence, as if they were little balloons just as happy to drift. Marooned on a tiny, tattered sofa, he gazed at the fire through the wee window of the small solid-fuel stove, at the cold half-moon streaming through the tall classroom windows, along with an occasional, yellow-blue flicker at the corner of his eye, like a backbeat to the music Nicole had put on, Talking Heads, now talking quite loudly from a cassette player on the table.

Jonathan was also given to talking, only more slowly, describing how he had crouched up on the hill behind the schoolhouse that afternoon, sheltered from the wind, and waiting for something to happen within the vast openness before him, only nothing had.

'It's more of a mute ecology,' Fintan heard Nicole say – or something like that – how vast sweeps of moor and mountain require a commensurate measure of time for anything to transpire. 'The sea works quicker though,' he then heard himself offer, telling how the Wee Strand at the bottom of the claddagh had entirely vanished, only for those words to become balloons too as he looked over at his brother, who he figured wouldn't give two fucks for Jonathan's account of a failed epiphany, but who clearly fancied the girlfriend Nicole. Yet guessing only, given how little he knew of Frankie now. Which then brought to mind his mate Wesley, and he puzzled aloud how he and his own brother could be pups from the one litter.

A while later he found himself standing on the road outside. Eyes shut, he listened to the sound of water everywhere, pitched high, low, hard, soft, fast, slow – audibly seeping from the boggy expanses on all sides and flowing into the roadside ditches – nothing but the sound of water everywhere.

He sat down beside Frankie once back inside, where Jonathan was holding forth on electromagnetism, a seeming obsession that Nicole informed them had driven her from bed to sofa at 3 a.m. the previous morning.

'But what's it like to leave a continent behind?' Fintan asked her, to which she replied how it was mostly Johannesburg she knew, that she hadn't grown up with the *National Geographic* plains full of the wildebeests and hyenas he had in mind. 'Mostly the light and air is what I miss. And yourself, what was it like to leave this island behind?'

'A blessing,' he said, though he knew it was never that simple.

'You fancy her?' he asked his brother on the way home, figuring it was Nicole who had prompted their long trek up to the schoolhouse.

'She's all right,' Frankie replied, 'but your man's a bollox. Have you a woman over beyond?' he then inquired of Fintan.

'Aye, I'm seeing someone,' Fintan said, leaving it there, given they'd never talked much of girls. His watch showed nearly 5 a.m., but there was not even the promise of a false dawn through the light rain that had begun to fall, the odd wee glint of light at the corners of his eyes all that remained of the acid, whose energy had by now given way to a world-weariness as old as the surrounding hills.

*

The wind was round to the east the morning Fintan departed, grass stiff with frost, the steeple on the small Church of Ireland beside the post office a brilliant white, as if its granite had been replaced with aluminium overnight.

'Safe home,' Jack Gara had offered when he called over to say goodbye.

'I'm headed back anyhow,' he'd replied, 'whatever about home.'

'Home, sweet home, and the fire out!' Jack smiled. 'Safe journey so.'

'You're doing OK?' he asked Packy back in the cottage, his bag already by the door.

'Never better,' his father said, though he looked anything but.

'I'll send you a few bob when I'm back working.'

'There's no need.'

'For your tablets, so.'

'The medical card takes care of them.'

'For another dog licence then. Should you change your mind?'

'I was never any good with a dog,' surprising Fintan with a half-smile.

'For a rainy day then. Should it ever rain here,' smiling himself now. 'Frankie has a number for me,' he added, his brother having headed off early to the Garda barracks to sign back on the dole.

Managing another awkward half-embrace, they left it at that then, Packy following him as far as the door to watch the Opel disappear down the lane. *Had I been playing the returned Yank again?* Fintan wondered at the wheel, promising to send on money from America, when truth was he seldom made much more than would keep himself. 'Is there any future there?' his auntie Eileen, herself home from Cincinnati, had asked when he called in to her the previous night. 'Ach, plenty of present anyhow,' he'd said, smiling back at her.

The sun was a large red ball in a dark cloudbank behind Molly's pub as the Opel began the long climb out of the Glen, passing a hooded crow on a fence post at the bend in the road, where the village below finally vanished from the rear-view mirror. Given the odd patch of black ice, he took it handy all the way to Donegal Town, where he tried ringing Carla again from the post office just off the Diamond, prepared to apologise for waking her an hour or so before she'd likely rise for her first class, only for the phone to once again ring out.

Ten minutes later, on a curve just south of Laghy, he hit another patch of black ice at nearly 50 mph and spun into the oncoming lane. He tried steering into the skid while feathering the brake pedal, only for the Opel, tyres screaming, to execute a further 180-degree spin, before slamming into a high, grassy bank where it came to a dead stop, once again in the lane he'd been in, only facing back now in the direction he'd come.

His seemed the only car on the road as he quickly reversed – his left leg shaking so badly he could scarcely manage the clutch – then slowly drove on until he was able to pull in at a gate. He sat there for several minutes, breathing deeply until the trembling subsided and wondering whether he had nearly played the returned Yank for a final time by not having bussed or thumbed up to the Glen. He got out then to look at the driver's side of the car, adding the undamaged door panel on the rental car to the list of his unbelievable luck – the dearth of any oncoming traffic, never mind a grassy bank flush against the road, which had kept the car from rolling into the field beyond – as if some guardian angel had been under orders to grant him an entirely free ride.

Better yet, the next morning in the Departures hall at Shannon, he thought for a moment he might be looking at her. A young woman, a few years older than himself, say thirty, with one of those faces you might remember for years – sallow skin, brown braids in a circle atop her head and faraway blue eyes that seemed to stare through whatever she took in – making Fintan wonder what she altogether truly saw. Dressed in a pair of baggy trousers and two jackets, the outer one of rumpled purple corduroy over which hung a battered backpack, and at her feet a large lilac-coloured case emblazoned FRAGILE – HARP, such that all he could think was *angel*, her wings folded within those jackets, while making out for some reason that she needed an airport.

And thinking of her suddenly again the following day, after he had failed to raise Carla yet again by phone and so had finally called Shelly, who, sobbing down the line, told how Carla had herself ended up on the wrong side of the road three days after Fintan had flown over to Ireland, the Ford Granada her mother had given her having encountered both black highway ice and a bank of freezing fog, into which an oncoming jeep had crossed over, clipping Carla so that she too spun round to meet another car head on, the rescue squad needing an hour to prise her remains and those of the other driver, a middle-aged woman, out of the still-smoking wreckage.

And while he knew it was a nonsense, he couldn't help wondering whether the angel back in Shannon had been sent there, harp and all, to give him the saddest news that morning, only to decide that another twenty-fours of ignorance would be the kinder act. Still seated by the phone, he felt his tears beginning to flow down towards his shattered heart.

**III**

# 11

Two years on from his lover's death finds Fintan in San Francisco, tending bar in O'Brien's, a small boozer near North Beach, then heading back after closing time to a red-brick rooming house a few blocks west beside the bottom of Telegraph Hill. Two years in which he has drifted between Texas and California, from one casual job to another – car wash, cashier, night watchman – working for rent and beer money. Living a stripped-down life, what little he hangs on to – a few changes of clothes, whatever paperback is on the go – stuffed into his olive-green army-surplus duffle bag, along with that black-and-white snapshot of Mary, and the colour one of himself and Carla on the steps of Lenox Place in St Louis, the morning they had struck out west.

There are no shortages of ad-hoc households in San Francisco either, but he is happier in what Uncle Condy might've called a flophouse than in another communal scene, prefers the anonymity that defines the gaff, down to an unsigned note – PLEASE DO NOT SING IN THIS KITCHEN AS WALLS ARE THIN AND IT KEEPS ME AWAKE – taped to the ancient Frigidaire. The wee corner of a red neon sign out his third-floor window reminds him of his mother's votive lamp beneath the Sacred Heart in the kitchen back in Donegal.

That said, he avoids his underheated room as much as he can, stays on some nights at O'Brien's, now drinking whiskey instead of the small beer he might've nursed at the end of the night at O'Connell's bar in Cleveland.

Other nights, and some days even, find him tucked into a corner of the laundromat just down the street from his room, Condy having been dead right about the wonderful warmth of the self-serve laundries in America. Still, he doubts his uncle ever took to reading a book therein, nor grabbed any shut-eye as Fintan can sometimes manage, though he takes care to stuff whatever cash he carries down into his purple Doc Martens, lest somebody mistake him for a down-and-out bum asking to be rolled. Plus chatting a couple of times with a French lass from Fougères, who scratches her crotch as easily as an Irish lass might her elbow.

*

He had made straight for California two years earlier, had fled St Louis twenty-four hours after learning of Carla's death, thumb out on the I-64, his body still half on Donegal time, but determined to keep moving.

'You can stay with me,' Shelly had offered. 'At least until morning?'

'I've work waiting,' he'd lied, Lenox Place – its sizeable, storied kitchen table and tiny bedroom under the eaves – the last place on earth he wanted to be now. Nor did he think, until months later when the Kodak print of Carla and him on the front stoop arrived in the post, of how he had never considered Shelly's own loss; of how she might've needed him to stay around for a day or two, and only now reflecting on the selfishness of his own sorrow.

A middle-aged couple had dropped him off around midnight at Kansas City, where he turned north towards Nebraska. Running on empty, he nodded off in the front seat of a Buick Skylark whose driver was nursing a six-pack of beer, opened his eyes twice to see Carla seated on the steel guard rail of I-29, yet failing to make out at 70 mph whether she too might've spotted him. Dropped off then at St Joseph, he walked down the entrance ramp and back onto the interstate, where Don, a US soldier on leave, offered him a field ration of smoked mackerel, which he declined. Two blokes thumbing ensemble were an improbable long shot, but he guessed Don's uniform might shorten the odds, and a VW van shortly proved him right, its beardy driver waving them aboard with a plastic bag full of popcorn, which he promptly insisted they share. Fintan fell asleep in the back, sprawled on a mattress beneath a birdcage with a parakeet. He woke a few hours later, the dawn's grey light filtering through the van windows as he lay there, listening to a blizzard alert on the radio, while John at the wheel finished telling Don how he'd named his parakeet JJ: 'So I could tell Joan, Jane and Jennifer, all of who I was dating then, that I'd called him after us!'

They dropped Fintan off fifty miles west of Lincoln on Interstate 80, which would see him across both Nebraska and Wyoming, skirting the Rockies, then down into Salt Lake City. A scattering of popcorn from the van lay at his feet on the blacktop, like a portent of the snow that began to fall a half-hour after three college girls in a Volvo station wagon had pulled over to offer him a lift. And who happily assented when he offered to drive the car, which had begun to shimmy and slide from one lane into another.

They stopped then for a quick burger at a roadside service area, felt the wind even higher when they came out. Lisa, a thin, brown-eyed domestic-science major, put on a Crosby, Stills & Nash tape, while Abbie and Susan in the back began to tot up the cars that had gone off the road, a Lincoln Continental crumpled against an overpass abutment, plus several more abandoned along the soft shoulder after having spun 180 degrees round to face back east, much as Fintan had done to the west in Donegal just three days before. Shortly after, a semi some seven cars ahead suddenly jackknifed, its careening trailer swatting the car behind like a fly onto the median strip, before fishtailing back to knock a second car down the embankment, as Fintan, swerving into the outside lane, managed to avoid the Mercury Monarch they'd been following for many miles.

The curtain of snow then suddenly parted, revealing yet another car dangerously close ahead, and a stand of towering trees beside a big red barn beyond the steel guard rails. Bowie had by now replaced CS&N on the car tape deck, as Abbie commenced rolling a joint in the back. Fintan passed when it came to him, only to end up snorting the smoke from the smouldering roach, which Lisa had held out for him in a bobby pin. Shortly after they passed another jackknifed truck, a tanker lying on its side this time, its cab twisted upwards, and its partitioned windscreen like two eyes of a giant insect gazing up at the sky.

An hour later then they broke into the blue, the sun now gloriously high in a huge Nebraska sky across which clouds still raced, and a snowplough, followed by a highway truck spreading sand and salt just ahead, the three co-eds giddy with relief, and Fintan with a hundredweight of lead for a heart.

*

He found work a week after he reached the West Coast, hired on as caretaker for a small motel up in the Santa Lucia Mountains above Monterey. The job paid little, but came with a small cabin behind the motel forecourt in a stand of Ponderosa pines, whose needles he marvelled at, inordinately large as so much was in America, and apparently long enough for Native Americans to have once fashioned baskets from them. He covered five night-shifts a week, taking money upfront and handing out a key to the occasional late arrival, then falling back asleep on the small cot at the back of the tiny office. The owners, Walter and Wilma Lingren, a first-generation Swedish couple in their sixties, bitched at one another around the clock, but were largely OK with Fintan – a potential ally – and he took care not to favour one over the other.

He also took care to keep to himself as much as possible, hiking for hours in the hills on his two days off, along with drinking little – a weekly six-pack of Miller High Life from the general store a mile down the road – while reading anything he could lay hands on late into the night by the light of a kerosene lamp in his cabin. 'A poor-will, not a whip-poor-will,' Walter corrected him when he mentioned the bird that had sung over several nights, 'a two-note, not a three-note nightjar'.

February and March were wet, the moist Pacific air turning to rain as it was thrust upwards by the mountains, but April proved mild and dry, the springs and streams singing from the winter rains, the ground bursting with wildflowers, most of which he couldn't name, and the wee ants on the Lingrens' wooden picnic table the tiniest insects ever. The oak-strewn valley and heavily wooded hills – Douglas firs and the occasional Sequoia – were also some of the loveliest terrain he had yet seen, but the verdant abundance on all sides did nothing for the emptiness inside, any hope he might've had of regaining that California high, the unbounded promise of that Sierra Nevada vista the previous summer, put paid to altogether.

'I feel hollowed out inside,' he wrote to Shelly on a card in late May, empty as the Butte open-pit mine he'd stared down into some six months before.

'It hits a hundred degrees here in summer,' Walter told him a week later. 'And you'll be walking less,' he added with a kind of perverse satisfaction, 'once the ticks, flies and rattlers are out in force.' Taking Walter at his word, Fintan gave him and Wilma two weeks' notice the following evening, figuring his hermit-like retreat had run its course.

\*

He headed down to Texas then, where he stopped first with Darlene. Darlene, whose head of cropped blonde hair he'd found on his shoulder, after awakening at the back of a Greyhound somewhere east of Amarillo, herself slumped against him, as he stared at her right wrist – a spider web of red scar-tissue – resting palm up in her lap.

'Don't ask,' she told him when she too awoke, not that he had, or intended to.

That said, she then informed him where she'd slept the previous night, something else he hadn't enquired into.

'On an operating table,' shaking her head at the memory, 'with a corpse dozing next door.'

'Better,' he offered, 'than sleeping with a corpse?'

'Nope, not into necrophilia,' she said, not a word he'd necessarily have expected to hear from her just by looking at her.

Survival was what he'd shortly gauge Darlene was mostly into, but for now he was happy to buy her a coffee at the roadside café into which the bus had pulled just as a big red sun was coming up over the flat yellow land. He could see her better too in the neon lighting: dirty-blonde hair as he now knew to call it, pale-green eyes not unlike his own, rings on six fingers, and looking like she weighed maybe a little more than seven stone. He noted too a slight imprecision to her speech – from whatever she was on or coming off that morning, he suspected – only it proved to be habitual, like tiny stripped gears at the back of her mouth, and not unfetching either.

Not that attraction was to prove their story, despite Darlene having invited him to crash for a night back at her apartment when their bus finally pulled into Dallas. He had some more of her story by then, if not precisely why she'd presented herself at the emergency ward of the small Kingman, Arizona hospital where, tired of waiting, she had wandered off to see where she might lay her head, opening three or four doors, including that of the tiny morgue with its dozing corpse, until she found a darkened operating room with its empty table down the corridor.

And she too had a mother story – *as if any of us don't*, thought Fintan – telling him how her own had walked out years back on her family in Denison, Texas, only to walk into the Red river an hour later.

He stayed for two nights on the couch in her efficiency apartment in a small two-storey complex above a tiny pool. Bought a quart of milk, a loaf of bread, a dozen eggs and a pack of tomatoes the next morning, leaving them on the kitchen table for Darlene still asleep in her bedroom, along with a scribbled note of thanks for her hospitality. He headed over to Wesley's then, where he would crash for three days only, Wesley having once again split up with Terri Ann, and not in the best of shape himself.

Next port of call, more or less by default, was San Jose, where a back tyre on the San Francisco-bound lift he'd caught in Bakersfield blew out shortly after midnight. And if there was little for him in San Jose, there seemed little on offer anywhere, and so he hustled any work he could find there till September, pumping gas, picking string beans, which paid peanuts by the bushel, flipping burgers in a joint on Los Gatos Boulevard, and humping refrigerators one weekend out of a large apartment complex being repossessed by a local bank, whose assistant VP and chief accountant worked two-wheelers alongside him, both big into Bob Dylan, and seeming anything but bankers.

San Jose, a college town, was awash with young women, half of them blondes it seemed, and one of whom every now and again brought his Carla to mind, if all too readily, like water down a well-worn stream bed. Yet what little stock she had professed to put in sex seemed his own way now, and he continued to sleep alone in the single room he rented from a Mrs Vitale, whose own husband had been struck down by a train twenty years before.

He gave house-painting a go then when summer ended, more honest graft than cheap plastic-vinyl, until one November morning when he awoke suddenly wondering how he was still in San Jose, when he'd been San Francisco-bound. 'Hang on to that, you might need it yourself,' Mrs Vitale told him an hour later, after he had offered her an extra week's rent in lieu of two weeks' notice, adding how she herself was thinking of selling up and moving to Salinas to live with her elder daughter.

\*

Two weeks later he was behind the bar at O'Brien's in North Beach, a small bar & grill with a pool table, and a LADIES sign on the inside of the men's-room door, which gave him a start on his first time leaving the jacks. The clientele were mostly regulars, the work more wearying than it had felt back in O'Connell's, working alcoholics for tips not entirely unlike the Kerryman back on a London building site, who'd boasted of having nicked the pennies laid on the eyes of a corpse back when he was a kid. Nor were the clientele the only committed boozers he discovered on his first Friday night, after Gerry, the short-order cook, exited the kitchen to demand a double shot of Jack Daniel's.

'Give him it,' O'Brien signalled over by the door, lifting his own empty hand to his mouth. 'De-oxygenation,' he told Fintan later. 'He'd have torn your head off, had you refused.'

The dishwasher, who answered to Batteries, only ever asked for a Coke, a small, quiet, moustachioed man in his forties, whom Fintan spotted sleeping on the grass one afternoon in Washington Square Park. 'As in missing a few?' one of the regulars offered, when Fintan queried the nickname. 'He wears two watches, for Christ's sake!'

But O'Brien himself was not the worst boss, and if Fintan never fell in with any of the regulars, the give and take with the drinkers across the bar, however hackneyed, did him arguably more good than working as a night-watchman, say. Bottom line, it was a job, a weekly check, a reason to haul his sorry ass out of bed most mornings.

That said, he kept to himself what few waking hours he spent at the rooming house, apart from occasionally calling in after an early shift at O'Brien's to have a drink with Sam Stevenson next door. Sam, who dressed a cut above the rest of the lodgers, departing each morning in a jacket, tie and straw hat, and leaving a trail of egg yolk one afternoon behind him across the tiled vestibule floor, leaking from the battered brown paper bag he had somehow managed to hang on to after a day's drinking in whatever haunts he had.

'Gin's better for you,' held Sam, who kept his own backstory to himself. 'Made from anise and coriander, and more like herbal tea.'

'More like drinking aftershave,' countered Fintan, who took pains to carry a six-pack or half-pint of bourbon with him before calling over.

He rarely heard anything through the wall from Sam's room, unlike the muffled 'Jesus Christ, another goddamn day!' which periodically sounded through the opposite wall as Victor, a heavy-set Italian American in his sixties, greeted the sunrise. And if only twenty-six, Fintan found himself already wondering what rooms might lie ahead, his current digs not unlike a London-Irish hostel to which he'd accompanied a Donegal workmate, who was visiting an elderly uncle there: a half-hour of desultory chat, punctuated by the faint sounds of coughing and tinny music seeping through the walls.

While the odd nocturnal cockroach might dart across the white-porcelained kitchen when the overhead fluorescent light flickered on, Fintan was in no ways prepared for what looked easily like a hundred roaches crawling all over the communal bathtub one February night, as he turned towards it from the toilet into which he had just upchucked what little he'd eaten earlier that day before downing nearly a fifth of Old Grand-Dad bourbon.

Such things were something altogether new, and, considerably shaken, he decided to check out an AA meeting two days later, where he listened sympathetically as an overweight tram driver talked about how hard it was to be sucking an ice cube at home, when the wife or grown kids were popping open a beer. However, he'd lasted but a further hour before the talk of a *Higher Power* sent him packing, telling himself as he walked back to his room how he hadn't drifted away from an Irish church in order to enlist in a Yankee one.

\*

He first saw Marianne in the laundromat that May, some six months after he hit town. Small, slight, short brown hair, sombre eyes. And first spoke to her the following week after her washing machine had suddenly stopped. 'The imbalance signal,' he explained, pointing to a small yellow light blinking like a traffic signal above the round door. 'You have to shift the clothes around inside.'

And, with a grin, 'A pity we don't come with a warning light like that ourselves? When things are out of whack?'

'You're not American?' she said.

'Nor you either.' Not German, he knew, but he had not as yet met enough Dutch to place her accent.

'Irish,' he then owned up.

'A fellow European,' Marianne replied with a shy half-smile – though Fintan doubted many heads from Donegal had ever self-identified as such.

They chatted for a few minutes more, then again two weeks later, after which they went for a coffee once Marianne had retrieved her laundry from the dryer. 'No, I carry it,' with another slight smile at his offer. And then for something to eat the following Friday, at a seafood place on Fisherman's Wharf.

'I came with flowers in my hair,' she said after he asked how long had she been in San Francisco. 'At least I had wanted to,' telling him how much she'd loved singer Scott McKenzie's hit when she was small. 'I arrived just three years ago, with my boyfriend.'

'Is he also from Amsterdam?' he asked, pushing the grilled swordfish around his plate.

'The Hague. He stayed just two months,' she then volunteered.

'It didn't work out,' Fintan said, more observation than query.

'He told me he was tired of my flirting with the unknown.'

'Sure, we all dance with that fellow daily,' he said with a smile, pushing his plate aside.

'What do you live on, Fintan?' she asked, frowning.

'Milk and alcohol,' he replied with a laugh. And he laughed again the following week after he drew the Temperance card at her flat, where Marianne had offered to read the Tarot for him.

'Yes, the Angel is pouring water into wine, but this temperance is more like tempering steel, you know? Bringing together two opposite qualities?'

'Balance, purpose, patience,' she continued, when she saw his interest.

'So I needn't worry?'

'Worry gets you nowhere. But your Temperance card was reversed.'

'Reversed?'

'Yes, upside down.'

'And?'

'It could mean not so good judgement at times? Or maybe not enough long-term vision?'

'No five-year plan à la Mao Zedong anyhow,' he admitted.

Yet he felt himself marginally opened up as he walked back to the boarding house that evening, their tête-à-tête a good cut above most of the conversation had at O'Brien's. They continued to see each other too, every week or so through the summer, most often at her place around the corner from their laundromat, a small one-bedroom flat where she often made them something to eat.

Else, on his way into O'Brien's, he might call into the flower shop on Stockton Street where she worked, bring her

229

a coffee or once a Dutch-chocolate ice-cream cone, already half-dripping down his sleeve. There seemed no successor to her ex-lover from The Hague, but Fintan doubted they were bedward-bound. 'We could have sex,' Marianne had told him on one of their first evenings together, 'but I think it better if we do not,' frowning slightly as she spoke, as if she were opting for a bowl of soup over an omelette for their supper.

\*

San Francisco wasn't just milk and alcohol though, and even a goer like Wesley, who blew through town for a week in late August, shook his head admiringly at the contents of the cigar box Fintan pulled out back at his room. There was weed from four different states – 'Though nothing as good as Colombian,' Fintan allowed – along with various pills: Seconal, Valium, amphetamines, plus something with codeine, most of which Fintan had scored from Vicki, an ER nurse he had chatted up in a bar shortly after hitting town the previous year. Vicki who eventually took him home to bed, until they both concluded a fortnight later that it wasn't really meant to be.

'The pink ones?' Wesley inquired.

'A painkiller her patients said made them feel like they were flying. Most of it's for a rainy day,' Fintan added. 'Or maybe the odd sunny day, if I'm not working.'

'Morning glories!' Wesley exclaimed two nights later, having spotted the vine of sky-blue flowers trailing across Marianne's kitchen window. Fintan had figured the pair of them might hit it off, given their mutual interest in separate realities – what Wesley described as 'a dozen intersecting vector sets' as he and Fintan walked back to the boarding house.

'And the Heavenly Blue variety are a great body high?' he continued to enthuse from the makeshift bed Fintan had fashioned on a corner of the floor. 'But make sure to ask her for the seeds off the plant, cuz any packet ones are coated with a mercury-based fungicide that'll make you puke like a dog before you get off!'

*

Marianne had Fintan harvest the seeds then, which he stashed in a small plastic baggie inside the cigar box and promptly forgot about. He was doing less stuff anyhow – 'Your good influence,' he teased Marianne one evening, after she remarked how he seemed to be eating better too. But she was having none of that. 'No person can change another, Fintan. We need to do that work for ourselves.'

'Sure, a change is as good as a rest,' he parried – as if *work* were the operative word, and hadn't he enough of that already?

But Marianne also brushed that aside in her default Dutch, forthright way. 'You treat life like you're at a party, Fintan, only you're seated on a staircase there, staring at a door that's permanently closed.'

'But nobody does change here,' he had countered, trying to deflect her yet again, the picture of himself on somebody else's bottom steps not altogether inspiring. 'America's all non-stop, everything in motion, yet nothing evolves underneath.' Or was it just California that felt like it didn't suit? The so-called Golden State making him feel far too wired – as if too much free fall were in play – whatever about living along the San Andreas Fault.

At the same time he was managing a bit better, hanging out less in the local laundromat and exploring more of the city itself, even finding an old chapel in the Mission District whose graveyard markers were rife with Irish surnames – a rake of McCarthys – many of whom had escaped the Irish Famine for the California Gold Rush, only to die ten or fifteen years later.

Still drinking true, yet a tad more measured now, and occasionally in the company of Stíofán MacTomáis, an Irish folksinger from Galway, who gigged the odd Saturday at O'Brien's, and struck Fintan as entirely sound. He also dropped into the City Lights Bookstore – to which Wesley had introduced him back in September – and where he in turn took Marianne to hear the American poet Ferlinghetti read that April, a few weeks before Fintan too split town. Not that he had planned to depart quite so precipitously – as if mimicking the Fool, its feet at the edge of a mountain crag on the Tarot card drawn at Marianne's kitchen table three days before he left, seemingly instructing him to eschew all sorrow and anticipation so that the Tarot could emerge.

'You are facing a fresh choice, so you must choose wisely,' said Marianne.

'And look before I leap?' he countered, taking in the bag hanging from a stick over the Fool's shoulder, and a small dog jumping at his feet. Yet only now thinking to tell Marianne of his great-aunt Cassie, with her own fortune-telling deck of cards back at the cottage above the sea in Pier, where the

King of Spades might represent an ambitious master of all trades, and the Queen of Hearts a faithful, fair-haired lover. Along with her bent for *tasseology*, as he now knew – thanks to Wesley – to call Cassie's tea-leaf fortune-telling.

He remembered the morning-glory seeds when he got back to his room that evening, and so ground them up on Friday morning, his day off, stashing the white powder with a small bottle of OJ and a sandwich in his jacket pocket. Hopping a bus across the Golden Gate Bridge to Marin City, he then thumbed a lift along the winding road through Muir Woods to Stinson Beach, where he downed all with the OJ at the Pacific's edge.

The fog had lifted off the sea by the time he too got off, less than an hour later, a bodily high as Wesley had promised, and the surf as it broke on the sand rippling in warm waves down the skin of his forearms, its sound made tactile. He headed down the beach, and then up onto a hiking trail through the woods overlooking the water. The sun was already sinking towards the horizon by the time he turned back, and night beginning to fall, when a car finally lifted him on the road back towards Marin City, dropping him at roadside diner beside which three or four semis were idling in the dark, the exhaust from their upright stack pipes pluming forth like winter's breath.

Still crashing from the crushed seeds, he decided on a short nap before grabbing a bus back, and espying a lone semi-trailer truck at the back of the lot, he quickly mounted the aluminium ladder bolted to its side. Giving the stars one last look, he then conked out flat on his back along its tarpaulin-covered roof.

It was a deep sleep too, so much so that the semi was already pulling out before he remembered where he had lain down, and it was another moment or two before he fully grasped what was in play. Rolling carefully onto his belly, he managed to crawl cautiously forward and grab hold of a rectangular brace along the front edge of the trailer roof as they pulled onto the road, thinking he might be able to clamber safely down the ladder at the first red light.

They hit a string of green lights, however, the truck just trucking on – until before he knew it they were on the Richmond–San Rafael Bridge, crossing San Francisco Bay en route, it would turn out, to Colorado. He thought he was headed for a sure death each time a sharp southwesterly crosswind tried to shift him off the roof, his hands clinging on for dear life. Head down, feet braced, he missed the panoramic view of the night-lit city to his right, never mind the sinuous, street-lamp-lit curve of the bridge snaking out ahead with its bright string of red-white car lights. The winds then eased once back on terra firma, and he managed to hold on for another hour or so, until the truck pulled in at a rest stop somewhere between Vacaville and Sacramento.

'Fuck me!' shouted the tall, brown-eyed, high-cheekboned driver, who was tightening one of the tarpaulin lines when Fintan slowly, painfully, crawled down the ladder. 'Don't tell me you've been up there since fucking Frisco?!'

'Fintan,' Fintan said, 'but I can't shake,' holding up two cramped zombie claws.

'Name's Roland,' said the driver, moving his head in disbelief. 'Man! I feel like I oughta turn around and take you back!'

'Where're we headed?' Fintan asked.

'Colorado.'

'Denver?'

'Nope, not that far, Grand Junction.'

'Can I get a lift?'

'Fuck me!' Roland said again. 'But in the cab this time, man, OK?'

*

*You were spot-on about the Fool,* he wrote to Marianne on Sunday, *and if you can send on the wee duds from my room, I'll send you the postage once I've work. The cigar box of assorted treats you can save for Wesley, who's due back in Frisco next month.* O'Brien he had already spoken to on Saturday afternoon, shortly before he was due to show up for his evening shift, ringing from the first public phone he could find after Roland had dropped him off on Grand Street, though it was nothing grander than he'd seen in Butte, whose mountains now loomed in the distance. Whereas Grand Junction sat in the middle of the Grand Valley – as if they couldn't get enough of a good thing when naming the place – which was just grand with him as well.

O'Brien had taken his two-hours-in-lieu-of-two-weeks'-notice surprisingly well, saying that the regulars would miss him, and telling him to 'mind yourself up there in the High Country'.

He found work by Monday, hired on as a janitor at St Mary's Hospital. Hired on the spot, he suspected, for being Irish, the personnel head, Mrs Sullivan, informing him how the hospital had been founded by two nuns from the Irish

Sisters of Charity, who had braved smoky saloons back in the 1880s, soliciting donations from cowboys and gamblers for a new hospital in town.

Nor was it the first time being Irish had given him a leg up Stateside, the curiosity factor of his accent helping out more than once when being interrogated by the police for hitchhiking – 'Are you carrying any weapons?' Or standing another time alongside a cruiser, blue lights flashing around his head, until a computer check over its shortwave radio came back: 'Negative on your subject.' Having his US-citizenship paperwork underway had likewise served him well. That said, he'd messed up a few years back – had brought a halt to his gallop en route from Texas back up to California when, half-tight, he'd parroted a state trooper's 'No fixed abode' back at him – and so got to spend a night in the county jail in Gallup, New Mexico.

Heartened by the hospital's history, he settled easily into the job, which came with a small room at the back of the main building with a single bed and hotplate, thanks once again to Mrs Sullivan. His supervisor Leo, a slight, taciturn World War II vet with a missing pinkie finger, informed him on his first day how the hospital incinerator could burn a body within three minutes. Leo looked and sounded like a drinker too, which hardly helped his embittered mien, but Fintan had by age twenty-eight encountered sufficient foremen to simply get on with the job and Leo both. What's more, the patent hardship manifest on the hospital wards offered a certain perspective on his own quotidian well-being, such that by July he had begun to feel himself cohere somewhat – as if the very wind that had endeavoured to pitch him off a semi-trailer-roof in May might've also dispersed some of the interior smoke and shadow that Marianne had told him he needed to dispel.

*The landscape here*, he wrote to her early in August, *is also helping me regroup*, describing the high-desert sunsets that looked like massive vermilion oil spills, or the majestic mesas on the horizon north and southeast of the town, which itself sat on the cottonwood-lined Colorado river. Plus the towering red-stone monoliths to the west, which he had explored several times – like hiking through a movie set – though the ubiquitous sagebrush up close, pale green and aromatic, looked nothing like the bleached, skeletal bits that had blown across his cinematic childhood back in Donegal. And the spiked yucca flowers reminded him of the foxglove his mother had loved back home, only ten times bigger, making him feel surprisingly at home on the range.

He was also drinking less, an occasional cold beer on a hot summer evening, then nothing more for days at a time, along with *keeping a lower pharmacokinetic profile*, a bit of St Mary's-speak he'd overheard on the wards and scribbled down by way of good advice on a postcard to Wesley, who, it seemed, had moved in with Marianne back in San Fran.

There was no woman in his own life now, though he got on well with most of the nurses he saw on his work shifts, while begging off politely both times his hospital benefactor, Mrs O'Sullivan, had invited him to a family supper. Nor did he see anyone closer than acquaintances outside work, including the dozen heads at a storefront Zen-meditation circle where he occasionally dropped in, having found a paperback on Buddhism at a nearby second-hand bookshop.

He took note too of a near neighbour on a front lawn not far from the hospital, a bloke in his fifties in a wheelchair with a plaid lap rug, even on the hottest days, such that Fintan couldn't gauge whether he still had his legs or not. And of course bringing to mind his St Louis boss, Will, whose now well-scuffed boots Marianne had posted on from San Francisco.

Still, Fintan didn't feel isolated – nor anything approaching lonesome – knowing that, once again, he was only passing through town, as trucker Roland might've been aiming his rig most anywhere. Grand Junction, in other words, being a town chosen entirely at random, a town that he felt – by the time he got the urge for going, the September aspens having gone all yellow and gold – had offered him a small, yet benevolent, junction of his own.

# 12

Picture Fintan once again, this time halfway down the Kaibab Trail in the Grand Canyon, where the faint sound of someone fanning themselves in the otherwise utter quiet stops him short, only to see that it is but a raven's distant wingbeat. The late-afternoon silence is a match for the stunning geological architectonics, the dark cloud-shadows that further fracture the tangerine rock face, or the trail dust that has coated Will Woodward's boots with a copper-coloured powder. It takes him two-hours-plus to cover the seven miles downhill to the wee suspension bridge across the Colorado river, then on to a small deserted campsite where he lays out his ground-cloth.

He wakes sometime after 3 a.m., having been cautioned by a National Park Ranger on the south rim – who'd also kindly gifted him a large plastic bottle of water – to start the four-hour trek back up well ahead of the blistering July heat. And so he takes in the stars on the river below some fifteen minutes later, startles two mule deer an hour farther on, and marvels at the sunrise that surfaces minutes later, its dry, rose-pink mist briefly colouring the canyon walls until, like the deer, it too evanesces.

Then, an hour or so shy of the top, he suddenly spots it – a supple, eighteen-inch string of yellowish-brown arabesques, making its way slowly down the steep trail just ahead. Sensing Fintan, it slides into the rocks on the canyon-side of the path, and pauses then with some seven inches of its tail still exposed. Thinking it makes no sense to have come this far out west only to watch it glide silently by, he leans down to ensure its head is sufficiently entwined within the rocks, before he gently touches its lower back, marvelling at the coolness of its scaly skin and how mad its rattles sound, not unlike the clappers on Uncle Condy's alarm clock back in Donegal. And he takes care too, ten minutes on, to advise a descending trio of Germans to keep an eye out for a pissed-off, poisonous sidewinder on the trail below.

*

Phoenix, Arizona had been first port of call upon departing Grand Junction the previous October. Its balmy winter weather proved a treat, but what felt like high-summer heat by mid-May saw him call it quits on yet another gig – delivery man for a furniture warehouse – then pack his bag the following night, as a locust rattled round within the lampshade overhead. Truth be told, he was not that gone either on the ubiquitous spiders in his rented room. Having to keep an eye out for black widows, while also trying to remember to check his shoes each morning for scorpions, who were given to sleeping in footwear overnight. Even the crickets, which had charmed his Wisconsin carney-nights, now sounded too stridently outside his window – as if reminding folks how the low desert they both now inhabited had once belonged to their kind alone, and might well again one day.

He'd knocked about the Southwest for several months then, including Santa Fe for a fortnight, before drifting down to Carlsbad. Then northwest up to Flagstaff by early September – high-desert country like Grand Junction, only a half-mile higher at seven thousand feet, the mountains to the north a mere ten miles away. He had smiled to himself upon seeing how Uncle Condy's Route 66 also doubled as Main Street – all but demanding that he pull up here. And so it did feel, if not like home, then like something approaching familiar: Ponderosa pines, autumnal aspens once again yellow and orange, and yet another storefront Zen centre thrown into the mix to help him remember to *be there now.*

*

The Zen centre was also where, six or so weeks later, he met a painter named Rachel. 'Today's my thirtieth,' she offered in an off-handed manner on their first night out – to a film, Wim Wender's *Paris, Texas* plus a single cocktail after. Fintan couldn't recall what Wesley had no doubt spouted about Libras, nor did the two years Rachel had on him matter in the slightest. Tall, light-boned, long brown hair and brown eyes behind tortoise-shell glasses, soft-spoken, yet quietly tenacious in what she voiced – all of it reason enough by the evening's end for Fintan to think about staying on in Flagstaff. He began so to look for something better than his half-time hardware-clerk post that just about covered his weekly rented room and some street-running money. And he shortly found something far better too – with a diesel-trucking outfit this time – which allowed him to upgrade from his single-room occupancy to a small one-bedroom flat with central air and a swimming pool.

He called by Rachel's studio a few days after their night out, a compact, squat adobe building with sliding, east-facing glass doors, plus three Velux skylights in the tiled roof. Rachel answered the door in a pair of striped denim overalls, its encrusted layer of acrylic paints like the variegated plastic skin of some brightly coloured alien life form – only in this instance, one with a genuinely welcoming smile.

Having asked him in, she proceeded to walk him round the studio space with its easels, cork boards, workbench with tins and tubes of paint, plus a corner bookcase crammed with art volumes. Captivated by it all, he tried not to ask too many questions, instead listened intently as Rachel spoke a few words about a large canvas propped against two wooden saw-horses in the middle of the floor. 'You need committed indifference when painting,' she informed him – albeit offhandedly, like she were talking of the best way to boil spuds. 'You don't want to always run with the first image.' After which she spoke as briefly about the colours – chartreuse, ochre, salmon and citrine – of what looked like a fractured cactus, two of its five arms at utterly loose ends, and the remaining trio more or less akimbo.

'But best to remember, if you want to make art, cut off your tongue' – advice from Matisse, it seemed.

'Who must've been having a Van Gogh moment?' Fintan had offered, prompting a laugh from Rachel, after which she brought out a coffee each from one of two small rooms at the back, where, he gathered, she ate and slept. They drank them on wooden folding chairs outside the glass doors, Rachel telling a little about her childhood, of a twin brother, Arthur, who now taught literature at some college back in Plattsburgh, New York, where they grew up, two cosseted kids of middle-class, non-religious Jewish parents. And of how she had felt so guilty about not attending a Saturday synagogue that she had stood up in Fifth Grade one Monday, along with two or three Christian classmates, when their born-again teacher asked who hadn't gone to church on Sunday.

Coffee finished, they made a date for the following Friday, Halloween as it happened, after which Fintan departed, along with a book on Edward Hopper, whose painting of a woman seated alone in an empty cinema had caught his eye in a San Francisco museum the previous year.

Walking back home that night, he thought again of how differently you talk with women – what he had first discovered with Carla back in St Louis. And wondering once more, had he a sister instead of a brother, would they have done some of that too? And if so, might he have penned a letter in lieu of the postcard he'd sent Frankie two days before, a few lines saying how he'd found more work, while hoping Frankie and their father were keeping well? Not a word of what he might've liked to ask – had Frankie managed any joy up at the old schoolhouse with the South African lass, Nicole? Or how in hell was he able to stick the Glen after his time away in swinging London? The kind of heart-to-heart stuff he and his brother had rarely indulged in – as if *indulge* were the operative word here.

Meanwhile he and Rachel took their time in becoming lovers – Fintan half-thinking they might simply remain friends, as Dutch Marianne and he had done back in North Beach. And so it was Rachel who made the first move, taking Fintan by the hand into the tiny bedroom at the back of the studio a day after Thanksgiving, where they lay together on the thickest mattress he'd ever encountered – a *futon*, Rachel called it – which she had unrolled onto the floor. And only afterwards, propped up side by side against several pillows, had he seen the wee tattoo of a bird on her stomach, its long beak sipping nectar from her navel.

'Yes, a hummingbird,' she confirmed, 'only they actually drink with a grooved tongue, not their beak' – after which she gifted him yet another word, *gorget*, for the ring of brightly coloured feathers around its neck.

'You actually drew it?' he'd then marvelled, a tattoo – no matter how finely drawn – being the last thing he might've expected to encounter beneath Rachel Kreiger's blouse.

'It seemed a healthier alternative than to carry on cutting myself,' she offered with a rueful smile.

'Cutting yourself?' he asked, the first he had ever heard of such a practice.

'With a razor just, no steak knife,' she replied, adding a gentle smile at his indrawn breath before pointing to a laddered series of faint, white scars higher up her abdomen, like the broken lines of an I Ching hexagram. 'Let's just say adolescence wasn't all that easy.'

'Did you use a mirror for it?' he quickly asked, pointing at the hummingbird.

'I did,' she said, brightening. 'A small round shaving mirror my dad kept in his sock drawer. Plus professional inks.'

'No hummingbirds in Ireland,' Fintan offered, 'just the odd hummingbird moth,' information courtesy of *Ireland's Flora Fauna*, which his mother, Mary had brought back from the used-books stall at the Carrick sheep fair.

'Kids didn't have time to be self-harming in Ireland either, I bet?'

'No way,' he smiled, tracing the tattoo with a forefinger, 'too busy cutting turf.'

'She sounds lovely, your mother,' Rachel said after they had dressed and, donning coats against the chill, stepped out for the last of the sunset.

'Aye,' he replied. Then 'heart failure' in answer to her next query.

And then as he was leaving: 'You must be joking. It was lovely, Rachel,' after she thanked him for following her to bed.

It began to snow lightly on the way back to his apartment, first of the season for Flagstaff, though snow had sat on the Peaks overshadowing the town since late September. The soft, flaky fall against the streetlamps put him in mind of home, in mind of Packy for some reason – thinking how he too had suffered in some fashion from heart failure – as if he were able to view his father with more clarity at this distance, with more charity even. Not only how often Packy had made a mess of something – no more adept at helping Mary rear their two sons than he'd been in training Shep the dog – but how he'd also lacked the wherewithal, courage or confidence to chance more of some undertaking that might've possibly rewarded him in turn.

Yet he spoke some more about Packy to Rachel through the winter months. And of Carla too, for the first time to anyone – never mind to another lover – even if both of them knew they were only passing through one another's lives. Telling her after the third time they made love, just before Christmas, how she was the first woman he had lain with since Carla's death whose caress hadn't made him contract, 'close up like that plant whose leaves furl when touched?'

'Mimosa,' Rachel said, running a forefinger along his collarbone as they lay on the spread futon. 'It's one of the stars in the Southern Cross too.'

'My mate Wesley and I saw that for the first time last year,' Fintan said. 'Lying flat on our backs in the Golden Gate Park one night after we'd smoked a joint.'

'But you can't see the Southern Cross from San Francisco!' Rachel smiled.

'Yeah, I read that later myself somewhere.'

'Carla sounds lovely,' Rachel offered after a while, choosing again the present tense.

'She was, surely' – as if he were once again lying half-naked with a sister in lieu of a lover, only it somehow seemed OK. And so he told of having bolted from St Louis upon learning of Carla's death three winters before, of seeing her then seated on a guard-rail stanchion outside Platte City, and how two nights later he had heard on the radio – high up in the cab of a kind-hearted trucker, Herschel, who'd lifted him half-frozen on I-80, east of Rawlins, Wyoming – some singer recounting how he too was on a Western highway, hearing his lover's voice on every radio station, herself promising they'd meet again, when standing by the sea.

And finally, telling before they both drifted off, of the pay phone later that spring, outside an Exxon garage in San Jose, where he had lasted a week only pumping gas. Of how that phone had rung late one night as he was locking up, and how this time he'd answered it – Carla not there to advise him against tempting fate, as she had done down Texas way. And how, blue handset pressed to his ear, he'd failed to make out through the static any trace of his lost love singing 'Wish You Were Here' down the line.

*

The diesel-trucking work went well, with plenty of overtime, enough anyhow to get himself another set of wheels in early January: a cherry-red, 1972 Oldsmobile Delta 88, which Fintan loved for its brand name alone – it being far from deltas that he'd been reared. Better yet, the fellow mechanic, Joey, who sold him it, told over a beer one night after work how his maternal grandmother had grown up in St Joseph, Missouri, next door to the house where, on an April 1882 morning, Jesse James had taken a bullet in the back of his head as he went to straighten a picture on the wall, and for all Joey knew, his granny, seven years old at the time, might've heard the shot as well.

That tale of course led to another round, during which Fintan told Joey of a story Texarkana's uncle Johnny, himself a returned Yank pedlar, had brought back to the Glen before Texarkana too went over beyond. A tale of yet another crowded boarding house, this time somewhere in Kentucky, whose proprietor had asked Johnny whether he would mind sharing a room. He'd have a bed of his own though – unlike

Fintan's great-granda on his last night alive in Missouri – plus a roommate with a Colt .44, who then proceeded to lay crumpled-up newspapers from the door to his own bed after Johnny turned in. And who was still propped up on his pillow, smoking a cigarette, revolver in his other hand, when Johnny briefly awoke a few hours later. In the morning they spoke some, during which Johnny alluded to your man's precautions.

'There's many a man who'd like to kill me.'

'And why is that?' Johnny asked.

'You've heard of Jesse James?'

'Aye, surely,' Johnny replied, 'but that man's dead?'

'You've heard of Frank James so?' Jesse's elder brother then inquired.

Fintan was no longer sure he believed the story, but a delighted Joey insisted on another pitcher of beer. However, it happened Joey had himself purchased the 1972 cherry-red Delta 88 five years previous from none other than Flagstaff's sheriff, and by the third time Fintan got pulled over by a deputy sheriff – curious as to who was now driving Sheriff Brown's Olds – he figured the car to be more trouble than it was worth, especially should he happen to have a joint rolled, or an opened bottle of beer in the front seat.

'Yup, guess I forgot to mention that,' Joey said with a grin when Fintan asked about it at their lunch break three weeks later. 'Had that same little sheriff problem myself.'

And so, come February, Fintan traded it in for a far smaller Honda Civic hatchback, which proved every bit as dull a car as it sounded. But then, hadn't Jesse James's older brother Frank gone the same way too, he told himself, having spent his final years working as a night watchman or shoe salesman, when not selling tickets to see the inside of the James brothers' family home at 50¢ a head.

The trucking job offered dental care too, of which Fintan availed after the nerve in an impacted molar had begun to sing out 24/7. Plus they had a bowling team, which he likewise signed up for – as if he'd grown up anywhere near a bowling alley.

Still, he thought often of Donegal, of what he might be missing there – like the two empty wooden crates that old Jack Gara's uncle Michael, fishing from the rocks below Scrigg Mor, had failed to lasso, either jetsam or flotsam from a ship somewhere far out to sea. And how Jack still wondered all these decades on just what those crates – which had washed back out on the following tide – might've contained. Not that there was much to miss there in the back of beyond, or so Fintan now told himself, as the memory of a skinned rabbit hung to dry inside Jack's turf shed suddenly flashed upon his inner eye, flesh slowly mutating from pink to reddish-black, a wingless fly stuck to its neck.

*

Rachel had simply laughed when Fintan asked early in March whether she might want to go bowling with him. Just like Jo-Ann had done back in Cleveland, how many years ago? He totted them up – eight – and thinking it a miscount, added them up again. Odd how he'd taken up with a primary-school art teacher and a practising artist both – or maybe not so odd at all? Yet he doubted Rachel and he would be an item, had he not first been tutored in the pictorial arts by Jo-Ann, those lazy

Sunday afternoons strolling through the Cleveland Museum, while she spoke of whatever caught her eye. He said little now to Rachel about her own painting, an occasional question only, but listened intently to whatever she too chose to share. Of how the Impressionists loved to paint scenes of snow – "Cuz they could put so much colour in the stuff!' Or how the hues of the early-spring Arizona landscape actually worked, say: the manner in which the grass on a Sunday picnic out towards the Humphrey Peaks had first looked golden and white, then brownish against the pale March sky.

'What colour would you call it?' he had asked Rachel.

'Yellow ochre – but it's only that colour on account of the colours around it. Those brown tree trunks behind,' she said, pointing. 'Plus the blue sky and the sunlight,' she added, pointing overhead.

'So something is a particular colour depending on its neighbouring shades?' he puzzled aloud.

'Sorta.' She smiled. 'Though opticians will tell you there's also such a thing as "colour constancy".'

She loaned him books from her studio too, a massive *History of Art* that he could at best thumb through, along with smaller works on individual artists: Georgia O'Keefe, Albert Ryder, Frida Kahlo and another on Kahlo's Diego Rivera, with colour plates of his Mexico City murals, his wife Frida holding a book of Marx and Engels, while a priest dallies with a prostitute next to a gaggle of the moneyed class.

Then, one evening, waiting for Rachel to change out of her paint-smeared gear, he discovered on her bottom bookcase shelf a slim, sky-blue volume on the life of the painter Randall Hart.

'He lived on a farm in upper Vermont state, not far from where I grew up,' Rachel said when he showed it to her. Then, 'You must be joking?' when he told her of Hart's time in Glenelg.

'I think I knew he'd lived in Ireland,' she said, shaking her head at Fintan, 'but I can't believe it was in your village?!'

'Not exactly in the village,' he said, describing for her the small townland on the sea where Mary Cunnea had grown up, and the further glen behind Pier Hill where Hart had stayed for a year.

'Did your mother know him?'

'Oh, aye,' he said, but nothing about the painting the American professor said Hart had done of her.

Taking the book back to his apartment, he read over the next several nights of Hart's peripatetic life, of forays to Alaska, Newfoundland and Greenland to live and paint, same as he'd done in Donegal, plus a sailing trip as far afield as Tierra del Fuego. There were few illustrations in the book, however, and nothing from his Glenelg sojourn. The book also made something of a meal of the various hats Hart had worn in his roving life, or so Fintan thought – sailor, lobsterman, farmer, flute-player, gravedigger and social activist, as well as painter, though you could say the same about many a man in Glenbay, provided you left out the painterly or revolutionary bent. Take his own old buck Packy even – weaver, farmer and fisherman, if less of a dab hand as a roofer, dog-trainer, father or family man.

It seemed Hart also had run afoul of the US government in the late 1940s, having made no secret of his admiration for the USSR at a time when many Americans were sleeping poorly for fear of the Commies hiding under their beds. Hart's passport had then been revoked in 1950, until a court case found in his favour the following year, shortly after which the painter had decamped for Donegal. Fintan for his part had learned a little about the McCarthyism of that era from Wesley down Texas way – the kind of simple-minded, black-and-white codology that many Yanks excelled in – and which a few decades on would see more than one Irish American dig deep in his pockets to support the Provisional IRA.

Fintan had then got word of Wesley the following day, a letter from Marianne in Oaxaca, Mexico, where she and Wesley had landed early in the new year: *I worry about W ... he's very low and yet just goes, goes, all the time ... and I'm afraid he will burn out ...* He wrote back to Marianne that night – of having read recently about a painter who'd put him in mind of Wesley – not just the left-wing politics, but the stripped-down life, the way Yanks like Hart and Wesley eschewed most creature comforts, never mind all the 'stuff' that Fintan himself, now nine years in America, still could not get his head around. The tonnes of crap people bought, half of it plastic, the purchases piling up between a self and a life as it might otherwise be lived.

After pausing to roll a spliff, he proceeded to describe for Marianne the four dead mice he had discovered early one morning at the Food Co-op back in St Louis, drowned in a five-gallon vat of honey that someone had forgot to close: *And America seems like that a lot of the time, too rich a mix, too much shite, too much, too easily accessed ...* And then: *Tell Wesley to pull out his chessboard and make himself a few bob under a palm tree in the park* before he decided to call it a night.

He rarely mused aloud over such with Rachel – herself well-practised in the positives of a stripped-down life – plus there were other things to talk of. Like what exactly was a *lithographer* or a *silk screen* when he, she or it was at home? – all of it lingo he had first come across in the book on Hart.

Whereas Rachel might occasionally inquire after his family, asking 'Did your dad drink?' one night as he walked her back from a bar and single nightcap as Rachel called it, following yet another film, *Five Easy Pieces* this time. 'More of a binger,' he told her. 'He'd go wild for a week, drink nothing then for a month or more.'

And 'What flowers did your mom like?' two days later, after Fintan had chanced looking over her shoulder at the large, floral-patterned canvas with its shards of desertscape, which had commandeered her for several weeks in a row. 'Daffodils,' he replied, seeing as he did so their yellow heads dancing either side of the cottage door where Mary had planted them, as if lording it over the diminutive primroses that also bloomed in March on the verges of the lane down to the road.

He knew better other days – her long brown, braided hair coiled atop her head – than to look over at her easel, sensing the work was not going so well. But she never said as much, would say little about anything then, though he could usually coax her out for an evening walk in the county park full of Ponderosa pines a few miles south of town.

*

The following Sunday they took in a spring equinox party at his workmate Joey's bungalow – or *ranch house*, as the Yanks called them. The party had been Joey's pencil-thin, shaven-headed girlfriend's idea – 'Suzanne's from California,' he informed the gathered party-goers, as if that explained everything.

'The equinox's eighteen hours earlier, this being a leap year!' Suzanne had in turn informed Fintan, who didn't mind either way, having happily passed up a Paddy's Day party thrown by another workmate, Paul, complete with green beer, three days before.

'The vernal equinox determines the start of Passover,' Rachel had then tutored him in turn, balancing a paper plate of barbequed ribs in Joey's backyard, which bordered the train tracks that more or less bisected Flagstaff. 'Along with your Easter Sunday.'

'Not really my Easter anymore,' Fintan replied, while robbing a rib. 'Nor ever really your Passover, was it?'

The party moved indoors once the moon rose, not long after a freight train had thundered past some twenty yards beyond the chain-link fence, a long line of multicoloured boxcars with an odd flatcar thrown in for good measure, its whistle evoking the 'wayward sound of the outward bound' of which Texarkana had sung back home in Molly's pub. The sound like a long drawn-out audio cue for the restlessness that had been slowly accreting within, and which now washed suddenly through him.

'You're one of us so,' Rachel said when he confessed as much on their walk back from the party sometime after 2 a.m. 'Just another wandering Jew.' Telling him then, before a goodnight kiss at her studio door, of some Hungarian novelist she had read, who argued how Jews were attached to what was international and therefore portable, be it theories, art or revolution – attached to anything but the soil.

'Better a wandering Jew than another Irish rover,' he smiled, as if the latter did not describe him to down to the ground. Still, her parting shot felt like a blessing of sorts as he made his way slowly back to his flat – the possibility that primacy of place might not pertain to him – for all his seeming belief that one more town in yet another state might finally sort him out. And if not, there was always the open road.

Whatever the case, the West he had first set his sights and heart on as a kid – and had criss-crossed since for nearly a decade now – no longer held him as tightly as it had. That said, he'd nonetheless stood stock-still earlier at the party when Josh, a pal of Joey's just blowing through town himself, told of how his 92-year-old grandfather had once travelled the riverboats along the upper Missouri, its banks either side still festooned with ten thousand tepees of the Lakota. And told too of a riverboat skipper, Captain Massie, who had shown his grandad a scar on his left arm – from the bullet that had passed through Wild Bill Hickok's skull at a Deadwood, South Dakota poker table, and into Captain Massie's arm.

'Aces and eights,' Fintan had told Rachel on their walk back. 'A dead man's hand.'

'Or alpha and omega. Or who knows – alpha and eternity sign, depending on how his cards spilled onto the table?'

'Eternity sign?'

'You know,' tracing it for Fintan on the night air. 'A lazy eight? *Lemniscate* is its proper name, I think?'

'Oh yeah!' he laughed, 'that's the word all right!' Only wondering again as they neared his apartment, whether the

Old West was arguably better apprehended from afar? From across the Atlantic Ocean say, back in the 1950s and '60s, than from America itself.

\*

Nor had he dreamt that night of freight-hopping a train – himself and Woody Guthrie sitting hobo-style – in an empty flatbed railcar leaving Flagstaff. Had dreamt instead that he was back high up in a tractor-trailer cab with Herschel, the kindly trucker of whom he'd again spoken to Rachel earlier that night. Herschel who had lifted him on I-80 near Rawlins, Wyoming, three years before, three days after word of Carla's death had set him running west. Herschel, broad forehead and prominent cheekbones, who'd pointed out the wind playing on the snow along a culvert, or the sun cutting diamonds on the ice-laced trees. And Herschel who'd been happy just to be moving, not caring what he was carrying. 'Freight!' he had replied when Fintan asked. 'As long as the wheels are turning, I'm making money.'

Yet Herschel also knew money wasn't really the answer either: 'It's what people want when they can't find what they need.' Fintan couldn't follow it all over the din of the cab-over engine, but he got the gist of it: of how the steering wheel was his weathervane, its play telling him which way the wind was blowing. And how the slipstream from a tractor-trailer bequeaths 10 or 15 mph to a car following in its wake.

Played out from the late-night party, he took a nap after work on Monday. Crashed in his clothes onto the unmade bed, to dream of someone slain by a rifle shot, their body falling into a river as several horsemen behind a shadowy tree suddenly splashed through the water to the nearer bank, their tunics a blood-red against a surreal, blue-lit sky.

He awoke shortly after, the light a yellow-green blend on darker cloud, as faint footsteps sounded across the apartment courtyard below, as if someone were trying to beat the storm home. Looking out, he saw the wind-tossed leaves of the courtyard acacia turning to greet the first of the rain – all of it as unaccountably strange and surreal as if he had not awakened at all.

The following evening after work, he drove his second-hand Honda to a landfill north of the city, backing it up to the steep, cutaway edge, before throwing down into the pit below those clothes surplus to requirements culled from his apartment closet, along with a yard-sale 8-track tape player, small portable ice chest, his bowling ball, plus a good-as-new pair of bowling shoes. He might've tossed in both swimming pool and central air conditioning from his apartment complex had he been able, but he stopped short of pushing the Honda over the edge, figuring he could leave it kerbside in the city centre, keys in the ignition for some enterprising pedestrian, once he'd removed the licence plates.

'If you've got the cash,' he told Rachel that evening, 'America's got the trash – isn't that how the song goes?' Yet thinking now how he might've given most of it to a charity shop instead, had his dream the night before – the wind on the window and the far-out light beyond – not spooked him so. Only for Rachel to slowly shake her head, hair swaying slightly, before taking him by the hand for the last time into her tiny bedroom at the back. Afterwards, over a coffee at the table in the corner of the studio, he told of what he'd read in the art book she'd lent him on Randall Hart – and of his intention to follow it up across the continent to coastal Maine.

'Whatever the reason, I'm at least less like Elvis the Mouse for once,' he offered, having already told her of his carnival summer in Wisconsin six years back, 'scrambling for whatever hole might hide me.'

'You take care, Finny,' Rachel said, hugging him at the door. 'And drop a line when you can.'

'Will do,' he promised – hoping that he actually might. 'And you mind yourself too.'

It took him another two days to ditch the day job, the chief mechanic Maddy less than best-pleased and workmate Joey sorry to see him go. Thinking he was unlikely to hop a freight train, he instead rang an auto driveaway outfit Wesley had mentioned, who happened to have a Ford Thunderbird in Albuquerque, New Mexico, belonging to a doctor moving to Little Rock, Arkansas. And it was his to deliver there – provided he could present himself by midday Monday, along with a valid driver's licence and $90 in cash as a refundable deposit. Albuquerque was 300 miles due east of Flagstaff, from where another 900 miles would see him and the Thunderbird in Little Rock by Wednesday afternoon, where there just might be another driveaway headed in the general direction of New England. And so by Sunday midday he was already as far as Winslow, Arizona, duffle bag over his left shoulder, right thumb out, on the road again.

# 13

It takes Fintan six months to get to Maine then, having still not shaken his rambling nature. Nor is there any driveaway car heading north when he hits Little Rock that March – just a flatbed Ford destined for a Gainesville, Florida, car dealer, which he duly delivers. Only it turns out the car dealer, Larry, also has a half-share in a Computa-Tune garage, which is looking for a mechanic – short-term if needs be. 'I don't know diddly-squat about computers,' Fintan tells Larry, lingo learned during his carney summer. But Larry allows in turn as how 'the computers are mostly a hustle', so Fintan signs up till early June – only to stay on till late September.

Florida proves hot and humid both, but he has a tiny rented lakeside cabin just outside the town, plus the use of an old Pinto from the garage, and so is happy enough to add a few dollars more to the roll of $50s he keeps stashed in a jar under the cabin steps. Meanwhile, the computerised car-tuning bit, even if mostly a wheeze, is also something new to learn, and his workmates are mostly a likeable bunch, not least Carmen, a raven-haired Costa Rican desk jockey who answers the phone and keeps the books, all at 85 miles an hour. 'Keep your shirt on!' Fintan shouts when she bugs him for the parts and labour on a repair bill, though he's not entirely sure he means it. But her shirt stays on either way – for Fintan anyhow – as Carmen has a Cuban fiancé, Carlos, with whom she's constantly quarrelling over the phone in Spanish.

He comes so to think of Florida as being in a different country to Arizona, the way one chunk of America can seem to another, the entire nation just too bloody big for starters. But Fintan falls big time for the southern Florida ethnic blend that he encounters on a quick skite down to Miami over the Memorial Day weekend. Then once again on a longer Fourth of July foray halfway down towards Key West: the mix there a mélange of Black, white and Caribbean, plus a smattering of those affluent snowbirds who used to migrate winters down from the cold northeast, only to forget to fly home one spring.

*

Still, his Maine mission began to tug at him again towards the end of September, and so, like a snowbird in reverse, he packed in the Computa-Tune gig and signed up to deliver yet another car – a Cadillac Seville this time, comfortable and smooth-riding as an ocean liner – clear up to New Hampshire. So comfortable is it that he had his shoes shucked on the second night somewhere south of Rocky Mount, North Carolina, having read somewhere how the additional sensory load generated by bare feet on petrol and brake pedals can help keep you awake behind the wheel, though he reckoned it were likely illegal in most states. He pulled in then at an all-night service station on Interstate 95 near Richmond, Virginia, where he winced at the thirst of the gas-guzzling Caddy, managing another eighty or so miles north before turning into a lay-by just above Ladysmith, Virginia, for some shut-eye.

The following midnight found him crashing on the sofa of retired North Conway, New Hampshire firefighter Daryl Smyth, whose sister Muriel had passed away down in Daytona Beach two months back, leaving him her Caddy Seville. He slept soundly too – until 3.17 a.m., per the red numerals on a coffee-table clock, when a freight train passing out back had shaken the entire tiny, wooden house, its whistle shortly after down the line sounding like a bird's cry on a breeze, as if trying to shunt him clear back across America to that Flagstaff backyard party.

Still awake, he wondered out of nowhere whether Condy had ever hopped a freight train, something he had never thought to inquire of all he'd endeavoured to prise out of his uncle about his time Stateside. Then, recalling, with a final, faint echo of the train's whistle, Wesley in Laredo telling of a Louisiana flatcar he had jumped in his teens once for a laugh – before the razor-wired railyards, sealed boxcars and mace-carrying railroad bulls put paid to a once-storied mode of transport.

*

The following Friday night found Fintan in the small back bedroom of a double-gabled farmhouse halfway down the St George peninsula in mid-coast Maine – its red scaffold-ringed barn and two Jersey cows out back, and out front a single, towering elm like no tree in southwest Donegal. One hundred and forty-odd miles east of North Conway, the last ten miles of which he had travelled in an old Volvo sedan with his present host, Karl Larsson, a short, bespectacled, moustached, first-generation Swedish American who was a secondary-school history teacher and part-time farmer both.

'Early New England poverty,' Karl said at breakfast the next morning, gesturing at the ramshackle kitchen décor, mismatched chairs and untidy pile of newspapers next to a sagging couch beside the range. 'Complete with Down East accent,' although Fintan had not remarked on a twang that would give the deep Southern drawl he'd heard in Mississippi a run for its money. Fact is he was already feeling remarkably at home, as Karl served him a bowl of porridge on the scarred wooden kitchen table, offering him a cup of tea instead of the ubiquitous American coffee, then topping it off by pulling out a pipe.

Better yet, the talk turned next to solid fuel, Karl keen to hear about turf-cutting – its turning, footing and bagging on the bog – though Packy had rarely bothered with the last, preferring to turf the sods straight into a trailer behind Rory's da's grey Ferguson tractor, which looked – whatever the odds – like an identical twin of the old grey Ferguson that Fintan would spot an hour later inside Karl's barn.

Karl had quizzed him some about Ireland in the car the day before – curious about its pre-colonial history – of which Fintan parroted what he could recall of Miss Carr's history class at the Tech. Miss Carr whose blonde ponytail and lively eyes had undoubtably helped focus most of the Fifth- and Sixth-Year lads. 'And the current state of things?' Karl queried, to which Fintan quoted Jack Gara from his last short visit home: 'Ireland is nothing but a den of thieves and robbers, hypocrites and hoors.'

Karl then told Fintan of another Irish drifter, Conn, who'd lived nearby in a small shack when Karl was a kid. Given to drink, he crawled one night into the local Protestant minister's Studebaker, wrapping himself up with a blanket found within. Outraged by the overgrown lump on his back seat the next morning, the minister had demanded, 'And who pray tell are you?!' 'I'm Cornelius O'Leary of County Cork,' countered Conn, 'and who might you be, sir?'

It happened that Karl had begun to replace the worn black-asphalt slates on his barn, so Fintan offered to give him a hand, though his stomach proved somewhat queasy as they worked their way up the roof, nailing down fifteen-inch batten lengths as they went. A glimpse of the iridescent water in a distant cove over the roof-ridge pole helped steady him, however, such that by afternoon he was moving as confidently as a cat on high, or near enough.

The rooftop talk meantime was mighty craic, Karl telling of the large rum boats that used to anchor off the coast in the 1920s and '30s during Prohibition, offloading to enterprising locals who stashed the bottles in lobster pots, to be hoisted up after each clandestine, neighbourly purchase. And how an out-of-state lawman had allowed as to 'how local smugglers were generally nice, though south of NYC they turn nasty'.

They called it a day then as the setting sun made a golden pool of the cove beyond the meadows and trees, climbing down to a supper of minced-beef burgers, boiled peas and spuds, over which Karl finally asked, 'And what brings you to this corner?'

'On the trail of a painter,' Fintan said, albeit hesitantly.

'Oh, we get your kind throughout the year,' Karl said with a smile. 'Only Andy lives across the river,' gesturing with his fork over his shoulder towards the back kitchen window. 'His studio is down the road though,' he added, his head tilting slightly towards the sitting room at Fintan's back.

'Andy?'

'Yes, Andy ... Andrew Wyeth?'

'Don't know of him,' Fintan said. 'It's a deceased painter I'm looking for – Randall Hart?'

'Ah, the commie Randall!' Karl smiled. 'It's Monhegan island you want then.'

'Yes, next port of call,' Fintan allowed.

'And do you paint yourself?' Karl asked, clearly curious now.

'Only the odd East St Louis warehouse.' Fintan grinned. 'Plus a handful of houses back in San Jose.' Then added, 'No, it's just a book I saw about him back in Flagstaff, which made me curious about where he had hung out up here.' Scant explanation for a journey of some 3,500 miles, but a seemingly satisfied Karl merely mentioned the boat out to Monhegan from Port Clyde at the bottom of the peninsula.

The nine o'clock TV news had pictures that night of a volcano erupting somewhere in Hawaii, putting Fintan in mind of Wesley, and Karl in mind of a small jar of volcanic ash – 'very fine-grained stuff' – that his great-grandfather had brought back to Sweden 'from some place near Java', and now stored 'somewhere in the house', though he gave up looking for it after a futile five-minute search. 'Lay not up for yourself treasures on earth,' he declared, settling back into his sitting-room easy chair, 'where moth and rust destroy. St Matthew,' he added as Fintan grinned.

The following morning, a Sunday, Fintan watched from the barn roof, its new shingles already hot to the touch, as the cove beyond slowly filled with the incoming tide, mirroring the darker green of the surrounding pines and scattered clouds overhead. 'Late for a whip-poor-will,' Karl remarked when Fintan mentioned having heard one from his bed the previous night, its repetitive call like an insistent reminder of something he'd not likely ever forget. 'They're usually en route back to Mexico by now.'

Karl's teaching colleague Walt joined them on Monday afternoon – also somewhere in his early forties, and a dab hand with both the chalk lines and capping shingles. Accepting a cold can of beer before heading home, he told of having no memory of commissioning the faded tarantula tattoo on his left shoulder during a US Navy shore-leave drinking bout in Jackson, Mississippi some twenty-five years before. No recollection at all until his scabbed, sore shoulder lifted the bedsheet too as he finally rose the following afternoon, only to moan 'Oh, no, no, oh, shit, shit, shit …'

'My fiancée dumped me our sophomore year of college,' he continued after declining a second beer, 'so I took my revenge by dropping out to join the Navy. Four years of overseas service, and I'm sure she's sorry still. My buddy Billy got a tattoo that same night in Jackson, of a dog in a navy cap on his forearm. We too were gonna be lifelong pals, though I only knew him for all of four weeks.'

On Wednesday morning Karl offered to show Fintan Cornelius O'Leary's grave, with its small metal marker, in the pauper's section of the local graveyard that afternoon when he got back from school, but keen to carry on, Fintan simply thanked his host for the five bed-nights and heartfelt hospitality. 'Call by on your way back,' Karl offered. 'Just lock the door when you go. Key goes under the stone,' he said, nodding towards Fintan's left foot.

He got a lift straight away then towards Port Clyde with Jonathan, a hippy blow-in from Rhode Island, who took him back to his place near Turkey Pond, its farmhouse dating from 1797, pointing out a gravestone beneath an elm tree in the drive for ALFONSO who died in 1824 IN THE FIFTH YEAR OF HIS AGE. 'Thanks, no,' Fintan then said to an offer of porridge with goat's milk, only to get the latter in a cup of coffee that tasted like pure meat drippings.

Jonathan also showed him the old barn out back, again pointing with pride at a portable, single-piston, gasoline sawmill. '1910!' he exclaimed, firing its engine until it finally engaged, its large circular blade whirring.

'What's that off?' Fintan asked, pointing to a dark grey, three-winged bone hung on the barn wall. 'A vertebra from a whale I saw beached, or its skeleton anyhow, in Newfoundland,' Jonathan replied, not unlike something Wesley might've stuck into his own backpack as a keepsake.

Jonathan and his girlfriend Leibe seemed sound enough, had travelled some themselves and knew America too had its past. But they were also clearly grafters, and not just at milking their herd of goats. Jonathan worked as a landscape gardener for the moneyed summer folks from New York and Philadelphia, plus as a part-time plasterer winters, while Leibe, long brown hair pinned back and floor-length, tie-dyed skirts swapped for slacks, headed off four days a week to her cashier's gig in a Rockland supermarket.

Fintan stayed over that night, with a vegetable curry *sans* goat's milk for supper, though opting this time for a mint tea in lieu of a coffee, along with a savoury slice of homemade carrot cake, another first. Followed then by a water pipe with home-grown weed, Fintan musing, nor for the first time, on all that American hippies shared with the rural Irish: from beards, tattered garments and local grub to a more open mind on the so-called mechanics of cause and effect, never mind a keen interest in the properties of whatever they smoked, the difference between Crowbar and Condor pipe tobacco, say, or Moroccan versus Colombian hash among the younger set.

After a final, communal pipeful, he made his way slowly upstairs to the large foam mattress his hosts had thrown onto an empty bedroom floor, managing to just about admire Leibe's hand-stitched, blue-patterned quilt cover, along with six moon-lit white tiles on the floor beside him, before Morpheus checked in.

\*

The following morning Jonathan dropped him down to Port Clyde at the bottom of the peninsula, passing en route a cluster of dark-red steers whose breed the ex-Rhode Islander didn't know, though he pointed shortly after to a string of Canadian geese heading south overhead, like the crest of a wave pulsing across the sky, as he pulled into the pier for the *Laura B* mailboat to Monhegan island, ten miles offshore.

Fintan's fellow passengers, a small mix of day-trippers, included a chatty Chinese American who told of visiting Dublin once, plus a handful of islanders, one of whom gave him the name of the less costly of the two island inns, were he planning to stay overnight. The sea proved choppy with a brisk northwesterly breeze, but Fintan had been tossed about on the same Atlantic often enough in Packy's far smaller skiff not to pay it any heed.

Monhegan itself then focused him entirely, its colossal granite headlands and wave-washed rocky shore like a sheared-off chunk of southwest Donegal, washed up some three thousand nautical miles east. Granted, the Glen lacked the thick stands of spruce above the sea, but the azure sky, salt air and sun-splashed light on all sides evoked a subtle sense of homecoming, reminding him of something Uncle Condy had once remarked – of only Maine and Ireland having stratified coastal ledges, or some such parlance, suggesting they might have indeed once been conjoined.

There was nothing familiar about the mix of accents on the harbour pier however, nor along the steep gravelled road that wound its way up through the tiny village, overlooked by a lighthouse to the northeast with a small graveyard in its lee. 'One night only, thanks,' he told Mildred at the dark-shingled Monhegan House, stowing his duffle bag in room No. 7 before returning to the reception desk to ask directions to the Herberts' cottage.

'They're summer folk only,' Mildred told him in turn. 'Back in Medfield, Mass, since Labor Day.'

Heart sinking, he tried not to start totting up the days, miles and dollars spent on what looked now like the proverbial goose chase. Tried not to imagine where else he might now be, had he not spotted that slim, blue-spined volume on Rachel's bookshelf.

'It's a painting I was hoping to see there,' he finally managed.

'Oh, you might be in luck yet!' Mildred said. 'One of the schoolteachers, Lynda, house-sits for the Herberts, and I don't think she went inshore this weekend.'

That too felt like the Glen – where the Mildreds and Mauras likely knew the whereabouts (and more) of half the village at any given moment. And sure enough, a short-cut, dark-haired woman a few years younger than himself answered his knock some ten minutes later, peering hesitantly at Fintan through the screen door on the wrap-around porch of the white-clapboarded house overlooking Lobster Cove, only to visibly relax when she heard his accent – as if an unheralded male stranger, possibly intending harm, would not intonate like that.

'It's not here now,' she told Fintan there on the porch. 'It's on loan to an exhibition of Hart's work that opened in California a year ago May, Santa Barbara I think?' Fintan tried calculating how close he'd been to it then, but the distances every which way were entirely too much.

'Would you like a cup of tea before you go?' Lynda then asked, as if having sensed his dismay.

It was a cup of Rolling Thunder, as it happened, having requested whatever she was having herself. 'It's got 23 per cent less tannic acid than tea,' she enthused as she poured, 'and 47 per cent more caffeine than coffee!'

'Yet you can buy it over the counter?' he said with a laugh.

'Absolutely legal.' She smiled back, handing him the box of teabags. 'Makes me feel like my feet are a quarter-inch above the floor after a second cup!'

He looked at the brightly coloured box with its picture of a charging buffalo, thinking what he might've given for it at age ten, of what tiny treasures it might've stored under his bed, out of Frankie's sight.

They spoke some about Hart's work then, of his years painting on the island, of which Fintan hadn't known, and the several paintings that he had gifted his close friends the Herberts, speaking long enough for Lynda to set it all to rights again.

'Boston?' he repeated, as if not trusting his ears.

'Yes, the exhibition was to close there, after Santa Barbara, Columbus, Ohio and Portland here,' pointing out the window as if Maine's onshore capital were only the next townland over.

'And is the Boston exhibition over now?'

'I'm not sure, but there's a brochure here somewhere,' she said, rising from the kitchen table where she'd been removing the seeds from a pile of sunflowers, before pausing to lightly blow the chaff off her palms like some latter-day Demeter.

'You're in luck!' then sounded from the living room – in luck for the second time that day. 'Museum of Art, Boston, September 27th to November 14th.'

Having accepted a gracious supper invitation for 7 p.m., he set out to walk a fair part of Monhegan that afternoon, past what had been Hart's former cottage, then down the rocks to tidal pools, the sea a dark, beguiling shade of blue. Taking care along the cliff edges, he proceeded through a thick pine forest towards the upper end of the island, and back to Monhegan House to read a further chapter of

Graham Greene's *The Comedians* before heading down to the village store for a bottle of red wine.

'Baltimore,' Lynda told him over a starter of crab toes, thanking him again for the wine, which she'd set aside in favour of a chilled bottle of white. Haddock and spuds followed, along with what he'd finally learned to call *zucchini* (not that he'd ever seen a courgette in Glenbay), fried with onion and sun-dried tomatoes. 'Though we moved from there to Pittsburgh when I was twelve.'

'I was already teaching on the mainland,' she said, when he asked how she'd found her way onto the island, 'in Thomaston, when I saw the position advertised.' And 'one year here already' in answer to his next question, 'but I'm not sure I'll have a third year in me!'

'Anything but!' she laughed when Fintan inquired whether she too were a painter. 'Though I'd love to maybe write a children's book someday.' Grounded, he thought, and a kind of gravitas beyond her years, along with a slight tinge of melancholy, but who really knew? She had her own story clearly, but then who didn't? A pair of keen blue eyes as well beneath her cropped black fringe, thin wrists and long fingers, though he tried not focus on any of that, lest he find himself once again in love for the want of it.

They had a slice of blueberry pie next in the living room, where Lynda had laid a fire in the Franklin stove, giving Fintan yet another proper noun for his lexicon, along with a new, gorgeous taste for his palate, the berries frozen from that year's harvest near Boothbay Harbor on the mainland, where she lived summers now till school commenced again, and the Herberts departed south.

He thanked Lynda for the evening, wishing her well with the new school year as a cuckoo clock somewhere upstairs called ten. Outside a smoke-like mist lay over a small meadow beyond, a large white moon on high as he headed back toward Monhegan House, along with a sharpness to the night air which he hadn't felt since Arizona. It had been months since he had made love – and love it had surely been with Rachel – and he wondered now, as he unlocked his door, was it ever the same for a woman, or were they simply able to enjoy a meal and a far-ranging chat without imagining themselves bedward? Or was it simply something he arguably had for schoolteachers – from Miss Carr at the Tech and Jo-Ann of Cleveland to his dearest student teacher, Carla?

\*

The local Maine mainlander who lifts him the next morning from Port Clyde up the peninsula has the name of its dark-red cattle – Devon – the same steers who'd pulled the covered wagons west, or so his lift informs him. It's slow-going from Thomaston then, as if those having passed the Maine state prison on the left as they head southwest are even warier than most about lifting a stranger by the side of the road.

It's past lunchtime so as he enters a diner in Brunswick, where he's only halfway through his burger when a series of phone calls at the check-out counter are followed by the offer of a free meal that had apparently been prepared for an incoming policeman, only for him to have died in a car crash en route. Nor is it surprising, thinks Fintan, that none of his fellow diners are keen to take up the offer of a dead man's meal.

A series of short lifts then sees him as far south as Laconia, New Hampshire, past an empty, snow-dusted drive-in theatre just as both dusk and flurries are falling, its low-cut projection shed, concession stand and smaller screen all the more intimate than its Laredo cousin back at the edge of Highway 35.

Two-plus hours later find him checking into the Boston YMCA on Huntington Avenue, figuring he qualifies still as a youngish man, whatever about the Christian. Only to shake his head at the play of things when the older bloke behind the desk the following morning tells him that the Boston Museum of Fine Arts is only just down the street. 'Go left out the door here, and keep an eye out for it across the way, less than half a mile.' There's no missing it either, its colossal granite-colonnaded entrance set back within right-angled wings to either side. Better yet, if less neoclassical, is the large bronze equestrian statue of a mounted Native American – head and shoulders thrown back and arms out-stretched – that he passes in the forecourt.

The grand stairway up to a massive rotunda with detailed murals is nothing but a pathway to *The Paintings of Randall Hart* for Fintan, who inquires of the first uniformed staff member he sees as to the whereabouts of the exhibition. The two hours that follow then are something dream-like, as he moves slowly through the three interconnected galleries, determined to take in every painting – mountains, seascapes, sunsets, many without figures within – even if a single canvas was what has brought him here. Hart's vast geographical range is nothing short of sprawling, and the placement of paintings mirrors same – Alaska, Greenland, Switzerland,

British Columbia, Tierra del Fuego, the American West –
and yes, finally Ireland as in Donegal, the first painting that
of the fabled nineteenth-century French shipwreck north of
Glen Head.

And then it is there before him, entitled simply *Mary
Cunnea*. His mother, lying barefoot on the brow of a sunlit
headland overlooking the North Atlantic, head propped in
her hands, brown hair tied up behind in a bun, her red frock
more sensuous slip than dress. He stands stock-still gazing at
it, then sits for a time on a wee bench back from the canvas,
wondering what might transpire were he to inform those
of his fellow museum visitors who pause at the canvas or
comment to each other, how said Mary was his mother?

Rising then, he slowly passes through the exhibition a
second time, pausing once more at a self-portrait of Hart,
sandy hair and blue-green eyes, not altogether unlike his
own. And thinking again of how his father, Packy, had never
spoken of the painter, along with a reserved obliqueness from
Jack Gara on several occasions next door, or the old Walsh
brothers, say, whom he had likewise queried about their
tenant Hart some three years back. If feeling lately like too
much of a Yank himself, was there any chance he was more
of one than he knew? Yet it was a pure dead letter either way,
as it had been Packy Doherty who showed up when wedding
vows were exchanged and a marriage covenant sealed.

Seated now back on a bench before one of Hart's earlier
landscapes – Colorado, he would wager – he considers how
his own lifelong western *grá* has seen him circle an entire
continent, as if seeking something he cannot yet quite
define. Yet small wonder either, his being in motion where

a great-grandfather, grandfather, uncle and mother had previously made their way? That said, he had no wish to join those souls who end up recounting countless road stories, having met a fair few already – like Wesley, say – who once spoke of having juggled Cairo, Moscow or Rome as his next port of call, prompting Fintan to cite the poet Rilke on our need for an inner resting place.

Seated once more before Mary Cunnea, reclining at ease back there in the home place, he considers how geography is perhaps not the answer after all – the fistful of years spent puzzling where next might he head – when not worrying over where he might've longer stayed? And wasn't Zen's exhortation 'To be here now' patently more about consciousness than locale? Standing up, he blows his mother a discreet kiss, then turns towards the exit.

# Epilogue

Picture Fintan one last time later that July – not in Cairo or Rome, but rather pumping gas into a chromed Harley-Davidson at Dubliner Mickey McKenna's garage across the Charles river from Boston, the motorcycle flashing him back to *Easy Rider* at the Killybegs cinema, which played on inside his head after he had thumbed back home to bed. Better yet, the bloke astride this chopper, somewhere in his thirties, could arguably pass for a second cousin of Dennis Hopper.

'Hope you didn't take a credit card from that bugger?' Mickey asked, once your man had roared off down towards Massachusetts Avenue.

'Greenbacks only,' Fintan replied, prompting workmate Lionel to ask what their boss had against plastic – only for Mickey to just shake his head. He lightened up though shortly after, asking Fintan did he not know that red-haired women were unlucky, after the lass, with whom Fintan had been chatting as he serviced her blue two-door Saab saloon, had pulled away.

'Sounds like you're in touch with your inner culchie?' Fintan grinned, before sharing a story Jack Gara had got from his own da decades back. Of having climbed up to check on his sheep one Easter Sunday towards the edge of Sliabh Cloch, which falls like a massive headstone nearly six hundred metres to the sea below. Only to see, sitting at its edge, a young woman with long red hair and a foreign frock – an outright stranger decades before there were tourists, never mind hostels, in the Glen. He greeted her with an upraised hand, only for her to wave him away. Jack's da turned so, but returning the following day with his brother, they found the grassy bank on which your woman had perched sheared off now into the sea.

'Wish You Were Here' comes on the office radio an hour later, the first Fintan has heard it since last Christmas Eve. Only this time it's not Carla but Wesley he first thinks of. Of Marianne's letter from Oaxaca some three weeks back, telling how *Wesley suicided himself by hanging.* He had puzzled too over the fractured syntax – given her customary fluency – as if grief had overridden language. And wondering too whether poor Wesley had ultimately run afoul of his own mantra on the over-examined mind?

At work the next day he spoke briefly of Wesley to Lionel, who having offered condolences, told of his own short-term gig as a mechanic at an MBTA bus yard a few years back. And of the body he suddenly saw hanging from the passenger rail in his rear-view mirror as he backed a bus into the garage on a late-night shift – only to discover it was only a cleaner's coat left behind.

The image of the hung garment had in turn brought to mind a McNelis lad from up the Glen, who had disappeared when Fintan was ten or so, having left his neatly folded clothes and wellies with a note on Leach na Ronnach, less than a metre above the tranquil sea. It's a memory, however, he chooses not to share with Lionel.

He gets on well too with Mickey at work and no surprise really, given his own early gravitation towards his elderly neighbour Jack Gara or Uncle Condy – and ever more so after his mother Mary's death – as if compensating for a father who did not, or could not, engage. And if Mickey himself occasionally waxes paternal in turn, that too is manageable.

Still, the east coast of America is not what or where he wants. He knows that too, and so smiles ruefully the following Thursday, when a car radio checks in with a female songstress suggesting 'he's been down in lowlands too long'. Better yet, it's sounding from a Ford Escort with Oregon plates at the petrol pumps – like a page out of Carl Jung's tome on synchronicity – lent him by Wesley way back in Laredo.

He sits down to meditate again that evening – a practice begun back in Grand Junction – as if searching for a self that often felt like it too now were missing in motion. A thirty-year-old self since February, which has him thinking as he lays out the small hessian matt, how Jesus had secured his own boat by the age of thirty-two? Only to think next of his mother Mary who might remark of some minor misfortune how 'Worse things happen at sea'.

Having fallen into bed an hour later, he lies there pondering the earnestness of America, its rampant verbalisation-cum-frequent-insistence on heightened emotion, compared to the patently more grounded correlations of daily life back in Donegal. The way, say, a pair of minks following fish guts one afternoon back upstream to where Uncle Condy had pitched them in, had managed to further feast on three of his hens.

Reaching over to turn off the bedside radio, he hears yet another folk-songstress singing, yet another voice he does not know. It's the lyrics though that have him marvelling once more:

*I'll be using all these stormy nights for rest*
*For my day-break journey*
*Way out West.*

# Acknowledgements

The author would like to thank Paul O'Gara, a true Donegal touchstone, and the superb New Island publishing team led by commissioning editor Aoife K. Walsh, whose steady hand at the helm, together with editor Neil Burkey, have superbly steered the book ashore. Heartfelt thanks also to long-time colleagues Edwin Higel and Dermot Bolger.